FOREVER MORE

THE SEQUEL TO SILKWORM SECRETS

RHONDA FORREST

Valeena Press

BOOK 1

SILKWORM SECRETS - Dark Secrets from a Distant Past

'The ancient trees with their rough bark wrap around me like silk cocoons. Their solid trunks and tendril roots grip the ground as if to say, I will hold you, I will not let go.'

SILKWORM SECRETS - Silkworm Secrets Series Book 1

In the 1960s the rural suburbs of Brisbane should have been an idyllic place for Ruby and Bobby to grow up. Their treehouse retreat, set high in a mulberry tree is a place to share friendship and watch the events of the yards nearby. However as the two become teenagers, the naive Ruby is exposed to the sinister events that Bobby has to deal with in his family life. As the years pass and the best friends go their separate ways, childhood events become a distant memory. Will the dark secrets remain uncovered or will Ruby and Bobby be forced to face up to what they witnessed so many years before.

This is a story about the secrets that children keep, the strength that comes from a childhood friendship and a special family love that overcomes the hardships of the past.

***

Mary – reviewer Goodreads - *Yes it's true this novel explores deeper and darker issues, - but life can be like that, complex, difficult, unfair. A rollercoaster ride of emotion but well worth it. This quintessential Australian novel is a must-read.*

Brenda – Reviewer Goodreads - *'Silkworm Secrets' absolutely blew me away! It was beautifully written - filled with deep emotion and heartache, love and abiding friendship.*

FOREVER MORE

WESTERN DOWNS, NEAR BOULIA - 1988

*T*he old man at the end of the table ran his fingers across his chin, flattening the thick beard that covered the lower part of his face. Even though she was only six, Sarah could tell he was thinking, the lines on his forehead deepening and stretched from one side to the other. He stared hard and she locked eyes with him, his blue eyes blazing back at her as she stuck her chin out and scrunched up her face. The man was her grandfather, her mother's father. Her mother, Leila, said Sarah had met him and Grandma when she was smaller. Sarah couldn't remember though, she'd only been a baby.

Mum said she'd argued with Grandpa and Grandma before Sarah was born. They'd tried to tell her how to live her life and she didn't need that added to all the problems she already had. In more recent years she'd only seen them a couple of times when they came into town. 'That wasn't fun,' she said, 'they didn't like Lyle.'

Sarah bit her lip. She did that when she was nervous. Lyle, the boyfriend, was the problem. Everything had been okay until he came along. Now he wanted to take Leila and move far away, up near Mount Isa. They were going to run a pub and that wasn't a good place for Sarah to live. She couldn't go with them. Phone calls had been made. Sarah had tried to listen but Lyle caught her and yelled at her to go to her bedroom and not to be sneaky.

'Your grandparents want you to come and live with them,' Leila told Sarah. 'You will love it there and Grandma will teach you how to read and write. Same as she did with me.'

It had been hard not to cry. 'I'll be really, really, good if you let me come with you. I don't want to live with them. I want to be with you.' Tears rolled down her face and her stomach churned when Lyle's harsh voice drowned out her mother's words. 'Don't be a sook. It'll be good for you. I'll give you a packet of jellybeans when you go.'

Pulling the meanest face possible, she scowled at Lyle. As if she wanted his stupid jellybeans. She wanted to be with her mother.

'How come we never visited them before and where are we going?' Sarah asked on the drive out.

'It's a cattle property called Western Downs, out past town. Now no more questions. Just do as you're told.'

Sarah clutched her bag on her lap. There were some clothes and toys in there that she'd been told to pack last night. Pressing her hands over her shorts, she smoothed the material, hoping that no one noticed the hole in her t-shirt. Sarah wanted to ask how come her mother had new jeans on. Even her shirt was ironed. But there was no more talking in the car. No words spoken the whole way to where they were going; a place further than Sarah had ever been before.

* * *

Now she was here, sitting opposite her grandpa while her mother spoke to Grandma.

She watched him as he sipped his cup of tea, his eyes leaving her for a moment to look through the doorway into the other room where the two women were talking. He had been told to stay in the kitchen to look after her.

'I need to talk without *her* listening,' her mother had said, tipping her head to the side as if she needed to point to who 'her' was. Why did she speak as if Sarah wasn't there? She could hear, there was nothing wrong with her ears.

Grandpa shook his head and looked angry when she'd said that. In fact, he hadn't looked happy since they arrived. Grandma smiled though and her face was pretty. She said her name was Eileen, but Sarah was to call her Grandma. Her voice was soft and she had even given her a hug. Grandma's arms had wrapped around Leila too, but she didn't hug her back. At least she could have put her arms out. There was a sad look on Grandma's face after that and Sarah thought how mean her mother could be.

It didn't matter that she was a meanie though. Sarah still wanted to live with her. Nasty or not. Putting on her grumpiest face she started to pick her fingernails. That's what she did when she was worried. Grandpa was watching her so she stopped and sat up straight, folding her arms and trying to look angry and not scared. She jumped a bit when he put his cup back down on the saucer and pushed a plate with some biscuits towards her, nodding so she knew she could take one. The best one was the one with icing on it. No one else was watching so she took it before picking up another one with her other hand. For a moment it looked like Grandpa was going to smile, but he didn't, he just kept staring. 'Thank you,' she said, hoping he wouldn't tell anyone that she had been greedy and taken two.

He nodded and this time he did smile as he replied. 'You're welcome.'

His face was a lot nicer without the cranky look on it and she noticed his teeth were straight, not crooked and missing like Lyle's were. She relaxed a bit more when he leaned back in his chair and sipped his cup of tea.

The biscuit was covered with pink and white icing and she ate that part first. The sweet sugar coating melted in her mouth and she was side-tracked for a moment from the conversation taking place outside. The different areas of the room drew her attention and she licked her fingers as she looked around. A huge wood stove took up the back wall, and on top of it was a stack of saucepans. That must be what dinner was made in, she thought, wondering what old people like her grandparents ate. Shelves lined one wall, their tops filled with rows of bottles and jars that were full of different types of food. Floral plates and cups filled the shelves of a large green hutch and when Sarah looked harder, she noticed there was a glass jar on the bottom shelf, filled with lollies.

Grandpa must have noticed that she'd spotted them. He made a funny, hmph noise, before twisting around in his chair and grabbing the jar. Sitting very still she blinked quickly as he slowly turned the lid. She held her breath, only letting it out when he reached over the table towards her. 'Quick, take a couple before *they* come back in here. You're probably not supposed to have sweet biscuits and lollies together, but they won't know.'

She didn't need to be told twice. As she reached in and took two lollies, he whispered, 'Liquorice Allsorts. They're my favourite.' He winked at her before taking two out for himself.

They sat in silence again, deep in thought, both chewing on their lollies. Luckily the liquorice was soft and she had finished eating them before Grandma, followed by her mother, came back into the room. Her mother's face was red and Sarah wondered if Grandpa would offer her a lolly. But he didn't and for a moment they all just stared at each other.

Grandma finally spoke. 'Leila has told me what she wants, Thomas.'

'I thought she might.' Grandpa looked up at Leila. 'Are you going to sit down?' he asked. 'You look like you could do with a good feed. You're thin.'

'I work hard. It keeps me fit.'

Leila didn't sound very happy and Sarah could tell she was cranky because she kept pushing her long blonde hair back behind her ears, just like she always did when she was cross. Grandma was no longer smiling either. Maybe they didn't want Sarah to stay with them. 'I won't, thanks. I need to get going,' Leila said. 'Lyle and I are leaving tomorrow.'

Grandma gave Leila a long look before directing her words at Sarah. 'Your mother is going to leave you here with us so she can pursue this new job. It could be for a while.'

Sarah sat up straight. This was the first she'd heard of the 'for a while' bit.

Grandpa's face was stern, and his eyes narrowed. His voice was deep, and the angry words that rolled out slowly made Sarah sit up straighter. 'And where do you think she'll go to school? We're a long way out.'

'Mum said she'd do that. Sarah hasn't started school yet. I haven't had time to enrol her.'

Grandpa made a growling noise. 'By my calculations, she should have been at school last year. She's missed a whole year.'

Leila glared back at him. 'Mum will catch her up. She can't come where we're going. There's no other option and I have to go where the work is.'

Grandpa stood up. 'There're jobs in town.'

'You've never understood me or what I've been through. It's my turn now. I need a break.'

They started to argue and Sarah put her hands over her ears. Grandpa's voice was getting louder and her mother yelled back at him, saying all sorts of nasty things.

Grandma took Sarah's hand and led her outside. She sat in a wooden rocking chair and pulled Sarah onto her lap and started slowly rocking. Lying her head on Grandma's shoulder, Sarah closed her eyes. Grandma smelled nice, a mixture of baking and a sweet smell that came from her soft skin. Sarah snuggled in, pushing her ear against Grandma's chest so she couldn't hear the fighting inside. She was tired of yelling and arguments. Leila and Lyle yelled at each other all the time. Then when they got sick of yelling at each other they yelled at her.

Grandma hummed a tune and held her tight, rocking slowly as she stroked her hair. Sarah closed her eyes.

Maybe when they stopped arguing and came out of the house her mother would change her mind and take her back home.

The humming and movement calmed her and she thought how she already loved her grandma. Maybe she'd get to see her again.

Eventually, Mum came out through the front door. She'd been crying and Sarah could tell that Grandpa, who stayed standing in the doorway, was still angry.

Her mother bent down and kissed the top of her head. 'Be a good girl now and I'll see you when I get back.'

Sarah sat up and Grandma held her tighter. She wanted to cry, to stand up and kick the chair and run after the car. But she didn't. She was confused. Was she coming back to pick her up later today or in the morning? What did, for a while, mean? Her eyes followed the car as it drove away, her mother and it disappearing down the dusty track. Tears rolled down her cheeks and she rested her head back on Grandma's chest, wishing that when she opened her eyes, everything would go back to what it had been.

CHAPTER 2

*S*arah's mum had not come back that afternoon or the next day, or the day after that. Grandma tried to explain what was happening. 'Come with me and we'll feed the dogs and horses.' She held her hand out and Sarah skipped to catch up to her. Grandma's hand was warm and it felt nice when it wrapped around hers. 'Your mum wants us to look after you. She's gone away and now you're going to live with us. We'll take care of you.' Crouching down next to her, Grandma gently pushed stray bits of hair back behind Sarah's ears. 'Everything will be alright. We love you and we'll always be here for you.'

She told Sarah they were her family now. 'Your mother never came and visited so we only saw her a few times when you were a baby. We tried to see her when we went into town but she didn't want anything to do with us or her brothers. It wasn't our fault and it broke our hearts the way she treated us. Now we can make up for the years that we didn't get to see you.'

Sarah studied Grandma's face when she talked. Her skin didn't have as many creases as Grandpa's and she smiled a lot more than he did. Her hair and eyes looked like Leila's; they were the same colour, although her blonde hair was shorter and sat just above her shoulders. The colour however was the opposite of Sarah's dark curls and Grandma's eyes weren't dark brown like hers but green like the leaves on her shirts. Most days Grandma worked on the property and although her jeans were always the same blue colour, her blouses were always different, each one with flowery patterns on them which Sarah loved.

Grandma also had quite a few pairs of riding boots and before the week was out, she had bought Sarah a shiny new pair that she said were a present to welcome her to her new home.

At first, Grandpa didn't talk that much and Sarah was a bit scared of him. When he yelled at the dogs when they did the wrong thing, his voice was deep and loud and she jumped when he cracked the whip to stop the cattle from going in the wrong direction. Grandma took her everywhere in her rusty old ute while Grandpa rode a horse. He sat very straight when he was in the saddle and it was fun to watch him as he kicked his horse into action and moved around the cattle, rounding them up and chasing them to where he wanted them to go. Sometimes Grandma also rode a horse and Sarah loved watching her, especially when she took her horse over some wooden jumps in the home yard.

'Your Grandma used to ride in the horse jumping shows. She was one of the best riders in the state. She still sits beautifully in the saddle.' Grandpa always looked at

Grandma in a different way from how he looked at anyone else. It was love. Grandma told her so.

***

Soon Sarah forgot that she had ever lived anywhere else. When the year ended and Christmas passed, Grandma started teaching her how to read and write. Other days they spent in the kitchen learning how to cook the meals and cakes that Grandpa loved to eat. Leila rang a couple of times and once she even visited, but she didn't stay long and only talked about herself and Lyle. She hadn't asked any questions and when Sarah started to tell her about the new pups down in the shed and how Grandpa had said she could have one once they were old enough to leave their mother, Leila just nodded and didn't even seem excited.

'Do you want to come and see them?' Sarah asked her. 'I've got one picked out already. He's the smallest one and I've called him Rusty. Grandpa says he's the runt of the litter but he'll be the best of the lot.'

She started to walk towards the shed but turned back when she realised that Leila hadn't followed. Instead, she was looking at her watch and had picked up her bag from the table. 'I don't have time. Maybe next visit.'

Sarah held Grandma's hand until her mother left. At least she could have come and seen the pups but all she wanted to do was to get back to Lyle. As they stood watching the car drive away she thought how she didn't want her mother to visit again. She liked living here, even though there were rules and sometimes she got in trouble. Unlike her mother, Grandma talked to her calmly and explained what she had done wrong. Grandpa sometimes tried to sound stern but he usually ended up smiling and ruffling her hair. 'How could I get angry with you. You have the face of an angel. Next time though, make sure to keep that back door shut. We don't want snakes inside again.'

Living here she also had a big bedroom and Grandma made her a patchwork quilt that she loved to run her hands over. Each square had a different pattern and it was hard to work out which one she liked best. Grandma also sewed her pretty dresses and blouses, and bought her books and coloured pencils. Last week when Grandpa went into town he had taken her with him and let her choose a colouring book and felt pens from the lady at the newsagency. When he paid she stood on her tiptoes next to him, peering over the counter.

'That will be fifty cents, thanks Mr Hartley,' the lady said. 'This must be your granddaughter. I hear she's living with you, and that Eileen is schooling her.'

The lady leaned over the counter and smiled at Sarah. 'You're a lucky girl.' She turned back to Grandpa. 'You're good people taking her in.'

Grandpa nodded. 'Thanks, Marion. She's a great kid. We love having her with us.'

The day in town had been special and even more exciting when they got to the main gate of Western Downs and Grandpa let her sit in front of him and steer the ute. He laughed when she hit some potholes, the ute bouncing over the dusty red track. 'We'll have you driving in no time. You're doing great.'

***

Most afternoons when her lessons were finished, she followed Grandpa around the sheds, helping him with the horses and watching as he fixed his tools. Sometimes she sat on his tractor, talking to him as he worked in the shed, jumping down when he needed her to fetch something for him. When she talked too much, or chose the wrong tool that he needed, he didn't even get cranky. He was patient and explained everything slowly so she could understand. It didn't matter what was broken, Grandpa was so clever he could fix it. The horses and dogs followed him and Sarah around, and Grandma said he looked like the Pied Piper with all of them trailing along behind him.

One day, Grandma made her close her eyes as she led her to the stables. When she was told to open her eyes, Grandpa was standing in front of her with a chestnut pony. 'He's yours, Sarah. His name is Banjo and he's ten years old.'

Banjo was the best present ever and every afternoon either Grandma or Grandpa spent time with her in the house paddock, teaching her everything she needed to know. It hadn't taken long before she was trotting around by herself, pressing her knees in tightly and sitting up straight as she held onto the reins and guided Banjo around in a circle.

'You're a natural.' Grandpa was pleased with her progress and before long, when he wasn't going too far, he let her go with him. She felt like the luckiest kid in the world when she rode beside him, listening as he talked and pointed out the cattle and horses that he'd bring back into the stockyards.

When she cuddled up between the two of them on the lounge at night, she'd whispered in Grandma's ear. 'I want to be a stockman just like Grandpa when I grow up. Or maybe a jillaroo or a rodeo rider.' Grandma giggled and squeezed her tight. 'You can be whatever you want. You're a smart girl.'

Sarah closed her eyes and lay between them. It was a warm feeling when she snuggled up to them, the scent of the perfume Grandma sometimes wore, mixed with the tobacco smell that lingered on Grandpa's clothes drifting across her. She loved being with them both. This was home.

CHAPTER 3

*O*nce Sarah was a bit older, Grandma enrolled her in Distance Education. By now she needed more than simple tuition and each morning she sat at the kitchen table, her books strewn in front of her as she completed her lessons. Science was her favourite and when her lessons were done and the three of them sat together at lunch, she relayed everything she had learned that morning.

When the studies for the day were completed it was time to work in the yards or some days to go further afield. She had become Grandpa's offsider and sometimes she travelled further with him, across the plains, rounding up cattle and sleeping out for a couple of nights. They'd lie side by side in their swags, the flicker of the campfire sending its light across them and the dogs who lay near them, Rusty always by her side. Grandpa told her stories about the olden times, when men on horses drove cattle for thousands of miles across the driest parts of Australia. He talked about stock routes he'd been on and about their life before she came to live with them. She listened carefully, the names of people and places, becoming part of her memories also.

He'd point to the heavens. 'Look at that, Sarah. You'll never see stars as bright as you will out here. They have no other lights to compete with.'

When she looked up, the sky was covered in millions of stars, the milky way stretching across the far reaches, the flickering lights joining together to create a waxy clump of brightness.

Often they watched the satellites tracking from one side of the vast expanse to the other and Grandpa told her what lay beyond the deserts and the ranges on the other side. She didn't want to go too far away from Western Downs though. 'One day you'll want more than these grassy paddocks and dry rivers,' Grandma said. 'There's a lot to see out there. When it's not so busy we'll have to take you to the coast or even to Mount Isa.'

Sarah was adamant. 'I don't want to go anywhere, especially not Mount Isa. That's near where Mum is.'

Once Sarah turned seven, the phone calls from her mother stopped. On her tenth birthday she received a card, the message short and the words showing it was from Mum and Lyle. After that, she no longer wondered if her mother thought about her or even remembered her birthday. Leila's brothers, Sam and Ethan, lived close by and they always came to visit on her birthday and sang loudly as she blew out her candles. They never forgot. That was enough family for her. She was happy.

***

Uncle Sam, Uncle Ethan and Aunt Josie, who was Ethan's wife, had all come to her fourteenth birthday dinner. They'd bought her a present, a fancy stockman saddle that smelled and felt like the best leather in the world. 'It's made by old Snowy in town. He's been making the best saddles in the country for over fifty years,' Uncle Ethan said.

Aunt Josie passed another parcel to her, a new horse brush and set of reins. 'I heard your last set snapped and you're always making that pony look the best.'

Sarah hugged them all and thought how lucky she was to have them as her family. She felt sorry for her mother who was missing out on her birthdays. Over the years on Western Downs, there had been plenty of family celebrations. On special occasions, her uncles and Aunt Josie would arrive in the afternoon and sit on the verandah or in the dining room. They'd stay until long after dinner and talk about so many different things. Everyone loved Uncle Ethan's jokes and Grandpa laughed so much one night that tears ran down his face and he started coughing. She had to jump up and get him a glass of water. Uncle Sam said something else that made everyone laugh even more and Grandma had rubbed Grandpa's back until he got his breath. It was strange how her mother's brothers and Aunt Josie treated her like she was their own daughter, yet her mother couldn't even find the time to ring anymore.

Sarah kissed Grandma on the cheek. 'I love you. This is the best place anyone could live.' Grandma got a bit teary and wiped her hand across her eyes. Reaching behind her she picked up a parcel and passed it to Sarah. Sarah looked into her beautiful face thinking how it would be impossible to love anyone more than she loved her grandparents.

She opened the present slowly, giggling when Grandpa leaned forward. 'Do you know what it is, Grandpa?' she asked, untying the pink ribbon that held the wrapping paper together.

He joined his hands together and leaned back in his chair, his brown hair and beard neat and combed especially for the night. 'Of course, I do. Grandma and I picked it together.'

Gently pulling the sticky tape away, she unfolded the pretty paper just like she'd been taught, making sure to read the card first. 'Oh, it must be special if you went into the shops in town,' she said, knowing that it was highly unlikely that Grandpa had stepped foot in a gift shop.

They all leaned forward as she pulled a small box from the wrapping. When she lifted the lid she inhaled sharply. Inside was a piece of jewellery she knew well. It was Grandma's engagement ring. A gold solitaire diamond surrounded by a filigree setting.

Grandma nodded. 'It's yours. Your Grandpa bought me that when I was only eighteen. I haven't been able to wear it for years because of my arthritis, that's why it's always in the jewellery box on my dressing table.'

'I know. We've looked at it together when I dusted for you,' Sarah said.

'Put it on,' Grandpa said. 'It's yours now.'

Sarah couldn't stop looking at the ring. She held her hand in different ways so that she could see what it looked like from a variety of angles and the changes in it when the light shone through it. It was the most beautiful ring in the world and she told them she would wear it forever.

'Til some good-looking bloke comes along and buys you a bigger one,' Uncle Sam joked.

She shook her head. 'I'm not ever getting married. I'm going to live here forever.'

They'd all laughed at that and Aunt Josie had taken a family photo. There had been plenty of banter and joking as she set the camera up on a pile of books, the timer going off early three times in a row before they were all ready. Finally, Aunt Josie got a photo of them that she was happy with. 'I'll do a copy for each of us and you can put it in a frame, Sarah. You'll always remember your four-teenth birthday.

CHAPTER 4

*S*arah could remember exactly what day it was when Grandma became ill. They had been getting ready to go on a ride. It was only a day after her birthday and she was keen to use her new saddle. Grandma and Grandpa were down in the stables, getting the horses ready when Grandpa asked her to run up to the house and get his other boots. Grandma called out after her. 'Take in the sheets that are on the line. Just in case we're back a bit late.'

Sarah skipped quickly towards the house, excited for the ride ahead. Grandma had worn her flowery blouse today and Sarah had worn a matching one she'd been given for her birthday. Grandpa had taken a photo of them together and said they looked like sisters.

She smiled as she reached the house. That would be another good photo she could put in a frame on her dressing table.

Heading towards the clothesline, she kicked her heels up to the side, calling out a loud 'yeeha'. Today was going to be the best day ever. She stopped being silly and was careful as she pulled the sheets down. Grandma wouldn't want any dust on them. As she walked towards the house she reminded herself to get the boots. She found them easily, they were always in the same spot. Grabbing them she dumped the sheets on the lounge chair before walking quickly back down to the stables. She thought that they'd both be waiting, saddled up outside the shed, but they must have decided to wait inside for her. Entering the shed she gasped loudly, shocked to see Grandpa crouching down next to Grandma, his arms around her as she lay lifeless in his grasp.

***

By the time the flying doctors arrived, it was too late. Even though they worked on Grandma for a long time, trying to resuscitate her, she never took another breath. They said it was most likely her heart. They'd do further tests to determine what had happened.

Grandpa's face was white and he kept shaking his head. 'She went so quickly. We were just about to go for a ride. She just grabbed her chest and my arm and then fell to the ground.' He'd broken down and squatted in the dirt, his head in his hands. 'It was Sarah's birthday yesterday. Eileen wanted her to try her new saddle. Sarah stood beside him, his hand reaching up to clutch hers. 'She knew. I could see it in her eyes. She knew she was going,' he said. 'She couldn't speak but I knew what she was saying.'

Sarah wiped her face with her blouse. 'I wasn't gone long. How could that happen? Are you sure she's not breathing?' Sitting in the dirt beside Grandpa, she started crying. She was still crying when Grandpa got on the plane with Grandma and the flying doctors. Two of the stockmen who had been down in the workers' sheds, stood beside her. They'd wait with her until Uncle Ethan and Aunt Josie came and picked her up.

They stood together until the plane was a speck in the distance. Rusty pushed his nose into her face and one of the stockmen helped her stand up. She picked up the dog and held him tight. He lay still in her arms and she pushed her face into his hair. It was full of dirt and she pushed her face in harder. She didn't want Grandma to be dead. 'How could it happen so quickly?' she asked the two men. They looked at each other and tried to offer some consolation but their words blurred into each other.

They waited with her on the verandah until her uncle and aunt came. When they arrived, Uncle Ethan jumped out of the car and ran to her. He wrapped his arms around her and then Aunt Josie hugged them both. The three of them stood huddled together, crying and asking the same question. 'How could this happen?'

CHAPTER 5

*T*he weeks after Grandma died, were long and filled with sadness. Grandpa was lost without her and seemed to get cranky with everything. Everything except Sarah. When he couldn't cook his eggs the right way in the morning, he yanked the frying pan off the stove and threw it in the big metal bin outside. It still had steam coming off it and when he slammed the bin lid down and swore, Sarah pretended she hadn't seen him from where she sat inside.

The washing and ironing pile grew higher and she tried to keep up with it, but the washing machine broke and when Grandpa tried to fix it he'd thrown the sodden washing on the concrete floor, cursing the machine and the people who made it. Thankfully Aunt Josie popped in a lot and helped with anything that needed doing. She drove Sarah into town and they picked up a new washing machine. For the first time since Grandma had died, Sarah laughed as the two of them followed the instruction book and put the machine into working order. 'Women power,' Aunt Josie said. 'Your Grandma would be looking down saying, well done, girls.'

It would have been good if Grandpa talked about Grandma like Aunt Josie did, that way it wouldn't make every day so hard. Her gut felt empty and she kept looking for her, expecting her to come around the corner of the shed or be sitting on the chair on the verandah after dinner. When Aunt Josie and her reminisced about all the happy times and what a special person Grandma had been it made her grief go away for a little while.

Sarah didn't talk about her with Grandpa though. He was acting as if she never existed and continued to be angry and depressed. He had even yelled at Leila over the phone when she rang. Nobody had seen her since the funeral and even that day she hadn't stuck around, she and Lyle making an excuse that they needed to get back to the pub and couldn't hang around for the wake.

Sarah had watched Grandpa through the doorway as he talked. His hands looked like they were going to crush the phone as Leila's words continued from the other end. She didn't give him a chance to interrupt and spoke quickly, as if she was in a hurry. When she finished talking he shouted at her and his face turned red. Sarah could hear the conversation clearly. Her mother was putting on her kind voice, the one where it sounded like she cared. 'She's older now, I can take her back if you want. Lyle says so as well. There's a spare room here for her and we can get her to do some of the cleaning work.'

Grandpa growled and it was the angriest Sarah had ever heard him. 'No one takes Sarah away from us. She belongs here. I'll ask her myself what she wants to do but I know what the answer will be.'

It was the perfect moment to walk in and speak her mind. She was old enough now to make her own decisions. She took the phone from Grandpa's hand, her words coming out through clenched teeth. 'It's me, Sarah. Don't ever mention me coming to live with you again. I'm not going anywhere and I never will. Grandpa and I are fine and this is, and always will be my home.' With that, she handed the phone back to him and stomped out of the room.

***

The first year had been the hardest. At least as the months passed, the time she took to do the kitchen chores improved. Thank goodness she'd been taught how to do most of them anyway and sometimes she thought she could hear a little voice guiding her from above. 'Give those cakes another ten minutes and make sure to put the tea towel over them straight away.' Maybe Grandma's spirit was there with them. At night when she lay in bed she waited to hear her voice again, but it didn't happen. Her body felt hollow and most nights her tears made her pillow wet. Grandma wasn't here and she wasn't coming back.

Aunt Josie talked to her about grief and that it was okay to be sad. She'd lost her mum only a couple of years ago so she understood how she was feeling. 'It's hard for Grandpa Thomas,' she said. We need to give him some space and let him come to terms with what's happened.'

Uncle Ethan and Uncle Sam called in a couple of times

each week and she could tell that the visits helped
Grandpa. When the men were together they talked about
the cattle, the weather and what needed doing on the
property. Her uncles had their own properties that
bordered Western Downs so at least they weren't far
away.

After a while, Sarah continued with her distance
education. It was hard without anyone to help her at
home, but the teachers were understanding and encouraged her to study hard. They regularly checked on how
she was going and if there was anything they could do to
help. There wasn't though and she worked through the
lessons, methodically ticking off her assessment and
making sure she passed everything. Grandma would want
that. After six months though she was ready to throw it
in. What was the use of continuing when she could work
on the property? It was all she had ever wanted to do.
She'd wait until the right moment to talk about it with
Grandpa. The thought of not having to be tied to lessons
each day made her spirits lift and she imagined what she
could do with the extra time.

It was hard to be happy though when Grandpa was so
miserable. One day as they sat and ate breakfast together
she realised that his hair and beard were now white and
not brown anymore. His face had also aged and the spring
that had once been in his step was gone. When they rode
together, rounding up the cattle, he was quiet and she
missed his stories and jokes.

She missed Grandma more than anything though. Her
voice sounded in her head sometimes, telling her that the
washing needed to come in before the night air got on it,
or to order the groceries before they ran out. So many

times, Sarah needed to ask her something, like how many cups of flour went into the fruit cakes, or how many times should she mend Grandpa's shorts before they bought new ones.

When the first anniversary of Grandma's death came, Grandpa cooked a special meal. They sat together at the kitchen table and Sarah tried to tell him some funny stories. He'd started to cry and that had made her cry also. They sat and sobbed and Grandpa passed her his big hankie. His voice was shaky. 'I miss your Grandma,' he said. 'This last year has been the hardest of my life.'

He'd put his hand on top of Sarah's as it rested on the table. 'The last eight years with you here have been some of the best. Eileen used to tell me nearly every night how much she loved raising you. You made our life complete. Don't ever forget how much she loved you.' He'd stopped talking and closed his eyes, and she could tell he was trying not to cry again.

When she went to bed she looked out her window and watched him leaning on the horse fence staring over the paddocks. There was a full moon and the yards were lit up by the moonlight that threw a milky warmth across the yards. The sound of dingoes far to the west sounded and night birds called out to each other from the sparse scrub down near the sheds.

She kept nodding off, the jerking of her neck waking her as she sat and watched him, the bright tip of his cigarette glowing in the darkness. Eventually, she'd laid down and fallen asleep, the words of Grandma coming to her in her dreams. 'He'll be right. Let him be.'

That night was a turning point and from that moment on, Grandpa regained some of his former self. The heavy sadness lifted a little for them both and he told Sarah it wasn't fair if he was always sad. 'You're young and Eileen wouldn't have wanted you to be down in the dumps and crying about her passing. Maybe you came to us for a reason. It's up to me now to make sure you get on with your life. That's what your grandma would want.'

CHAPTER 6

*T*his morning, Sarah lay thinking about that night when Grandpa had rounded a corner and decided to get on with his life. It wasn't that he didn't love Grandma or had stopped missing her, it was just he knew he was responsible for raising Sarah.

Shards of light filtered in through tattered curtains, the yellow flowers that had once coloured their folds, faded into a muted dusty colour. The dullness matched the grey walls, the only brightness in the room, a peacock blue door that someone long ago had splashed a coat of paint on. Sarah lay on her back looking at the ceiling, the peeling paint and bulging surface a mottled canvas that never seemed to change. Rolling onto her side she cast her eyes through the ajar door and across the hallway. Grandpa was in his usual morning position, placing items on the kitchen table. She closed her eyes and smiled, the familiar tunes he loved to whistle, a pleasant first call of the morning.

He'd be eighty next year and still worked most days

from dawn to dusk. 'It's just a number,' he'd tell anyone who questioned how old he was. 'Plenty of work life left in me yet. A stockman never hangs up his boots until he's dead.'

There was no stopping him or even trying to slow him down. Every morning he rose before the sun, cooked a big breakfast, and readied himself for the day ahead, his boots parked outside the front door waiting for him to start the day. Sarah couldn't remember him ever being sick. Sure, he'd been injured plenty of times. Working with cattle and horses, there was always bound to be accidents. Only last week one of the young horses had thrown him and he'd been catapulted over the horse's head before landing with a thud on the hard ground. She'd held her breath as she watched, his body motionless for a couple of seconds before slowly but surely he began to move each leg and arm. He'd glared at her out of the corner of his eye and she knew better than to rush over and try and help him up. Eventually, he'd scrambled up off the ground and dusted himself off.

Anyone else that age would have ended up with parts of their body broken, but not Grandpa Thomas. 'Got nine lives, just like those wild cats down the shed.' He'd winced as he straightened up and she knew he'd be bruised and sore. Under the fine dust cover, the ground was as hard as steel and he had narrowly missed a large piece of farm machinery. He moved a bit slower and limped for a few days, but then, just the same as other times, he'd come good, carrying on working as if nothing had happened.

She curled her legs up under the sheets, listening as he moved around the kitchen, making eggs, porridge and boiling the jug for his cup of tea. He would have already set her place at the table, the chipped plate that was her favourite and the delicate teacup that had been Grandma's, set in the same position every morning. Sarah was similar to him, methodical and rarely rushed. Grandpa said they were kindred spirits, bound together naturally, due to sharing the same birthday. He loved to tell anyone who would listen that they had come into the world on the same day and time, fifty-eight years apart.

She stretched her arms high above her head, the tune of Tennessee Waltz filling her ears, the words playing out in her mind. Who else her age knew the songs from long gone eras? Even people twice her age wouldn't be familiar with the music her grandfather had immersed her in since childhood.

'Good for the soul and good for the spirit,' he loved to tell her. 'Much better than that whining yodelling country rubbish or the crashing bashing noise people listen to.'

As she swung her legs over the side of the bed and reached for her jeans she smiled to herself, his whistling tune coming to an end as he broke into a loud rendition of Moon River, her favourite. She yelled out, 'Grandpa, you're singing loud enough to wake the workers down in the bunkhouse.' She should have known she was wasting her breath. There was no way he'd hear her over the whistling kettle and the sound of his voice.

Pulling her dark wavy hair back into a ponytail she looked at herself in the tiny mirror that sat above her chest of drawers. Dark brown eyes stared back as she pinned a tendril of hair back with a hair clip. Even though she was never without her hat outside, her face was tanned, matching her arms and hands, the only other parts of her body that were subjected to the harshness of the outback sun. She peered up at her reflection, wondering if her mother, Leila, had looked the same at this age. As much as she'd tried over the years she couldn't find too much in common with her mother. Maybe her height, but that was about where it stopped. Some people said she looked a bit like Grandma, but Grandpa said that was rubbish. 'You look like you. Don't you go worrying about all that talk about who you look like and who you don't. Just be who you are.'

Standing on her tiptoes she turned her head to the side, wishing that her eyebrows weren't so dark and thick. It was a constant battle to keep them plucked and shaped. Just because she lived a million miles from anywhere didn't mean she didn't care about her appearance. She straightened the mirror. Grandpa had put an extra nail in the wall and lowered it for her, after all, she wasn't that tall and the person who had lived in the room many years before—most likely her Uncle Sam— had been six foot two and as Grandpa liked to say, built like a brick shit house.

Turning away from the mirror she pulled on a blouse and found her socks, making sure to pick up her hat as she wandered out into the kitchen. Today was mustering day and like every other day since she'd left school seven years ago, she knew there was no use lying around in bed or spending time in front of the mirror daydreaming or thinking about how she looked. As Grandpa said, 'Get up and get going. There's work to be done.'

***

Sarah kissed him on the cheek, as she did every morning. 'Morning beautiful,' he said, 'your eggs are nearly ready and the tea is just about brewed.'

'Thanks Grandpa, I'm starving. We need to have a good breakfast, it's going to be a big day.'

'Too right. I hope those fellas down at the sheds are up and at it. We need to move stock out of those southern areas, back up here to the yards.'

She nodded as she ate. Western Downs had been in the family for generations. It was just over twenty thousand hectares of cattle plains, east of Boulia in far western Queensland. Like everyone who lived out these parts, the family had suffered their share of damaging fires, severe droughts, and floods that stretched from one end of its boundaries to the other. It was the way of life here and they were luckier than some, because Western Downs continued as a working family property, thanks to its flowing bores and a natural water system that flowed through it. Grandpa's house was the oldest building on the property, built not long after he'd returned from the two years he spent in New Guinea during World War II. He'd married Grandma, not long after that.

Sarah poured her tea, watching Grandpa as he sat opposite, eating his porridge. His white beard was still thick and she noted that he had trimmed it this morning. He was proud of it and kept it neat, much like the sparse covering of white hair that covered his head. White bushy eyebrows moved up and down as he ate and she stifled a laugh as he looked up at her. 'What?' he asked. 'What's so funny?'

Leaning back in her chair, she giggled. 'You are. You've trimmed your beard again and you look like you could go out on the town. Even though I've patched that shirt a million times it's still as blue as your eyes.'

He ran his hand across his beard. 'Nothing wrong with looking good. Don't want to let myself go. My Eileen always said I was the best-looking bloke she'd ever laid eyes on. Mind you this wasn't white back then.'

Sarah reached across and put her hand on top of his where it rested on the table. 'She was right.'

'And what about you?' He pushed a plate of toast towards her. 'It looks like my training has paid off. I see you have a clean shirt to match those new jeans.'

She sighed, 'They'll be filthy within the hour. Where do you want me to start this morning? Will I go with the first lot or hang back with you?'

He twisted his face like he always did when he was thinking. 'You won't want to ride out with us once you know who's coming in to look at that crook horse this morning.'

Her hand tightened on her cup and she sat upright. 'The vet's coming isn't he.'

Grandpa got up and started clearing the table. 'He is. You can stay here and talk with him, see what he says about sorting that horse out.'

She got up and placed her arm around his shoulders. 'Thanks, I'd like that.'

'I knew you would.' He turned around and faced her. 'While he's here, pick his brains a bit. Ask him about courses and how you'd go about studying.'

She sighed and turned away, busying herself with the dishes. 'It's no use. I've asked a couple of the fellas who've passed through here. You need to have your senior high school certificate. I left when I was fourteen. Plus, it's six years at uni and all the places to study are in the cities.'

'If you remember, I did try and talk you out of leaving school at the time. As usual you were stubborn though. Now maybe this time you should listen to me. I'm not stupid, Sarah. The main reason you aren't looking into the study is because you're worried about me here by myself. I know you love home, but there's more out there and if you even have an inkling that you'd like to do something then we'll make it happen. You're twenty-one. You've gained skills here, it's time to look at what you want to do for the rest of your life. Is this where you want to be in ten years? Moving stock and riding out along boundary fences?'

She cast her eyes down. 'You've always done it. You say yourself it's the best life anyone could wish for, plus you're right, I don't want to leave you. It's always been me and you.'

'I know that. But I'll be here. I'm not going anywhere. I think it's time to look into it a bit more.'

He bent down and started putting on his boots. 'You make sure to find out what the vet knows about options. I'll be asking you when I get back.'

*D*ust followed the ute that drove in through the gates of the yard. The driver headed towards the shed behind the house, pulling up right next to where Sarah stood waiting. She pushed her hat down on her head and spoke to Rusty. 'Sit. It's okay. Stay.' The dog whined as he sat, looking up at her as she scowled back. 'Sit.'

She glanced back at Rusty once as she approached the car. Her training had paid off and he hadn't moved. Two men got out of the ute and she held her hand out to welcome the local vet, Tom McGrady. Tom's large hand gripped hers and she smiled at him as he introduced the other man. 'G'day Sarah. Thomas said you'd be here. It's good to see you.'

'I thought I'd hang around and see if you needed anything. Thanks for coming out. The horse is in the shed.'

Tom tucked his shirt in before grabbing his bag out of the back of the ute. 'Sarah, meet Bill. He's visiting from

Winton and in his early years of practice, so he's come to watch what we're doing today.'

She shook Bill's hand. 'Pleased to meet you.' Bill was tall and stocky and she noticed the roughness of his hand when he shook hers, his arms and face tanned.

'The pleasure is mine, Sarah. It's great to meet you. I've never been to Western Downs before.'

'I'll have to show you around once you've finished.' She was curious. Bill looked to be about forty. 'How long have you been a vet?' she asked.

'This is my second year out. I'm forty-two this year. It was a late change of career for me but the best thing I've ever done.' He walked beside her as she led Tom over to the shed. Rusty followed, stopping when Bill bent down to pat him. 'I've got one just like this.'

'What did you do before you became a vet?'

'I was a stockman.'

Tom interrupted, 'Sarah's mum is Leila. You'd probably have known her, she worked at the local shop in Boulia for a while. Not far from where you were working in your younger days.'

Bill's eyes lit up and a wide grin crossed his face. 'I know Leila. Well, I used to. It's been years since I've seen her though. She was only young when she worked in the shop.'

Sarah kicked her boots in the dust and crossed her arms. 'She's never talked about her younger years.' She looked up at the men. 'I've always lived with Grandpa, and Grandma when she was alive, here on Western Downs. I came to them when I was only little. Mum hasn't been around, she's been busy getting on with her own life.'

'Your Grandpa is a lucky man to have you here,' Tom

said, 'and might I add he's done a bloody good job of raising you.'

She gave him a warm smile and continued towards the back of the shed, pointing to the horse lying down. 'Thanks, Tom. The two of us are close.' Tom unlatched a wooden gate and walked slowly towards the horse, talking to him as he neared. He crouched down, patting him on the neck and ruffling his knotted mane. She loved watching Tom work, he was calm and the way he interacted with animals seemed to come so naturally. Bill also watched him closely, asking a few questions every so often. After a while Bill joined him next to the horse and Sarah stood transfixed, trying to hear what they were saying as they worked out what was wrong and discussed medication.

When they were finished she chatted with them as they headed back out into the sunlight. 'Your grandfather was right. Cellulitis. That mixture I've given him should fix him up,' Tom said. 'Let him lie there for an hour or so, but then get him up and walk him around the yard. I'll give you a ring in the morning to see how he is. I can always come back out if need be.'

'Can I offer you a cup of tea and something to eat before you go? I could show Bill around a bit.'

'We'll have a quick cuppa,' Bill said. 'Our next stop is a couple of hours from here so that'd be great.'

The two men sat on the verandah while Sarah prepared a pot of tea and a plate of food. Grandpa and the other workers had left long before the vet arrived and the kitchen was quiet as she bustled around, making sure to get the best cups and saucers ready for the two visitors. She pondered on the fact that Bill had studied so late in life. A run of questions filled her mind and she remembered Grandpa insisting that she ask about vet courses.

***

As she poured the tea she listened to the men talk. She waited until they finished, enjoying their company and knowledge about animals. 'You make the best cup of tea,' Tom praised her.

'Grandpa likes it so strong it could stand up by itself. I baked the cakes and biscuits early this morning when I knew you were coming. There's plenty there.'

'I don't know what your grandfather would do without you out here.'

She laughed, 'He says he'd survive fine. I do look after him though, even though he won't admit it.'

Bill leaned forward in his seat, picking up another piece of fruit cake. 'It doesn't appear that there are too many females here on the property from what Tom has told me. You only seem young? I hope you keep those fellas straight if they give you a hard time.'

'I'm twenty-one. Don't worry about me. I put anyone in their place who steps out of line. Occasionally we get female cooks or jillaroos. Most of the workers are men though. We're a long way from anywhere so this life doesn't suit everyone.'

'It was always like that, even years ago. Nothing much has changed,' Bill added.

She stretched her legs out in front, pushing her boot up and down on Rusty's neck as he slept. 'Was it hard studying at a later age? There would have been a big gap since you were at school?' she asked Bill.

He turned to her. 'It wasn't easy. I left school when I was fourteen so there was over twenty years gap between finishing school and studying again.'

'You mean you didn't go to grade twelve?' She sat up straight, her eyes fixed on him. 'How did they let you into uni?'

His face creased up into a smile. 'I was pretty rough as a youngster. There were a lot of wild years in there and you might say I went off the tracks a little. I met someone though, a girl, a wonderful person who I'm lucky enough to call my wife.'

Tom grinned. 'There's always a girl.'

'She came out to be a governess on a property I was working on. I was thirty when I met her and she straight-ened me out. We fell in love and the rest, as they say, is history.'

'What did she do to help you become a vet?' Sarah was intrigued and tried not to ask a million questions at once.

'She recognised that I had always wanted to do that. I thought I was too stupid because I hadn't finished school. She started teaching me writing and grammar skills at night and then tutoring me in other subjects that I'd need to get my senior pass. I did a lot of it through remote learning. I worked during the day and studied at night. It took two years to complete years eleven and twelve. I wouldn't have been able to do it without my wife's help.'

'That would have been hard. I left school at fourteen also.'

Bill's eyes narrowed. 'That shouldn't happen these days. Why did you do that?'

'It wasn't long after Grandma died. I wanted to work on the property. Grandpa tried everything to make me continue but I was bored and not enjoying it. I'm stubborn when I want to be. I just wanted to work.' She offered them more biscuits and cake, delighted when they both took a couple of pieces each. 'So, once you got your senior pass, what did you do?'

'That was the trickiest part. My wife and I moved to the city. We rented a tiny flat and she found work at a local school. I enrolled in uni and started the course. It took years but look at me now. I'm working for the vet in Winton and my wife is a teacher at the local primary school. We're young still, so plenty of years ahead to enjoy our jobs.'

Sarah thought about his words and leaned back in her chair. Steam swirled from her cup, the strong black liquid pleasant on her throat as she sipped her tea. 'You said before, you knew my mother when she was younger. What was she like?'

A smile crossed Bill's face as he remembered. 'Leila was the life of the party. When we went to dances in town she'd always be the first one up on the dance floor. Always full of fun.'

Sarah rolled her eyes. She didn't have any kind thoughts about her mother. In fact, she rarely thought about her. 'She runs a pub now, up near Mount Isa.'

Tom stood up and rested his hands on the verandah rails, looking out across the plains. A whirly wind twisted across the far paddocks, picking up bits of grass and sticks as it went. Cattle lifted their heads to watch and a flock of galahs squawked noisily as they jumped across the ground out of the way of the wind.

Sarah stood up also, shielding her eyes against the sun as she also looked across the paddocks.

'We'd better get going if we're going to get to that next job,' Bill said as he came up next to her and held out his hand for her to shake. 'It's been a pleasure to meet you, Sarah. You know talking about Leila has brought back memories of younger years on Astral Station. My mate Ringo knocked around with your mum for quite a while. They were pretty tight. I wonder what ever happened to him?'

'You mean they were a couple?'

'Yeah, they went out together. He was a loner though and I think he took off and the relationship ended. He was a good mate of mine and we worked together on the boundary fences. Best seat on a horse I've ever seen. He told me once that Ringo wasn't his real name. He'd left home when he was a kid and changed it so no one could track him down.'

'What was his real name?'

Bill thought for a long while. 'You're taking me back a few years now. I'm good with names though. I remember him saying it was Bobby Carlon or Carlton, like the beer. Something like that. He'd had a hard life before he came to Astral Station. There were bad marks on his back. Said his old man used to belt him.'

'She's never told me about him. How long ago was that?'

'They were there the night of my twenty-first. We had a big shindig at the local pub. I can still see them standing there, Ringo with his long scruffy beard and dark hair and your mum looking as pretty as ever with some flash dress on. She tried to get him to dance but he wouldn't. He was a bushman and it was rare to get him to those sorts of events. I'm not sure what happened, but he left a couple of months after that. Your mum worked at the shop for a while but then she also left town.'

Sarah's heart thumped hard. 'Did she have other boyfriends apart from this Ringo?"

'No way. They were an item.'

She clenched her teeth. Her mother had never mentioned a man called Ringo. When she had tried to get her to talk about those days she said she couldn't remember much. Sarah's birth certificate stated, 'Father Unknown' and she had always gone by her mother's surname, Hartley, same as Grandpa's. She did the maths. Bill had said that he was nearly forty-two and it had been his twenty-first birthday. That left twenty-one years in between. Her exact age.

CHAPTER 8

'Grandpa, did mum ever talk about a man called Ringo or Bobby? She would have known him when she was young and worked at the shop? Before she had me.'

Grandpa didn't look up, instead, he focussed on making his cigarette. He held the Tally paper in one hand while carefully placing strings of tobacco in the middle of it. She waited patiently as he rolled it between his fingers before twisting one end, pushing a matchstick into the open end, and pushing a little more tobacco into the cylindrical shape. 'Nope. Never heard of them. Why?'

Sarah sat next to him on the front steps, brushing the dirt from her shirt. 'It's not two people, it's one person who went by two names. Another vet came out with Tom yesterday. His name was Bill.'

'Yeah, Tom told me he was bringing him with him. He's new to the game. I hope you asked a heap of questions. That's the sort of people you need to talk to about uni. A fella who has just finished studying.'

'He was interesting to talk to and he was older than you might think. He's forty-two and only just graduated as a vet in the last couple of years.'

She repeated the story of how Bill had gained his qualifications, Grandpa's eyebrows moving up and down with each new piece of information. He wiped his forehead with his hand. 'You and I need to have a more serious chat about this. It's time for you to make some decisions. If you don't I'm going to.'

She looked down at her feet. 'I don't like cities.'

'Sometimes you just have to bite the bullet and step out of your comfort zone.'

'We'll see. I want to talk to you about something this Bill fellow said.'

'Go on.' Grandpa placed the cigarette between his lips and lit it before standing up, his eyes roving over the plains in front of them. 'I reckon there's rain coming. I can smell it.'

'Let's hope so. Those paddocks could do with some.' She moved back to the topic she wanted to discuss. 'This Bill reckons he knew Mum when she worked at the shop. He seemed to know her fairly well.'

'Well,' he said, pausing while he took a long drag of his smoke, 'she lived near where that shop was for a while. She was always social. Never listened to any advice from me or her mother. She went her own way. When she came back here to us we didn't even know she was pregnant with you until she started to show. Your Grandma picked up on it first. Leila wouldn't tell us much. I'm not sure what she told you about her life back then. She's only had a few conversations with you since you moved here. To tell you the truth I'm happy that she doesn't visit.'

'All she ever told me was that my father wanted nothing to do with me. That he left as soon as she told him she was pregnant. When I've asked her before, she reckons she couldn't remember his name.'

'I'm sorry to say, Sarah, she wasn't the greatest mother. We also tried to find out who she'd been going out with, but there was no way she was telling us anything and we decided if that's what she wanted, well it was her business. The trouble was after a couple of years or so when you were a baby, she got real unsettled again. That's why Eileen and I took you in when you were only six. We never discussed who your father was. He wasn't around so we didn't ask questions.'

'Well, I've asked her a couple of times when she's rung. Back a few years ago I became curious and wanted to know but she always told me the same thing. Now I have a lot of questions. If what Bill said is correct, this Ringo is more than likely my father.'

Grandpa's eyes opened wide. 'Jees, are you sure?'

'The dates line up and it sounds like this fella was the only one she was going out with at the time. Bill was certain that they were together for quite a while.'

'Bloody hell. This is all news to me.'

'You and I,' she replied. 'The question is, do I want to know him or find out for sure?'

Grandpa drew back on his cigarette, blowing the smoke high in the air before replying. 'The question is, does he know about you?'

Sarah stood up, her dark eyes flashing. 'Mum said he didn't want anything to do with her once she was pregnant and Bill said he took off and didn't let anyone know where he was going. It's the same time, so it sounds like Mum's story is right.'

Placing his arm around her shoulders, Grandpa squeezed her gently. 'Your mum might be right that he left her because she was pregnant, but I know from over the years that you shouldn't always believe everything she says.'

*I*t didn't take long for Sarah to find records of a man named Bobby Carlon who had once worked on properties near Boulia. Last year Uncle Ethan had bought a computer for her. It was to check the weather and news, and to learn how to do the accounts for the property and help with ordering. It had taken her months to find her way around it and in between waiting for it to respond, she could patch Grandpa's clothes and make a cup of tea.

Sometimes she looked for ways to finish high school or get into a course at university. The internet was frustratingly slow and she became bored with it, throwing a piece of fabric over it to keep the dust out.

Now she started it up, persevering with her searches, putting in different words and waiting to see what it came up with. Her body tensed and she pushed her face closer to the screen when a newspaper article appeared in front of her. It related to a court case in 2002.

Bobby Carlon had been a key witness. The man who was up on charges was a politician and had been charged with child abuse and the murder of a small girl called Sally, many years prior. She gasped out loud. The murdered child had been Bobby's younger sister and the man responsible was his uncle. She scrutinised the reports, flicking back and forth between different news articles, jotting down information as she went. When a picture of Bobby flashed up on the screen, she put her hand over her mouth in astonishment. It was a photo of him and another lady—noted as Ruby—as they emerged from the courthouse after the final day of the court hearing. Another woman grasped Bobby's arm, her head down, her long hair covering her face. Her name was listed under the photo as Theresa Carlon, the sister of the deceased child. There wasn't a photo of the young girl who had been murdered, but all the details were there about how she had been killed by the uncle and then buried in the backyard of the family home.

The evidence and then the outcome of the trial were detailed and she held her breath as she continued to read. This had not been what she had expected to find. Perhaps this was as far as she should go. Maybe family connections were better left unknown. This family had a dark past and she wasn't sure if she wanted to know any more about them.

She peered closer at the photo, looking straight into the eyes of Bobby who was staring at the camera, grief clear on his face. Dark eyes peered back at her and she reached up and traced his eyebrows. They were hers. His eyes and brows were hers. Admittedly his were more masculine and thicker, but the shape of his face, the dark hair and broody eyes belonged to her.

She called out. 'Grandpa. Grandpa. Come here.'

The sound of the television echoed along the hallway and she called louder. He would be watching the nightly news and would try and ignore her for as long as he could. It was his nightly routine. Shower, news, and then dinner.

She yelled again, 'Come here for a minute. I want you to see something.'

The sound of him getting up from his chair and coming towards her made her sit up straighter. She enlarged the picture waiting for him to appear.

'What is it? What's so important that you're making me miss the sports report? I want to see how the footy went last night.'

'Look at this. Look at this man and tell me what you see.'

Grandpa adjusted the glasses that he wore for reading and watching television. Leaning over the computer he muttered, 'Should I know him? Is he famous?'

'Have a close look and tell me who he reminds you of?'

Grandpa took off his glasses and wiped them on his shirt. He peered over the top of them. He put them back on, closing his eyes before looking again. He looked at Sarah and then back to the screen. Standing up straight he replied. 'I don't know, you tell me. Who does he remind you of?'

'Grandpa! Tell me what you think?'

'What is that fella's name and how did you find that?' His eyes followed the print as Sarah scrolled down, revealing the writing under the photo.

He read it out loud. 'Theresa Carlon, Bobby Carlon, and Ruby.'

He stopped and took off his glasses. 'Okay. Okay. So, he looks like you and you're telling me you think this is your father. So what? He's never looked for you or wanted anything to do with you. Do you know what? I remember that murder case, it was a couple of years ago and it was all over the news. Happened back in the seventies and that mongrel politician had killed a small girl and buried her in the backyard. He went to jail for it. Do you really want to be mixed up with that type?'

'I know. I've read about it on here. It was the uncle though, not this Bobby man. By the sounds of it, they brought him to justice nearly thirty years after it happened.'

Grandpa turned to walk out, his words ringing in her ears as he returned to his nightly shows. 'Ring your mother and ask her. It's about time she told the truth about this. If that's what you want. Ring her.'

Sarah looked for a bit longer before going into the lounge. She sat down next to him. 'Do you mind if I follow this up? I don't want to upset you. I'm curious though. Does he think about me? Does he wonder what happened to me? Maybe I have half brothers and sisters I don't even know about?'

'I'd rather you looked at a vet course to tell you the truth. This other matter is probably a waste of time.' He looked away from the television, his tone sympathetic as he turned to her. 'If it means something to you though, follow it up. You'll never know if you don't. I'm telling you, if it's in your heart to find out, then do so. It doesn't bother me in the least, but I'm not sure your mother will be keen on it.'

'I don't care what she thinks,' she said, agitated when she thought about having to contact her. 'I will ring her though. I want to know what she has to say. Why has she never told me about him?'

*G*randpa had been right, and Leila tried hard to avoid Sarah's questions. 'Yeah, yeah, alright, so I did go out with Ringo for a while. He left though. Didn't even come and see me or explain why. Why the hell do you need to know anything about him?'

'Mum, I want you to be honest with me. Is this man my father?'

Silence hung in the air and Sarah repeated the question. It took a long while for her mother to answer. 'Yep, he is. I went out with him for a while. He was just like the others out there though. They were only interested in work and moving on when it suited them. Nomads, wandering around the countryside and not caring about who they left behind. He even went by a different name. He told me that Ringo wasn't his real name.'

'I met a vet called Bill,' Sarah spoke slowly, trying to keep the conversation calm. 'He knew you when you worked at the shop. Ringo was his mate. He said his real name was Bobby.'

'I remember a fella called Bill he was friends with. He was wild, a big drinker. Did you say he's a vet?'

'Yes, he came out with Tom to tend to one of the horses. That's how this all came up. He remembered you.' Sarah used her words carefully, a gentler tone to her voice. 'Mum, I know it can't have been easy, you were only young and by yourself. I need to know what he said when you told him you were pregnant?'

Her mother avoided the question and Sarah took deep breaths as she listened to a run of complaints and woes about how difficult her mother's life had been and how she liked living where she did today, well away from family and her past. Sarah gave the sympathetic replies when needed, cajoling her mother into talking more. 'So, Mum, tell me what he said?'

Her mother's tone bristled with annoyance. 'I've talked enough about this, Sarah. I don't want to discuss it again. I really need to go, the bar is busy, and Lyle needs me to help serve. We work hard you know. I've carved my own life up here and what's in the past is best left behind.'

'Maybe for you, but I want to know. For years I never bothered you and you've had your life to yourself and with Lyle. We've never asked you for anything, not even after Grandma died. But now I've found a photo of this Bobby in a newspaper article, and I look exactly like him. Did he have other kids? Do I have half brothers and sisters out there that I don't know about? You must have had some sort of contact with him over the years.'

'I didn't. I never saw him again after he walked out. Now, I need to go.'

Holding her patience in check she kept her voice even. 'I will ring you again and again until you answer the question. What was his reason for not wanting to stay with you, or help support a baby? Please, Mum. Answer me and I will never bring this up again. I won't bother you.

Her mother coughed and her voice came out squeaky. 'He never knew. He left when I was only five or six weeks pregnant. At first I tried to find him to tell him, but it was too hard. No one knew where he had gone. I never told anyone else at the time about the situation and not long after that, just before I started to show, I left town. There, that's it!'

Sarah could hardly speak, her voice a whisper. 'Thanks, Mum. I won't bother you again.'

*G*randpa sat opposite Sarah at the kitchen table, sipping a small glass of scotch. He rarely drank alcohol but he'd agreed to have a glass with her as she went over the information she'd gathered. 'It's easy to track people down these days,' she said, pointing to photos and information she had printed out. 'These are the paper clippings from the court case a couple of years ago.' They looked closely at them as Grandpa picked one piece of paper up and read it before placing it back down again. 'It doesn't sound like he had a very good childhood. You know you'll probably go to all this trouble and find out he's a real mongrel. I hope you're prepared for the worst. He may deny the relationship with your mother, or he might not want to see you or have anything to do with you.'

'It seems he left home when he was a kid. One of the articles said he ran away to avoid what was happening at home.'

'A lot of the fellas who worked out here were running

from something. They wanted to avoid the law or someone chasing them for something wrong they'd done. Back then there was hardly any communication, and you could blend into the dust and do your own thing. No one asked any questions. Everyone had a story and it was often troubled.'

'I've given all that a lot of thought. This is really eating at me and for some reason I need to have some closure around what happened and find out if he knows about me or not. You're right about Mum, who knows what's the truth and what's lies.'

Grandpa made that 'hmph' noise that showed he agreed and wanted to say more but didn't. She continued talking as she passed him another sheet of paper, a photo and information from another newspaper. 'It's like I need to complete this chapter of my life, find out who he is and what he knows. Then I'll draw a line in the sand. It will be the start of something new for me.' She looked up into Grandpa's eyes, 'Once I've got this sorted out I'll follow up on those vet courses. Talking to Bill the other day not only started this string of events, but it's also given me hope that I can find a way to do some study.'

She held her hand up, knowing that was all that mattered to Grandpa. 'Ease up, don't get too excited. It might be too hard to do but I promise I will look into it.'

He mumbled into his glass. 'About bloody time. I know what Eileen would say. Forget about him and find out about the course.'

She wriggled in her seat, ignoring his words and trying to think what Grandma would advise. 'She'd probably say it was up to me. To make my own decisions. Now let me read this one out. This leads me straight to where he lives. Nothing is secret these days.'

The paper clipping showed a photo of Bobby and his 'partner' Ruby, whose property had been transformed into an organic vegetable farm. The photo was of them at a market stall and the by-line touted – *Based in the hinterland of the Sunshine Coast we have the best produce around - Fresh, organic, and ready for you to purchase in seasonal crates or individually sold. Drop in for a visit or find us at the local markets every Sunday.*

She waved it in the air. 'See, it says, drop in for a visit.'

Grandpa shook his head and downed the last of his Scotch. 'I wonder if this fella has a clue what's in store for him? It's not every day that your grown-up daughter you never knew existed, pops into your life.'

***

It took the rest of the week to make arrangements for the trip to the coast. The furthest she had ever been from the property was north to Mount Isa and south to Charleville. Apart from that, she'd never left the inland area and if there was one thing she was going to make sure she did, it was to see the ocean. 'Even if this man doesn't want to know me, at least I'll get to see a bit of Queensland. I just want to put my feet in the sand and watch dolphins.'

Her ute was packed, and she promised not to travel too far each day and to check in with Grandpa. 'I'll give you a quick ring once I settle in for the night.'

Tears welled in her eyes as she hugged him goodbye and he gave her even more instructions about driving safely. They hadn't been away from each other for more than a few days over the years, and it was a wrench to leave him by himself. This was the reason she had never bothered going anywhere before. She belonged here with him.

Standing in front of her he placed both his hands firmly on her shoulders. 'Now, get that sooky look out of your eyes, and no tears. You're not going that far away, and your Uncle Ethan is going to be over this way moving stock and working on the fences for me. There's a big wide world out there and you need to get on your horse and go and see it. Plus meet this Bobby fella.'

She giggled and wiped her hand across her eyes. 'It would be a long way to ride on a horse. Thanks, Grandpa. I wouldn't be going except for your support. I promise I'll be careful.' She gave Rusty another pat on the head before getting into the ute. As she drove away she held her hand high out the window, the vehicle turning out through the gate and onto the dirt road that would lead her into town and then on further to the highways that stretched in different directions across the vast state of Queensland.

It was hard to leave but a sense of excitement filled her as she thought about the road ahead. Not only was she going to find out about her father, but while she was on the coast she would check out some options for studying. Surely one of the two things she was looking into would work out and fall into place.

CHAPTER 12

SUNSHINE COAST HINTERLAND – 2004

*R*uby closed her eyes and leaned back in her chair as gentle hands wrapped around her shoulders from behind. Contentment filled her as Bobby bent down and kissed the top of her head. 'Good morning Ruby-Rose. I see you've already had your breakfast.'

She squeezed his hand and held it to her cheek. 'I have. I left you sleeping. You looked so peaceful.'

When he came to sit beside her his dark eyes settled on hers as she placed a cup and saucer on the table in front of him. She studied his face, his curly hair tousled from where he'd slept on it. A wave of emotion washed over her, and she leaned over and kissed him, her lips lingering on his. As she pulled away a broad smile lit up his face. 'I love you, Bobby. I still wake up every morning and can't believe that you're here with me.'

He reached out and poured himself a cup of tea. 'I can't believe it myself some days. Who would have ever thought that I'd be living on top of a hill amidst green pastures with fat healthy cows and not a spot of bull dust in sight.' He looked under the table. 'And a sleepy pup that is looking at me with one eye open and one closed.'

Smiling, she offered him some toast. 'I think the dog knows it's a sleep-in morning also.' She looked across the valley, the mountains shaded with hues of purple in the morning light. 'Who would want for anything more than this? Mum and Dad must be looking down on us, saying, who would have ever thought those two kids would end up together.'

'You read my mind,' he said. 'They must have laughed at us when we were little. I can still see you lying on your stomach on the floorboards of that tree house counting silkworms. Skinny legs sticking out from that dress you always wore and dirty bare feet.'

She stretched her legs out, grateful they'd remained slim and shapely over the years. Bobby's eyes followed her movements, and she tapped his foot with her toes. 'Are you checking out my legs?'

'You must admit, Ruby, they're great legs.'

She giggled and put her head on his shoulder. 'Thank goodness they've filled out a bit since our silkworm days. Do you remember how bossy I was and how I used to get cranky when you didn't put things back in the right place? Those orange crates that we used as shelves. You never put anything where it was supposed to go.'

'I did that just to annoy you. You'd stack those old suit-cases up and then put all the shoeboxes on top of that. Always organising me even back then.'

'You need organising sometimes. Remember Dad made that spinning thing out of wood for me. I'd get the cocoons, find a thread and wind it around the wooden spool.'

He laughed. 'What the hell did you ever think you were going to do with the silk thread. Make a golden dress out of it or something?'

'Dad always built things for me. They must have laughed at how I thought I was going to make such fine clothes out of tiny pieces of thread. I was only thinking about Dad before you got up. He used to love this time of the morning. That view.' Her gaze turned back to the mountains, remnants of fog still drifting across the valley floor.

'I think about him and your mum. They were good people.'

'They were.' She wrapped her hand around his arm. 'You had a good sleep this morning. I knew it wouldn't be too long before you got up.'

He sat up straight and stretched his arms above his head. 'This lifestyle is making me lazy. Fancy sleeping in until after the sun is up. I'd be sacked out west.'

'The slow pace is perfect. Those markets are early morning starts and long days. We need to have some sleep-ins during the week.'

Reclining back in his chair, he sipped his tea. 'I must admit I've enjoyed those mornings in bed. Sleep comes so easy these days.'

'Is it just the sleeping you enjoy?' She threw him a cheeky grin. 'I thought there might be other activities that you enjoy on those mornings.'

He laughed. 'You have ruined me. I've taken up with a seductive country girl who is fattening me with good food and leading me astray.'

She watched as he bent down and picked up the pup who snuggled in on Bobby's lap. Bobby no longer looked like the wild stockman who had come and stayed a few years ago before disappearing. Back then he'd run away from her and his past for the second time in his life; vanishing once again to the sanctity of the outback and the remoteness of the properties he worked on.

For a while, she thought she'd lost him forever and at the time believed he had no feelings for her. She'd doubted he even thought about her. But the death of her father, Francis, had sent Bobby back to her, in time to support her and then drag her out of the depressive state she fell into after the funeral.

She still missed her dad. There wasn't a day when she didn't think about him. So often she wanted to share something with him, to tell him what she and Bobby were up to and how her life had changed in yet another direction. Sometimes the tears flowed, the memories and grief overwhelming. Now though, the sad times didn't linger. She was getting on with her life. It was what her dad would have wanted and with Bobby by her side, moving on became a bit easier.

Bobby drew his eyebrows together as he looked back at her, his rugged face covered in a neatly trimmed beard, his dark curly hair making him look as handsome as ever. She loved it when he wore jeans and riding boots. He was ready for a day of work, the habits, and dress from his years spent on properties out west still part of his character. Even though he socialised a bit more these days and had embraced life on her smaller property, some of the traits from his outback life remained.

At times he was quiet, happy just to relax and listen to her talk. He still wasn't good at sitting around for too long though and was happiest when he was working with the crops, fixing a piece of machinery, or building her new fences or sheds. She watched him stroke the pup. She'd surprised him a couple of months ago with an eight-week-old red kelpie who he'd named Rusty. The pup followed him everywhere and in no time he'd trained him to do exactly what he wanted. When he rode his horse, Astral, the pup trailed along behind.

She thought about the day he'd told her he didn't want to go back out west. That he wanted to stay here with her, and yes, he would love to work on the property as a team and build a business together. The night she had crept into his bed, just before he was about to return to Western Queensland had been the turning point for them both. Feelings were now out in the open and their life was together.

'I want to grow old with you,' he'd often whisper to her. 'Just you and me. Forever more.'

Life settled and they'd started the new business, Tall Trees Produce; growing and selling organic vegetables. It was a joint project and after a year of working out the best processes, they had reached a point where the only direction was forward. Other growers in the area were quick to offer support and they'd become part of a cluster of farmers, determined to supply fresh, organic produce.

The best part was it was just the two of them. Ruby leaned over and scratched Rusty under his chin. The pup yawned lazily before closing his eyes and nestling back into Bobby. 'I've become so selfish,' Ruby said, resting her feet up on another chair as she sipped her tea. 'This has to be the ultimate. Just you and me and whatever we want to do. No one else to worry about.' She pushed her hair back from her face, feeling Bobby's eyes on her. She knew he loved the tiny denim shorts and t-shirts that were her typical day attire, and she twisted her legs around, pointing her toes to accentuate their slenderness.

He ran his hand over her leg. 'You're beautiful you know.'

She placed her feet onto his lap, enjoying his hands as they caressed her legs. They both laughed as Rusty stood up and stretched before jumping down. He didn't go far, the door mat providing a warm spot in the sun for him to resume his sleep.

'Now you've upset the dog,' Bobby said. 'You and your legs. Poor thing. He's waiting for us to go and feed the horses.'

Throwing him the sexiest look she could muster, she looked straight at him. 'The horses can wait. Is it too late to go back to bed?

'You're a minx you know.' His voice was husky as he put his cup down and pulled her over to him, her legs straddling him where he sat. As her lips pressed down on his, he muttered. 'Never too late to go back to bed with you, Ruby Rose. I'm not passing that offer up.'

Bobby hoisted her into his arms, stepped over the dog, and carried her back into the house. Rusty stared at the closed door for a while and then sighed. He lay his head back down on the mat. He'd have to wait, it didn't look like they were going to go down to the paddocks just yet.

CHAPTER 13

*S*undays were Ruby's busiest day. The local
Maleny markets had proven to be the perfect
option for selling their produce and all week they worked
on the farm, getting ready for the weekend. Everything
needed to be in the van and ready to go by four o'clock on
Sunday morning. It didn't matter if it was torrential rain
or blowing a gale – Sunday was the day they made their
money.

It wasn't always easy. Some days the rain kept the
customers away and only the regular locals came out to
brave the weather and get their fresh supplies for the
week. Other Sundays were so windy they spent half the
time making sure the marquee didn't blow away or that
the tables didn't fall over. You had to take the good with
the bad though and overall the markets were proving to
be a reliable regular source of income.

Sometimes customers bought directly from them at
the farm or rang and ordered over the phone. The variety
of cafes and restaurants at the nearby Sunshine Coast had

also become regular customers and Bobby now did a delivery service, spending one day a week transporting produce to the local community.

Life wasn't all about work though. Ruby had fallen into that trap when she was younger and now she made sure there was plenty of down time. They had settled into a routine of relaxing afternoons and nights together, just enjoying each other's company. 'We took a long time to find each other,' Ruby told him one night when they were snuggled up together in front of the fireplace. 'I don't want to waste any time. I want you all to myself.'

'I don't need anyone except you,' Bobby said, his voice shaky with emotion. 'You're everything to me.'

Bobby had brought up the subject of having children not long after he'd decided to stay. 'It doesn't worry me that much, but if you wanted to try I'd be happy to go along with whatever you want. You're not too old, you're not much past forty.'

She thought about it for a few days, making sure she knew exactly what she wanted. 'I don't want to have kids this late in life. I know some do but we have such a great life together. I don't want anything to spoil it.' He'd prompted her again to make sure, but she was adamant. 'I would have loved to have kids when I was younger, but it's too much to go through now. You're my priority and now we have the business. Life can't get any better.'

*O*ne of their favourite pastimes was to ride and some afternoons Bobby doubled Ruby on his horse. Although they often rode their own horses there was something special about being bareback on Astral together. She loved the way he moved with the horse, almost as if they were one. A mutual feeling of peacefulness enveloped them as she wrapped her arms around him, hanging on tightly as they made their way down through the paddocks.

The local cemetery was not far from the house and an easy ride together on Astral. Francis had been buried there at his own written request and Ruby's mother's ashes were now scattered over his grave. Her father had left instructions on his desk. He'd kept Mary's ashes all those years and he wanted to make sure that even in death she was next to him. *I learned how to be organised from you, Ruby Rose,* his note said. *Bury me in the ground at that cemetery near your place and scatter your mum's ashes over me. We will still be together. Put her headstone next to mine.*

Bobby's younger sister, Sally, was also buried there and today just like the day she had been placed there, the jacarandas were out in flower, their purple hues covering the ground.

Ruby jumped off Astral, landing on the carpet of fallen petals. Her riding boots disappeared under the leaves and flowers, and she looked up into the spreading canopy of the huge trees that towered above. Bobby jumped down beside her, also looking up.

'Every time I see a tree like this I remember our childhood,' she said. 'I was so naïve back then.' A melancholic sadness filtered through the branches and she clung to Bobby's arm, the wind picking up and pushing the purple flowers on the tree back and forth.

'Children are supposed to be naïve,' Bobby replied as he reached for her hand. When they neared the graves he took a deep breath. 'The air is clean, and I always feel like I can breathe easy when I'm near these magnificent trees.' He ran his hand over the bark. 'Do you remember the day I went to get up when I was lying down in the treehouse and I kicked the box of silkworm moths over? I can still hear your little bossy voice – Go down and get those moths Bobby Carlon and don't come back up until you find them all.'

'I don't know how you put up with me back then. Being an only child, I guess I just wanted everything my way.'

'You were my only solace. I don't know what my life would be without you. Both now, and back then.'

She closed her eyes. 'I can still smell the mulberries and see the purple stains that covered our feet and clothes. They were fun times. We had each other.'

'You had your mum and dad. You know your mum used to sneak me biscuits when your back was turned. She'd say you couldn't have one because your dinner was nearly ready, but she'd always put a few in my hand and whisper, quick don't let her see them.'

His face fell and she knew he was thinking of other traumatic times, a life that had forced him to run as far away as possible at a young age. It was over thirty years since Bobby had fled the violent household of his childhood. Dark sinister secrets from that time had stayed hidden for many years, a recent court case in 2002 revealing the murder of his sister, Sally, by an uncle who had often stayed with the family. The same uncle had committed other crimes, the repercussions causing Bobby's mother to be placed in a home and his sister Theresa to live a tormented childhood full of trauma and abuse.

Ruby pulled on his arm. Come on, let's put some flowers on Sally's grave. I love that she and my parents are buried near each other. It's almost like it was meant to be, as if they're taking care of her.'

***

They stood for a long while, talking to each other and reminiscing. A fresh breeze drifted across and Ruby thought how serene the area was. She looked up the hillside, past the border of towering bunya trees and beyond, to the slopes that rose gently further out.

Large paddocks stretched between straight borders of fences, the cows that dotted the landscape, fat and content as they grazed. A hawk circled above, its eyes tracking down as it watched for prey. In the distance a tractor on a nearby farm chugged along a track, making its way to the far end of the valley. It was paradise and she still felt blessed that she had found the property and started her new life here, not long before her dad passed away. He had loved it too and she had fond memories of him visiting and talking about her plans for the farm. It had been his idea to call it, Tall Trees Hill, and the name had also become part of their business. Now she had an added blessing, Bobby. Her rock and soulmate. They had created a tranquil lifestyle together, with no stress or rush. It was what she had always dreamed of. Her house on the hill, a calm existence, shared with the man she loved. Perfection.

CHAPTER 15

arket day was the busiest, but also Ruby's favourite day of the week. After a long week of weeding, picking and packing, everything was ready for an early morning start. The van Bobby had purchased and fitted out with shelves, trays, and stacking racks was packed up before dinner time the night before and their clothes ready for the day. She stood in front of the full-length mirror, scanning her face as she massaged her arms with moisturiser. She was happy with the way she looked and loved that her eyes crinkled in the corners much like how her dad's had.

Although she was forty-two, she didn't feel any different from how she had felt at twenty-one. Dark green eyes stared back, her wavy brown hair, thick and shiny, and a smattering of freckles across her cheeks and nose.

A knee-length floral dress was ironed ready to wear and her sneakers cleaned and stacked near the doorway. The forecast was for a fine day with no wind, so hopefully it would be a good day with plenty of sales. They had a range of vegetables in season and it was getting close to Christmas so there were plenty of tourists around, their different coloured number plates easy to spot when she had been into town earlier in the week.

The area was popular with visitors. The fresh mountain air, the scenic walks and waterfalls, along with cafes, parks and small shops, enticed visitors from near and far. Tomorrow held the promise of a busy day and she locked up the house, double-checking everything was ready before turning off the lights.

Bobby was already in bed and she cuddled in next to him, resting her head on his shoulder as he wrapped his arm around her and pulled her in close. 'Night Ruby-Rose. Early start in the morning.'

She closed her eyes and twisted her legs between his. 'Night Bobby. I love you.'

***

Setting up their market stall was easy. They had done it so many times before. Each week the same stalls were positioned in their spots and over the last year they had become friends with the market people around them. Some, similar to them, sold fresh produce; avocados, bananas and pineapples filling the tables on either side of theirs. Others only sold one type of food. Across from them was a stall with twelve wheelbarrows full of watermelons that would most likely sell out in the first couple of hours. Next to that, wide tables were filled with bananas, the large bunches also hanging from the supports of the stall holder's marquee. The smell of freshly baked bread wafted across the space and Ruby breathed in deeply as she waved to the bakery owners who had one of the busiest stalls, two up from them.

She smiled at those who walked past, all bustling and chatting as they prepared for the busy day ahead. 'Ruby, move those zucchinis around further so I can fit this box of beans in there.' Bobby called out, before joking with a busker who was setting up to the side of their stall.

Pedro the busker, was a regular and his banjo and he were always perched just to the side of their stall. Some of the stall holders became annoyed with the musicians, complaining that the crowds gathered and blocked the way into their shops. 'Good to see you, Pedro.' Ruby called out. 'No rain today, thank goodness.'

Pedro was eighty and fit as a fiddle. He warmed up his instrument, strumming a tune for Ruby. 'I'm always here because both of you are. This is my favourite spot.'

Bobby passed him a coffee. 'We love having you there. It means music all day for us.'

Eventually they were finished setting up and Ruby stood out the front with Pedro, surveying the tables. 'Where are the cucumbers today? Pedro asked.

'That restaurant in Noosa bought the entire stock yesterday. They have a huge food festival further north, plus a busy weekend at the beach. Lots of tourists. They took the lot. We'll have to grow more.'

A little boy wearing shorts and a t-shirt came up beside Ruby. She tousled his hair and crouched down to say hello. He was the son of a stallholder further along and he always came to talk to them on market day. Everyone watched out for the kids that came every Sunday, many of them sleeping for the first couple of hours in the back of vans or cars, snuggled in beside bags and boxes; it was the life of a market kid and some of their parents had driven four hours or more to get here.

'What have you got in the box, Hamish?' she asked him. He was the cutest kid and her heart melted when he smiled at her, two of his front teeth missing.

'The tooth fairy came last night, and I have a dollar to spend today.' He held out his hand to show her two fifty-cent pieces.

Bobby called out from behind the stall. 'You're rich Hamish. Maybe you can give us a loan.'

'You got more money than me.' He tucked it back in his pocket, sending a toothless grin Bobby's way. It was at times like this that Ruby sometimes wondered what it would have been like to have had children. Imagine having a miniature version of Bobby. A little boy with dark curly hair or maybe a girl who would follow him around everywhere, just like Rusty did. 'What's in the box,' she prompted Hamish.

'Mum said you'd like these. She said you might have something to feed them.' He slowly opened the lid of the shoe box, revealing a box filled with mulberry leaves and fat, wriggly silkworms. Their white bodies moved up and down as they ate, the leaves quickly devoured as the silkworms left their dark green droppings scattered around the box.

Ruby squealed and a couple opposite them stopped hanging sets of chimes and looked over her way. 'What's he got in there?' Cheryl from across the way called out. 'A snake?'

Bobby came to stand behind her and Ruby stood up, the shoe box in her hand as she waved to Cheryl. 'Look at these Bobby. Silkworms. Big fat silkworms. Wow, Hamish, these are beautiful.'

'My older sister hates them. She keeps saying she's going to throw the box away and feed them to the birds. That's why I brought them to the market today. Dad said I could, to keep them safe.'

Ruby tried not to laugh. 'Rearing silkworms is a serious business. You've done the right thing. Silkworms are very important and need to be cared for.'

'Do you like them, Bobby?' Hamish turned his gaze to Bobby who put his arm around Ruby's shoulders. 'I love them, Hamish. You know, when Ruby and I were little kids like you, we had a huge mulberry tree with a tree house in it. We spent all our days up there and had lots of boxes just like that one, full of silkworms. Ruby was in charge of them, of course.'

Hamish was excited and jumped up and down. 'No one ever knows anything about them. I knew you would like them.'

They looked at them for a bit longer before Hamish's mother beckoned for him to come back to their stall. She had his breakfast ready for him. She waved at Ruby who watched the boy holding the box carefully as he walked back to his mum. 'Sometimes …'

Bobby squeezed her arm. 'Don't say it. Hamish is cute and I know how you feel. Sometimes when I see him I wonder what it would be like if we had kids of our own.'

She looked up at him. 'I'm happy with us. Come on, let's sit down. It looks like the customers are starting to come in.

The first rays of sunshine filtered in through the trees, and stalls that cooked food began their menus for the day.

The smell of coffee brewing in the van up further infiltrated where they stood, and Pedro played a soulful tune on his banjo. Ruby waved to Hamish before turning to talk to her first customer of the day. The markets were open for business.

CHAPTER 16

*A*s expected, it was a busy day and Ruby didn't stop serving people all morning. At one time she looked up and the crowd in front was three deep. At this rate they'd be sold out before lunch. Good weather always brought the tourists.

Bobby served the customers also, chatting as he worked and enjoying telling those who asked, how the produce was grown. Eventually the crowds started to thin and she took the opportunity to slip away and get something for their lunch. As usual, she stopped to chat with a few of the other stallholders as she went. Sundays were not only a work day but also a fun time to socialise. She spotted Hamish tucked up in a hammock strung between two trees at the back of the family's stall. His shoe box was cradled in his arms, and she thought about how much delight a box of silkworms could bring. By the time she returned, Bobby was sitting behind the table, reading the morning newspaper. Customers were still roaming around but many were now either sitting at tables, eating and drinking or gathered around Pedro and another couple of buskers who were jamming on a small stage further up the laneway.

She bent down and kissed Bobby on the cheek, waving a tasty hamburger in front of him. He loved his meat and although she was a vegetarian there was no way he was going to conform to her ways. Sitting down beside him she breathed a sigh of relief. 'What a morning. Look at that, we've hardly anything left to take home.'

He munched on his burger, placing the newspaper on the ground as he enjoyed his lunch. 'That's the day nearly over. Just a few stragglers left. We'll give it another half an hour and then we can start packing up. I've been talking to some of the others and they've also had a good day.'

They both looked up as a young girl wandered up the laneway. She looked up at the cloth banner hanging from the top of their marquee— *Tall Tree Organics*.

Ruby's eyes followed her. She was only young and looked like she was trying to find someone. Bobby returned to reading his paper as Ruby stood up.

The girl ran her hand over some of the produce. Something was intriguing about her. Her hands and arms were tanned, as was her face. From the country, Ruby thought. No fancy makeup or the usual beach outfit, just neat blue jeans and a collared blouse. She walked up and down, looking at what was left.

'Can I help you?' Ruby asked.

The girl came to stand directly in front of her. Her eyes were dark and her hair hung in curls down to her shoulders. Ruby looked closer at her hands. They were working hands and she wondered if she came from one of the farms further out the back of where they lived. When she spoke, Ruby was reminded of people she had met from out west. A slow pattern of speech with a colloquial twang to some of the words.

'G'day, is this Tall Trees Organics.'

Ruby smiled at her. She seemed nervous. The name of the stall was on their sign. Maybe she was going to ask if they had any jobs going.

'It is. We're just about to pack up and there's not much left. Were you after something in particular?'

The girl glanced over to Bobby and then back to Ruby. 'Are you the owners?'

'My partner and I own the farm and stall. Are you looking for work?'

She spoke so quietly Ruby could hardly hear her. 'Is that Bobby?'

Ruby turned around to look at Bobby who was still head down, reading the paper. She squinted, unsure where the conversation was going. 'Yes.' She looked over her shoulder. 'Oye, Bobby. Someone here knows your name.'

He looked up. 'Do you need me?'

The girl straightened her shoulders and directed her words at Bobby. 'Could I please talk to you for a minute or perhaps I could come behind the stall where you are.'

The girl's hands were trembling, her face flushed and Ruby ushered her into a chair next to Bobby. 'Are you okay, you seem a bit shaky?' Bobby poured her a mug of water, passing it to her. He looked down at her boots and a smile lit up his face. 'I used to have a pair of boots like that once. Where are you from? They look like well-used riding boots. Are you after a job?'

She drank the entire mug of water without stopping,

only looking up once she had finished and handed him back the mug. 'I have something important to talk to you about. I'm not sure if this is the right place or time. But here goes.'

They waited for her to continue, both intrigued and still thinking she was looking for a job.

Her question was like a bolt out of the blue. 'Did you used to work out on Astral property, near Boulia?' She took a deep breath before continuing. 'And is your name Bobby Carlon?'

Bobby was silent, his eyes narrowing as she waited for an answer. He looked towards Ruby, confusion written on his face.

Ruby waited for a moment, then answered for him. 'Yes, Bobby did. Has someone sent a message for him? He hasn't been out that way for a few years now.'

The girl went to speak but it appeared she was having trouble getting her next words out.

Finally, Bobby broke the awkward silence, his voice low. 'What are you chasing? What's your name?'

'My name is Sarah Hartley and my mother is Leila Hartley.' She looked up at Ruby, twisting her mouth as if she wasn't sure if she should continue.

'It's okay, Sarah. Bobby and I have known each other for a long time and there aren't any secrets between us. Does this have something to do with the court case from years ago?'

'No. Nothing to do with that. My mother is Leila Hartley and I've been told that you went out with her for a while.'

Bobby nodded. 'I did. She worked at the grocery store in town.'

'I recently met a fella called Bill. He said he was a friend of yours during the time you were there.'

Furrows appeared on Bobby's forehead as he thought hard. 'I once knew a Bill. Wild fella who loved to ride the bulls at the rodeos. We were all friends, mind you most of the time was work, not much time for socialising.'

'Bill told me about you and Mum.'

'There's not much to tell. We went out for a while and Bill knocked around with us. I don't understand what you want to know. I left Astral Station over twenty years ago and I don't think I've seen anyone from there since. I've worked in a lot of other places all over Queensland since then.'

Ruby looked from Bobby to the girl. It was a strange conversation and she couldn't work out why Sarah had come to find Bobby. Maybe this Bill fella wanted to catch up with him.

Sarah leaned towards Bobby. 'You left my mother and never told her where you were going. That's what she said.'

Bobby mumbled something before standing up, his eyes narrowing, a confused look on his face. 'Look. It wasn't meant to be. I know it wasn't the right thing to do but I was a loner back then and I think she wanted more than I was ready to give. I had a lot going on and I left. It's also many years ago. I guess she moved on and obviously things worked out because she has a daughter. You. Don't tell me she married Bill?'

Sarah also stood up and Ruby recognised a glint of anger in her eyes. 'No, she didn't marry Bill. I need to know something.' She pushed her shoulders up and pushed her chin out. 'When you left, did you know my mother was pregnant?'

Bobby's eyes opened wide and he took a step back. He crossed his arms and a wave of panic crossed his face as he looked to Ruby for support. She came to stand beside Sarah. 'That's a big question to ask. What exactly do you want to know?' Bobby said.

'It doesn't get any simpler than what I'm about to say. I'm twenty-one years old and mum always told me that my father left because he didn't want anything to do with her or the pregnancy. She brought me up on her own for a short while but then she left me with my grandparents. Recently I met Bill who told me you two went out. He gave me dates when you left the area. He remembered because it was just after his twenty-first. I've done the maths and Bill said Mum wasn't with anyone else except you at that time or after. She left the shop a couple of months after you disappeared.'

Bobby flopped back into the chair and ran his hands through his hair. 'Are you asking me if it was me your mother was pregnant to?'

'My grandfather told me that when she came back in 1983 she was pregnant and wouldn't say who the father was. All she would say is that the man didn't want her or the baby.'

Ruby finally found her tongue. 'Bobby, when did you leave Astral Station? I remember you saying that you had a girlfriend around that time. Is this possible?

Bobby shook his head. 'How can it be possible. She's twenty-one. Don't you think I would have known about this before now?' His voice was stern. 'Did your mother ask you to come here? Is she chasing money or something?'

Tears filled Sarah's eyes. 'She doesn't have anything to do with me. She left me when I was six years old. She's always told me that you left because you didn't want a baby. It's only that I ran into Bill the other week and he mentioned you. I rang her to ask her about it. I told her I wanted the truth and I wouldn't give up until she told me. She eventually admitted that you had left before she knew she was pregnant. It was only early days and she didn't realise until after you'd gone. She looked for you but couldn't find any trace, so she gave up on finding you. I've lived my entire life thinking that you didn't want her or me.'

Bobby stared hard and Ruby looked from his eyes to the similar dark eyes of Sarah. She could tell he was working out dates in his head. 'What date is your birthday?' he asked Sarah.

'October 12th, 1983.'

He blinked hard. 'Are you sure?'

Sarah repeated it, looking at Ruby, her expression anxious. 'I don't want anything from you and I know this is completely out of the blue but I didn't know how else to tell you. I thought it was better to come and see you in person than write or ring. I'm happy to get a DNA test done if you want it proven but it doesn't really matter. Like I said I don't want anything, I just need to find out who you are. It's a step in a new journey for me.'

Bobby blinked a few times as if he thought the situation might disappear. 'This is hard to comprehend. I find it difficult to think that I haven't known about you all this time.'

'My mother isn't the best person for communication. She should have found you and let you know.'

His face was downcast. 'No, don't blame her. She wouldn't have found me no matter how hard she tried. When I left Astral Station I went to numerous places, plus I went under different names. I'm surprised you found me because I went by the name of Ringo when Leila and I were together.'

Ruby noticed that Sarah bristled at Bobby's comments and she interrupted. 'Bobby doesn't mean that he's sorry you tracked him down, do you, Bobby? He's just surprised that's all.'

Sarah bit her lip, trying to hold her emotions in check. 'I'm sorry that your trick didn't work. Your mate Bill told me you had two names. You must have told him once. He even remembered your last name.'

Bobby held his hand out, his voice shaky. 'Give me your hand.' He held it firmly and turned it over. 'You have a stockwoman's hands.' He said her name softly. 'Sarah. Sarah.'

When she looked up into his eyes, her tears overflowed and she wiped them away with her other hand. 'I've worked on the property since I left school at fourteen. I live with my grandpa. It's just him and me, and this is the first time I've ever left the western area in all these years. It's been hard for me to come here today, but it was something I had to do.'

He squeezed her hand. 'I'm so glad you did.'

Ruby clutched his arm. 'This is amazing. You have a daughter, Bobby.'

He laughed, rewarded by a wide smile from Sarah. 'I do.'

*R*uby talked with Sarah while Bobby packed away the remaining boxes and tables from the stall. There wasn't much produce left and it didn't take long. He came to stand beside them. 'So, you'll follow us back to the house? We have a lot to talk about.'

Ruby stood up and folded up her chair, placing it in the back of the van. 'We have a spare bedroom you can stay in tonight. There's plenty of room and that will give us time to get to know you properly.'

Sarah stood. 'I'd like that. This all seemed like such an easy idea when I first thought of it, but now I'm feeling a bit overwhelmed.'

Bobby passed her an apple and biscuit to eat on the drive. 'You're overwhelmed. I feel like I've been in a washing machine for the last hour. What an emotional day!'

***

Ruby listened to Bobby talk for most of the drive home. 'What a mix-up,' he said. 'It's my fault. All I wanted to do back then was to run away from everything. I thought that Leila was nice when I first went out with her but after a while, I knew she wasn't for me. What a mongrel I was, just to up and leave like that.'

'Would you have stayed if you knew she was pregnant?'

'Of course I would have. I had morals even in my mixed-up state back then.'

'Your life would have turned out completely different.'

'It would have, and you and I would have never been together like this. Strange how everything works out.'

'Dad always said that. I would love to be able to tell him this. I can hear him chuckling.'

'What do you think of her?' Bobby glanced sideways, checking the rear-view mirror to make sure that Sarah was still following.

'She's lovely,' Ruby answered. 'Well brought up I'd say, by her grandparents. What do you think?'

Bobby's shoulders rose up and down as he took a deep breath. 'It's like looking in the bloody mirror. Did you see her hands, they are miniature versions of mine?'

'She has your eyes and similar characteristics. I don't think you need a DNA test.'

'I feel the same. That could be something we can talk about tonight. I hope she stays a couple of days. This is all a bit crazy. This morning it was just you and me, now I have a daughter.'

Ruby rested her hand on his leg. 'A dark-haired beautiful daughter who reminds me very much of you.'

***

Sarah slowed as she drove towards the house on the hill. A swinging timber sign announced the property as 'Tall Tree Hill'. Besides that, was another larger sign that showed it was also the business of 'Tall Tree Organics'.

She stopped as she neared a cluster of trees, their thick boughs creating a canopy of shade that spread like an arch over the track. When she put the window down and inhaled deeply, the air was fresh and crisp, an aroma of blossoms drifting in through the car. Under the largest tree was a log bench and she longed to get out and sit on it, to take in the tunnel of trees, the sweeping vista of rolling hills behind her and the colours that were so different from where she was from.

Her body was tense and she felt the start of a headache. Apart from the apple and biscuit Bobby had given her, she hadn't eaten all day and the fact that her stomach was empty, along with the emotional morning, made her feel like all she wanted to do was curl up in a ball and go to sleep.

Lush green vegetation surrounded the driveway and she looked back up into the trees, unable to draw her eyes away. Birds called out and flitted between the branches, and a fat cow standing underneath continued chewing its cud as it stared at her. The trees formed a tunnel entrance to the yard, the ground covered in leaves and the purple flowers of the jacaranda trees that were dotted in amongst other foliage. She held her hand out the window, the air cool on her skin, even though it was summer. Dappled sunlight filtered in through a few small gaps on the edge of the grove and she looked ahead to the windy driveway.

Who would have ever thought that vegetation so green existed?

Drawing her attention back to the car ahead she took one last look, before continuing. After a while, the canopy thinned and she peered up at the house perched on the small hummock ahead. It appeared at one with the landscape, like it had been there forever and was a sentinel, looking out over the entire area. Its style was similar to some of the houses out west. Wide verandahs wrapped around the outside walls, and a few stairs led up to the front door. A corrugated tin roof shimmered in the sun and a cluster of sheds and other buildings stood next to it.

Ruby and Bobby were already out of their van and stood shielding their eyes against the sun as they watched her drive towards them. She wondered what Bobby's partner Ruby had made of the surprise announcement that he had a long-lost daughter. On the surface she appeared to handle the information with ease and seemed like a nice person. Her words were smooth and elegant and Sarah could tell she was well educated. Bobby on the other hand reminded her of the men who worked on the properties. Rough hands, a rugged face, and eyes that didn't miss anything. He hadn't tried to run from the truth of the matter and it was as if he understood how she felt about finalising her family ties so she could move on in life. When he held his hand out for her, her heart had lurched and it had been difficult to keep her emotions in check.

He was not what she had expected and far different from what he looked like in the newspaper articles. Back then his hair had been wild and long, his beard hanging down on his chest and a hat pulled low over his eyes. He might still look like a rugged stockman with well-worn riding boots and the typical Akubra hat, but his hair was short and he was neatly dressed. He also spoke with wisdom and a softness that instantly drew her to him.

His eyes had held her attention. At first it was like looking in the mirror, the same dark brooding look that was hers. But there was also a hint of sadness, and when she had initially spoken to him she could sense fear, a dread that she was going to tell him something bad. His demeanour had settled though the more she explained why she had come to see him and with Ruby adding a little to the explanations, she felt the meeting had gone well.

As she got out of the ute a sense of excitement and nerves filled her. Hopefully they could talk some more and even make plans to meet again. Now that she had found him she wanted to know more about him. It was strange but she felt an immediate connection to him, a longing to hear him talk again and to sit next to him. Wait until she rang Grandpa and told him that her father, Bobby, wasn't anything like her mother. He was calm and welcoming and perhaps she would continue to see him in the future.

CHAPTER 18

*R*uby walked toward her and Sarah once again admired her elegance. A stylish dress clung to her body and her thick brown hair was pulled back by sunglasses perched on top of her head. 'Welcome to Tall Trees Hill. This is where Bobby and I live.'

A kelpie pup bounded out from behind the house. It yapped with excitement until Ruby talked to it. Although its tail wagged non-stop, it did as it was told and sat obediently at her feet.

'Oh, my goodness,' Sarah said. 'He looks exactly like our dog at home. How old is he?'

Ruby gave the dog permission to move. 'Only a few months. I bought him as a surprise for Bobby. His name is Rusty.'

'Rusty! That's our dog's name.'

They smiled at each other. Thank goodness her father's partner was such a pleasant person. Every time she spoke she made Sarah feel at ease.

She patted Rusty, her gaze drawn back to the view in

front of them. 'It's beautiful. I've never been anywhere like this. It's so green and the cattle are fat and content.'

'It's a lovely farm. I've been here for about four years and Bobby came to live here with me a couple of years ago. It's a long story how that came about, but we were friends as small children growing up, so we've known each other for a long time.'

'Do you have children?'

'No. I was married before, many years ago, but no, no children. Just Bobby and me.'

Sarah stopped and looked back over the valley. 'That view is incredible.' In front of them was a cleared paddock, to the side, three trees that stood in a row. 'What are they called? I've never seen such tall trees and what are those mountains? They're such a strange shape. You must have one of the best views in the world.'

In front of where they stood the grassy slopes dropped off, and three trees with symmetrical conical domes stood tall, like sentries guarding the edge of the valley. Further over the volcanic plugs known as the Glasshouse Mountains rose majestically, craggy steep pinnacles thrusting upwards in a variety of different shapes.

'The trees are bunya nut trees and their fruit comes in the form of very large cones. Ruby held out her hands to show how big they were. 'Each cone has a heap of seeds you can break and eat. We roast them on a fire when they fall.' Ruby turned her gaze to the valley floor. 'The mountains have different names. She pointed to two of them. 'That one is Mount Tibrogargan and one over there is Mount Tibberoowuccum. They're traditional names given to them by the Aboriginal people.'

Sarah was drawn to the mountains. There was a tranquil feeling that floated across the landscape. 'It's magical. Almost like a wave of calm comes over you when you look out.' She closed her eyes, enjoying the cool breeze on her skin. 'It makes me feel at peace. I've only ever seen places like this in travel magazines.'

Ruby touched her gently on the arm. 'Bobby often says the same. He finds peace here too. Although this has been a shock to him today, it's a wonderful moment for you both. He's a gentle soul, Sarah, and you have a lot to catch up on. Come inside and ring your grandfather. He'll want to know you've arrived and everything is okay.'

'Thank you. You have no idea how much it means that you've both been welcoming. I had no idea what to expect. I just knew deep down I had to come and find out.'

CHAPTER 19

*R*uby showed Sarah to her room while Bobby unpacked the van. She didn't seem to have brought much with her, and Ruby imagined how difficult it must have been for her to approach them today without knowing how they'd react. 'You've done a brave thing, driving from where you live to here, without knowing how your story would be accepted. I love that you've been strong enough to do that. Imagine if you hadn't, Bobby and I might never have known about you.'

'It was almost as if someone was guiding me here. A voice in my head that kept saying, just do it. Worry about what happens when it does and if he doesn't want to know about you then so be it. Nothing ventured, nothing gained.'

***

Before long they were all sitting on the verandah, Bobby with a beer in hand and the two girls with a glass of wine. A platter of food was welcomed after the day out and Sarah was quick to eat the delicious spread Ruby placed in front of her. Ruby kept passing her more food, noticing she was obviously hungry. 'You poor thing. You probably haven't eaten much today.'

'Yes, I'm starving.'

Bobby smiled at her, shaking his head. 'I'm still in shock to find out about you, Sarah.' He held his drink out. 'I think we should have a toast.'

They held their drinks high as he spoke, his eyes turning from Ruby to Sarah. 'Here's to our new family.' He paused, struggling to speak. It was an emotional day and there was still much to talk about. 'I hope we can catch up on the years that we've missed.'

They clinked their glasses. Sarah was the first to speak. 'I think I might call you Bobby if that's okay.'

He nodded. 'That sounds fine. Let's take it slowly. We need to get to know one another first.'

Ruby passed more food around the table. 'Tell us about your Grandfather. It seems like he's an important person in your life.'

***

There was much to talk about and the chatter continued long after dinner was served. It was obvious from the way Sarah spoke that she was close to her grandfather and had been with him for nearly her entire life. Bobby fired question after question and wanted to know about where she lived and what work she did on the property.

'Do you miss that life?' Sarah asked him after she'd

explained all the details about the size and scope of Western Downs. 'I've only seen a bit of this place, but to me it looks like the opposite type of farming and country-side than where you would have been.'

'It is. I was in awe when I first came here. The cattle don't search for feed, it's pushing up under their noses. Horses are fat all year round and there aren't so many flies to bother them. As for missing out west. No, to tell the truth, I don't. Once Ruby and I decided we were going to be together here, it was another direction for me. You might say another fork in the road. By the time I came back after Ruby's father died, I'd spent most of my life out west and don't get me wrong, I loved every minute of it. Just like you, life was all about being on a horse every day and working with the stock. The dust and heat never bothered me. It's just part of it.'

Ruby looked out across the darkness, the sound of noisy cicadas rising and falling from the trees nearby. 'I've always lived on the coast and this place was starting to come together when Bobby came along. Everything just fell into place.'

Bobby's arm wrapped around her shoulders. 'Ruby lost her dear dad, Francis, not long before I returned. He was her soulmate and maybe us finding each other again after so many years, saved both of us.'

'Didn't you have a mum that cared about you either?' Sarah poured herself another cup of tea.

Ruby passed her the milk. 'Oh no, I had a wonderful mother. She was the best. She died quite a few years before Dad though, so it was just him and I for a long time.' Tears came to her eyes, just like they often did when she remembered her parents. 'Dad's death left a huge hole in my life. I miss him so much. But …' she drew her hand across her eyes, 'he had a good life and he wouldn't want me to mope around. Once Bobby and I worked out what we wanted to do we started growing organic vegetables on the flats here behind the house. It took a while to get the business going, but it's full-on now and we love it.'

Bobby added, 'We run a few cattle too. Like I said though, that's easy to do with these paddocks.'

'It's so different here than where I come from.' Sarah looked up into the sky. 'I'll remember this place forever.'

Bobby sat up in his chair. 'I hope you aren't in a hurry to leave. We have so much to talk about.'

'I told Grandpa I'd be gone a week. My aim after contacting you was to see the ocean, and hopefully some dolphins before I go back.'

'Have you been to the beach much?' Ruby asked.

'No. I've never been to the coast. I was supposed to come in a couple of years ago. I went out with a fella once who'd travelled around Australia. He wanted to bring me to the coast and see the waves. We broke up though and he moved on.'

'Do you have a boyfriend now?' Ruby asked.

Sarah laughed. 'Oh no, not me. I only went out with him for a while.' She looked up at the sky again. 'I don't know, I've just never met anyone I like that much. My life has been working, and Grandpa, since I finished school.'

'You have to let us take you to the beach,' Bobby said. 'Ruby and I will take you out for a day, show you some of the coastline. We have some favourite spots and I can assure you there will be dolphins there.'

Sarah sat up, her eyes lighting up. 'Really? I would love that.'

Bobby added. 'We can go for a swim.'

'I can't swim very well.'

He looked toward Ruby and laughed. 'Neither can Ruby.'

'I'd love to feel the water. Saltwater, it just seems so strange.'

Bobby crossed his arms and looked at Sarah across the table. 'I'm intrigued why you left school so young. I left when I was that age. There were several reasons why. I'm surprised that you did though.'

Ruby interjected. 'It's late and it's been a long day for Sarah. We can talk about it in the morning.' She turned to Sarah. 'We'd love you to stay as long as you want. That way we can get to know you. You're part of our family now.'

'Thank you.' Sarah's voice was quiet and Ruby could tell she was tired.

'C'mon and I'll make sure you're settled for the night.'

***

Bobby stood silently on the edge of the hill. He rubbed his hand over the rough bark of the bunya tree, staring up into the boughs silhouetted in the darkness by the light of the moon. To the side of the trees, the grassy paddock stretched down to the bushes below. A group of cows lay together, their legs tucked up under them as they settled in for the night.

He loved his cows. There was something about them that was homely, reassuring. Even as a kid he'd loved Ruby's cow. He could still remember the cow's eyes, the thick dark centres that used to stare into his, like it understood the torment of his home life. Ruby on the other hand had a love, hate relationship with cows. The yard cow from her childhood had enjoyed chasing her whenever the opportunity arose and to this day she was still nervous to walk past the placid cows that roamed up and down their hills.

The small herd of cows was his project. There had been a few on the property when he arrived but over the last couple of years he'd built the herd up and it was a highlight of the day to be able to walk amongst them or sit on the verandah and watch them.

He could sense the same love of animals in Sarah. He spoke her name quietly, 'Sarah.'

Who would have imagined that in the space of twenty-four hours his life could change so drastically? The morning had started the same as any other market day, but now, everything was not the same. The last twenty-one years were not what he had thought they were. While he had been working and roaming from station to station, a baby girl had been born, reared by her mother for a short while and then left for her grandparents to bring up.

He turned away from the tree to stare out across the valley. The moon was three-quarters and its shape rose slowly in the east. The golden glow filtered across the countryside and he closed his eyes and breathed in deeply.

It had been what he loved most about Ruby's place when he had returned from out west. His mind settled and the trees wrapped around him like a cocoon. The churning panicky feeling that he used to experience regularly, barely surfaced. *Why did so many kids have dysfunctional lives?* he thought. Even Sarah's had not been ideal.

Luckily she'd had her grandparents, who seemed to have done an amazing job. But fancy a mother leaving a small girl. He tried to think hard what Leila had looked like when they had gone out together. They were distant memories though and so much had happened in between. Back then, they'd been young and she had been full of fun and laughter. It had been comforting to have someone love him like she did, someone who cared and made him feel like he was worth something.

He remembered she'd wanted more though. She'd talked about marriage and kids and just like he always did, he packed up his swag and moved on. He figured she'd get over him. There were plenty of young fellas chasing her. It was for the best anyway. His moods swung like the pendulum on a clock and in the end, he'd only be a burden. There was a swag of childhood baggage hanging on his back and at that age, he had no idea how to handle it. Even when he was older it had been hard enough. The best way when he was a young man had been to not get close to anyone. To keep to himself and be happy with his job and the animals that he worked with.

That had been enough, until he met Ruby-Rose again. She had complicated his thinking and forced him to look at where he'd been and where he was going. To add to that, they had fallen in love. They'd sit for hours and talk, about everything. Sometimes they'd talk about the dark moments in his life, but not that often. It wasn't what defined him now and it affected him less and less. When the dark clouds started to gather in his mind he recognised the warning signs and dealt with them, just how Ruby had taught him to; to leave the evil behind and to concentrate on the positive.

The branches above him rustled as a possum jumped from one limb to another. The night was still and his mind settled. He had surprised himself with how well he dealt with the events of today. In previous years and when he was younger he would have run a mile from anything that threatened to tie him down or reveal itself as family connections. As a teenager and after, he had re-invented himself with false names and kept his distance from anything that threatened to come close to his emotions.

Ruby had saved him and over the last couple of years, his real personality had been allowed to shine. He was no longer the morose, moody man she had brought back from out west. Now he liked to sit and chat, be part of discussions and make decisions.

Now there wasn't just Ruby, there was a girl who was his daughter. He went over the conversations of the day and night. So many years he hadn't known about, times he had missed, moments when he should have been there.

He battled with a wave of conflicting anger at Leila for keeping the pregnancy and baby a secret, but just as quickly a pang of guilt pressed down and he knew she wouldn't have found him anyway. He was to blame, not her. Ruby was right when she said there was no use looking back. He couldn't change the past and he needed to appreciate that Sarah had made the effort and found him. It wasn't too late. They had time to get to know each other.

He sat on a stump positioned to take in the view. In the darkness, there wasn't much to see, but the moon threw some light and he could make out the shapes of the mountains in the distance. He visualised Sarah, her dark eyes and tanned face. He felt an instant attachment to her, a need to see her again and an overwhelming reaction to protect her. She was still so young. She'd said she would be around for a week before heading back out, but he needed more time than that. Standing up he took one last look at the moon. A few clouds scuttled across it, the surroundings darkening as the light from it dimmed. Ruby would know what they should do next.

CHAPTER 20

*S*arah slept soundly, the long drive, good food and wine, sending her into a deep sleep. When she woke in the morning it took a moment to work out where she was. The events of the previous day replayed in her mind and she sat up looking around. It was a lovely room and Ruby obviously had a flair for making interiors look nice; the dressing table, bed and wardrobe all matching in a golden timber. Timber VJ boards lined the wall, the golden floorboards wide and polished, and a wooden door that reminded her of home. She ran her hand over the bedspread and sheets that were all in the same pattern. The material was soft and pretty, nothing like the ill-matched sheets and old woollen blankets that were on her bed back home.

There was a lot to learn. This place was a different world from where she came from. The most important part was that she had found her father, a man who wanted to get to know her and hadn't pushed her away. And to top it off, his partner wanted the same.

The smell of bacon cooking wafted in through the open window and a dog barked outside as she threw her legs over the edge of the bed, excited about the day ahead.

'Good morning,' Bobby said from where he sat at the outside table. He stood and pulled a bright yellow chair out for her as she bent down and patted Rusty's head. 'He's excited to have someone new joining us for breakfast. I'm still training him. He's a good one, but only young.' Bobby clicked his fingers and Rusty promptly came to sit beside him.

She took a seat and pushed her hair behind her ears. It was thick, and wavier than usual this morning, the humidity of the coastal region far different from the inland dry. 'My hair is out of control here, it must be the moisture in the air.'

Ruby placed a plate in front of her, beckoning for her to help herself to other food in the middle of the table. Sarah licked her lips, the crispy bacon and eggs a delicious mixture on her plate. Adding mushrooms and fried tomato, she nodded at the offer of coffee from a pot Ruby held. 'Oh, my goodness, thank you. It smells amazing. This verandah is the perfect spot.'

'We usually eat here,' Ruby replied. 'Bobby likes to be outside rather than in and we spend a lot of our spare time on the verandah.'

Sarah ran her hand over the chair she was sitting on. They were old wooden chairs that had been brought to life by glossy paint. 'I love this colour.'

'That's my colour. Nice and bright,' Bobby said.

She noticed Ruby and him exchange a look and she pondered the connection between the two of them. Sometimes they didn't seem to need to talk out loud. It was as if they knew what the other was thinking. Grandpa had told her that he and Grandma had been like that. Kindred spirits, together for so long they understood each other's thoughts. It would be nice to be that close to someone. Over the years she hadn't had many boyfriends. It didn't interest her and although plenty of young men had tried to gain her attention—she was after all often the only female worker on the property—she had never encouraged them and had often been abrupt in declining their offers for dates.

It worried Grandpa that she never went out with any of them. 'Before long you should think about finding a nice fella. Someone who'll treat you well.'

She had been sure in her response. 'I'm not interested. I'm happy here with you and not once have I ever thought of any of those fellas as more than another worker or friend. It's not a priority for me.'

It had never interested her, the whole romance, falling in love and getting married thing. Now as she watched Bobby and Ruby she felt a tinge of regret. What if she never felt that way about anyone. Would she end up old and alone, never experiencing what her grandparents had? She sighed, jumping a little as Ruby spoke. 'Penny for your thoughts.'

Sarah finished her mouthful of food before answering. 'There is a lot to think about. I wanted to thank you both for such a lovely welcome. I'm so glad I came.'

'We are too. Yesterday was one of the best days of my life. Thank you,' Bobby said.

***

They sat on the verandah for hours. Sarah plied Bobby with questions and Ruby was impressed with how he opened up and talked about his years out west and the times he had spent with Leila. These days he was happy and fun to be with. The seriousness of his former life was left behind. Ruby watched him, talking to Sarah, his voice animated, a smile constantly on his face.

Having this young girl come into their life was also a big step for Ruby. She was full of energy and positivity, reminding Ruby of herself at that age. Sarah's relationship with her grandfather was also much like what she had with her father and hopefully they would meet him one day. She spoke her thoughts out loud. 'Do you know what Bobby? It might be a good idea for us to meet Sarah's grandfather. Perhaps he could come for a visit.'

Bobby's eyes lit up and he looked at Sarah. 'Do you think he'd like to meet us?'

'He sounded excited when I spoke to him on the phone last night. I would love you to meet him. He won't come to the coast though. He's like me and doesn't venture far from home.'

Bobby didn't reply and they waited as he rubbed his hands over his beard. Ruby knew that it meant he was thinking, throwing an idea back and forth. Eventually he spoke, his deep slow voice holding their attention. 'How about I go with you when you drive back out. I could hitch a ride with you and then find my own way back here. There'll be a truck coming this way or I can fly back. What do you think? Ruby could come too if she wanted.'

A look of excitement swept across Sarah's face. 'I never thought about that. I didn't know you'd be interested in meeting him. I'd love you both to come out home.'

Ruby placed her hand over Bobby's. 'I might leave it to the two of you. I've got a few counselling jobs coming up and it will be better if I stay and run the business as usual.' She held up her hand as Bobby started to talk. 'I know you'd like me to come, but I also think it's important the two of you make the trip together.'

Sarah was beaming. 'Would you really come out and meet him? I mean, it's a long way from here.'

A wide smile crossed Bobby's face. 'That's not far for me. I'd love to.'

***

They'd spent the next hour putting plans in place. Sarah rang her grandfather. He had been speechless, 'beyond joy' were his words. Plans were discussed and they would spend the next few days showing Sarah around, making sure she wet her feet in the ocean and saw some dolphins. After that, Bobby would drive out with Sarah. He could spend a week at her place and then return.

Ruby watched the two of them as they saddled the horses. They were so alike and she admired the calm demeanour of the young girl. Her grandparents had done a great job bringing her up and she could tell that Bobby had formed an instant attachment to her. She also felt a special connection and typically had started to think about how she could help her in whatever she wanted to do.

They'd both tried to draw her into a discussion about why she had left school so young and was she happy doing what she was. 'I love where I live and being with

Grandpa. It's just him and I. We like it like that. He misses Grandma every day, but I'm there to work with him and we're company for each other.'

It was so much like the relationship Ruby had had with her father, that similar bond and reliance on each other for company. From experience she knew that although it seemed like a perfect situation at the time, as a young person you should also be fulfilling yourself with other pastimes and acquaintances. Sarah had answered their questions about boyfriends and relationships over the years. 'No, not me. I stay away from all that. Just Grandpa and me.'

Bobby glanced Ruby's way a few times and she knew he shared her unspoken view that living in such an isolated spot and not mixing with many people was sometimes not a great option. It could become an easy way out. It was fine if that was what you wanted, but at twenty-one years old Sarah should be looking ahead to what she wanted to do and experiencing a bit more in life.

They'd let the conversation slide, not wanting to press too much about her private life. One step at a time.

**

Bobby rode along the track that led away from the house and down to the main gate. He stopped under the canopy of the trees that formed a tunnel above them, watching Sarah as she stared up. Coming from out west, the sight of the heavy dark green foliage was something unique, a vastly different growth than the spikey spinifex grass and spindly dry scrub that grew where she came from.

Her voice was clear and youthful and he was filled with emotion when she spoke. How could such a beautiful young girl be his daughter? What a wonderful thing it was. She caught him staring at her. 'You'll get used to me, Sarah. I get a bit emotional sometimes.'

'Do you get upset easily? Maybe that's where I get it from because I cry when I'm sad, and also when I'm happy.'

He cleared his throat. 'I was upset a lot as a kid. Always crying. Not Ruby. She was tough as nails.' He swivelled in his saddle, looking up into the branches, blue flecks of the summer Queensland sky poking through the gaps in the leaves. 'As an adult though, I'm hopeless. It doesn't take much to set me off. Ruby-Rose has taught me that it's okay though. As young men we were expected to be tough, not to show emotion. That's all bullshit, excuse the language, but that's the only explanation for it. C'mon, I want to show you somewhere special.'

They cantered side by side down the track, Sarah as comfortable in the saddle as he was. She rode Ruby's horse, Tap, her poise drawing his attention. When they stopped at the gate he commented. 'You've got a lovely seat on the horse. Do you train them out home?'

Her face was animated. 'Oh yes. That's my favourite thing. I train the horses and the dogs that work with us. Grandpa says I have a magical way with them. That they're at one with me and my skills are like no-one else's he's ever seen.' She patted Tap on the neck. 'That is apart from himself. Like him, I love animals. Perhaps that's why I don't bother with humans so much.' She looked wistfully across the valley. 'You might understand that.'

He jumped down to open the gate. 'Sure do. Sometimes you can trust animals more than people.'

***

The horses walked slowly down the winding path, stopping now and then as Bobby pointed to different parts of the farm. Sarah was fascinated by the strangely shaped mountains that jutted up from the valley floor that she'd observed the night before and she practised the names, sounding them out slowly as Bobby repeated them for her. Before they reached the bottom, Bobby turned off through another gate, the track he said, a lesser-known way that led to where they were headed. This track was narrow, a well-beaten path that the cattle followed to get to lusher pastures. Thick grass grew along the edges, flanked by towering gum trees on either side. Bobby talked as they went, explaining all the different plants and answering Sarah's questions about the cattle and adjoining farms.

Eventually they came to a cleared area. 'We'll tie the horses up here and walk in,' he said. 'This is the local cemetery and I want to share a story with you and show you something.'

Sarah came up beside him as they walked in between the headstones. Some had fresh flowers on them and they stopped to read some of the older ones, dating back to the 1800s. When they came to an area where the ground was covered in purple flowers from the jacaranda tree, Bobby stopped and took his hat off. He stood looking down.

Sarah spoke quietly. 'I think I know why we're here.

This is how I found you. I read the newspaper article about the court case.' She knelt and read the inscription on the marble headstone. 'This is your little sister's grave, Sally.'

Bobby stood upright, holding his hat, his hands gripping the rim. She stood up facing him. 'You don't have to tell me what happened. I know. I read all about it. That's why you came back, isn't it? You came back to testify and put your uncle in jail.'

He leaned down and brushed some leaves and flowers from the flat marble surface that covered the grave. His voice was barely audible. 'It is. Ruby made me come back. If it wasn't for her I wouldn't have. I would have run as far as I could in the other direction. She's an amazing woman.' He stood up and looked Sarah in the eye. 'If I hadn't come back I may never have found you either. I wanted you to see this. Sally would have been your aunty.'

'This is a special place. It's very restful and she must be at peace here.'

'That's exactly what Ruby says. Yes, she is at peace.'

They stood for a while, neither speaking, both lost in their thoughts. After a while, Bobby beckoned for Sarah to follow as he led her to Francis and Mary's grave. The two headstones stood next to each other, rows of bright flowers bordering the plot. 'It sounds like Ruby had lovely parents,' Sarah said.

'She did. They were good to me as a kid and Francis meant a lot to me as an adult. If it wasn't for him I would have lost contact after the court case. He would love it that Ruby and I are together and I reckon I can see him smiling, knowing that you're here now too.'

***

They were quiet as they rode home, Bobby leading the way back through the narrow path and onto the main track back to the house.

He always felt nostalgic after a trip to the cemetery and he only nodded in response when Sarah talked on the way back. It had been a big couple of days and he was talked out, sitting happily that afternoon as he listened to the two women chat about the business and property. They turned in early that night, the promise of getting up and watching the sun rise over the ocean a good reason to go to bed early and be fresh and ready to go in the morning.

CHAPTER 21

*S*arah lay in bed going over everything from the day. The ride had been the highlight and she was humbled that Bobby shared the events of his past. He had been quiet on the way back and after a while she stopped asking him questions and let him be. His childhood had been tumultuous and watching him at the graveside of his little sister was unsettling, a sadness lingering for what had occurred.

Mixed up lives, Sarah thought. At least she had been given a stable childhood. In the end it hadn't mattered that her mother or Bobby hadn't been there for all those years. She had been safe and loved. Grandpa was her rock and tonight she missed him. He was a long way away and she thought about what he would be doing, sitting in the lounge room by himself and probably falling asleep in his chair like he often did.

It would be quiet in the house without her and a pang of homesickness made her count down the days. Just a few more and she would head home, and with Bobby. She snuggled down into the bed. How exciting, taking her father home. Then they would all know each other. Maybe Bobby and Ruby would come and visit regularly. She fell into a deep sleep, a minor storm not waking her as it threw leaves and small twigs against the windows. Not even Rusty barking at the thunder, or the sound of a branch hitting the roof woke her. She was dreaming about rolling waves and dolphins.

CHAPTER 22

*M*ist covered the valley in the early morning, only the very tip of one of the mountains poking through the heavy carpet of white. Ruby handed Sarah some bathers and a beach towel and she felt very conspicuous as she got in the car with only a flimsy cotton dress thrown over the top. 'Wear this,' Ruby said. 'Take your shorts and shirt with you and then if you want you can get changed after the swim.'

She pulled the dress down, uneasy as it came to above her knees. 'It's a bit short,' she said to Ruby. 'I don't wear dresses. I don't even own one.'

'Show off those legs.' Ruby giggled and swirled in her attire, also a short flowery dress thrown over her bikini. There was no way that Sarah was wearing skimpy togs like that. She had asked Ruby to keep looking through her drawers until she found a respectable one-piece. 'There's no way I'm showing that much skin.'

Ruby laughed as she handed Sarah a straw hat and pair

of thongs for her feet. 'We'll make a beach girl out of you yet. I do like your tan line.'

They'd both giggled at Sarah's reflection in the mirror. Years of wearing jeans and work shirts had left a definite line around her upper arm. 'Sometimes I wear work shorts but mainly jeans. I can't believe how clear that line is or how pale my body is.'

Ruby handed her the sunscreen. 'Get that on you. The summer sun will love your white skin.'

***

It was a perfect day, with blue summer skies and just a light wind. Bobby led the way to their usual spot, stopping at the headland and pointing beyond the breakers. Sarah squealed and jumped up and down like a little kid, grabbing onto Ruby's arm. 'Oh my God. Look at them. They're right there.'

Sets of waves broke on the rocky headland below, the white foam splurging up before smashing onto the jagged rocks that lined the point. Further out where larger waves rose, board riders waited patiently, turning where they sat before catching a wave, standing to ride the wave in towards the shore. In between the riders, the grey bodies of about twenty dolphins speared through the waves, heading in the same direction as the board riders. As they neared the beach, the dolphins disappeared, the riders lying back down on their boards as they hung on amidst the washing machine of frothy white water.

'Where did they go? Where are they? Sarah looked carefully through the dim light of the early morning. Bobby pointed out further.

'Just wait, they'll re-surface back out there. They won't come in too close to the beach. They turn and zip back out.'

The tip of the sun appeared and the colours of the water turned from a dark blue to a lighter shade. Pinks and yellows splashed across the sky as the sun peeped up over the horizon. In front of them in the calmer waters the dolphins cavorted and one spun in the air, dancing on its tail before splashing back down again. The group of about twenty, played, rising up and out of the water. Sarah clutched Ruby's arm again, her face flushed with excitement. 'I'll never forget this.'

They eventually managed to drag her away, the dolphins heading further out to sea, only a splash now and then to see where they were. 'You'll have to come back another time and we'll take you to see the whales. They're just as spectacular,' Bobby said.

'I can't even imagine what that's like. It makes me realise that I've missed out on different experiences.'

'That's right, however most people never get to experience what you and I have, working out on the properties. The sunsets, the dust storms and being with the people out there.'

Ruby added into the discussion. 'You would have seen and done things that I've never done but you should try to not limit yourself. You're so young and you have time to experience all that you want. It's a big world out there and if there's something you want to do you should do it.'

Sarah was quiet as they walked along the track and Ruby could tell she was thinking about what they'd spoken about. There was more to the young girl than met the eye and Ruby had the feeling she was holding back talking to them about what she wanted in life. She said it was just to continue working and living with her grandfather, but she sensed something else. Every now and then it was as if Sarah was looking at what was around her, her eyes wide. Was she wondering if she was missing out on something, or was there something particular she dreamed of doing?

Perhaps Bobby would talk to her on the way out west. It was a long drive, there would be plenty of time for conversations.

***

Sarah walked gingerly down towards the water. She had been shy about taking her dress off and walking around in her bathers and Ruby had laughed at the young girl's wariness of showing so much skin. Ruby closed her eyes as Bobby rubbed sunscreen on her back, his hands warm and firm on her skin. She thought back to when he had brought her to the beach and let the water wash away her grief.

'Watch the waves,' Bobby told Sarah, 'Ruby has been dumped here numerous times. It's quite funny to watch.'

She opened her eyes and glared at him. 'Someone was supposed to be holding my hand but they let go. My advice is don't turn your back on the water.'

Sarah looked nervous, her eyes locked on the waves that continually rolled in. There were a few other people around but the sun had only just come up and most people would wait until later to arrive. Ruby beckoned for Sarah to come with them as Bobby walked ahead. His broad back was tanned, his legs even darker. These days they came to the beach regularly and he had even started to learn how to ride a surfboard. His muscly legs strode out and when he reached the water he bent down and threw handfuls of water over his curly black hair. He turned to them. 'C'mon you two.' With that he waded out, stepping out over the waves until he was in deeper water. They watched as he dove over the top of a wave, swimming out further until only his shoulders and head were visible.'

'I'm not going out there,' Sarah said. 'No way. I can hardly swim. Those waves are huge.'

'I'm not a strong swimmer either. Just stand here. You don't have to come out with us, just enjoy the water.' With that Ruby waded out before swimming out to join Bobby. She clung onto him, jumping on his back as they splashed around, rising up and down with the swells that rolled in from the east.

***

Sarah watched them as she walked a bit further out. Tiny waves lapped at her feet, her toes squishing into the soft sand and the touch of the cold water refreshing on her legs. She folded her arms as a couple of men walked into the ocean near her. They called out hello and she lifted her hand and gave them a quick wave. It felt like being naked and she pulled the sides of the bathers down, making sure her backside was covered.

Ruby had strutted around in her tiny bikinis, her slim body tanned and lithe, long legs striding out confidently as she followed Bobby into the ocean. To her right a family sat at the water's edge, the young mum, similar to

Ruby, wearing only a tiny bikini. The dad wore blue board shorts, just like Bobby wore and she was fascinated by the different attire for a day at the beach. The couple sat with a baby in between them, the small waves licking over its chubby legs, its little squeals of delight a happy sound on such a beautiful morning.

Other families started to arrive further down the beach and she watched as parents applied sunscreen to kids, passing them their boards, or buckets and spades as they walked down to the water with them. A young couple arrived and set up near the family, the girl who looked to be about the same age as she was, taking off her bikini top and sunbaking topless right there next to everyone. Sarah's cheeks flushed and she kept her eyes down as the man who was with the girl ran past with a board under his arm.

He talked to another two girls who also had boards under their arms. The three of them entered the ocean to the right of where Bobby and Ruby were and quickly paddled out past the breakers. Was this how young people spent their days, playing in the water? She rarely had a day off work. Usually only when Grandpa insisted or when the rain came. Even then, there was always something to do. Inside jobs were also plentiful and she had a routine for the cleaning and housework on those days off.

Grandpa often tried to get her to go to social events in town and had even accompanied her one night when a well-known band played at the town hall. But she had been happy when they left and went home. That was where she was most content.

Today, watching other people her age, left her confused. She sat down in the water, letting the small waves lap over her. A bigger one took her by surprise and she stood up as it banged hard against her. They just kept rolling in. They didn't stop and out further the white foam on top rolled over and smashed down hard. She'd held her hand over her mouth as huge waves approached some of the swimmers. But they'd put their hands in front of them, and just like the dolphins, disappeared underneath the wave, coming up the other side and waiting for the next one. The ocean was powerful and there was no way she'd go any further. She waved back at Bobby and Ruby, shaking her head when Bobby beckoned for her to come out to where they were.

They looked so romantic together. She hadn't seen a couple act like them before. They loved each other. It was clear by the way they spoke and how they looked at each other. Their conversation was interesting and she hung off every word, intrigued by the different topics they discussed. They were good people and now she would get to introduce Bobby to Grandpa. Everything had fallen into place.

CHAPTER 23

*B*obby and Sarah took turns driving when they returned to Western Downs. Bobby had to admit that Sarah was a good driver, and her skills showed she had been well-schooled in traversing country tracks. For her age she was adept at most things that were important when living where she did. He'd joked with her about her water abilities though, reminding her that learning to swim was a priority. 'You never know when you'll need it. We always swam in the waterholes and creeks. You need to learn.'

He'd enjoyed being with her and it was good to sit in the passenger's seat and not drive for once. It was however the start of summer and the temperature nudged forty degrees as they approached the town. 'Halfway between Darwin and Melbourne, we used to say,' Bobby joked, looking at the large sign that welcomed them to the small township of Boulia. 'Welcome to Boulia, home of the Min Min Light.' He looked at Sarah. 'It's a while since I was here.'

'Nothing will have changed. The town's always the same. I don't come in that often, mainly to get supplies.' She turned off the main road, following a dirt road that led out to Western Downs.

'Only another hour and a bit now. We're nearly there.'

*G*randpa was waiting for them on the front steps, Rusty at his feet. It was surreal to see him and Bobby together and she watched as they shook hands and spoke to each other. From that moment on, it was as if they had always known one another. They spoke the same language, cattle, horses and the weather. Bobby also knew some of the local people Grandpa knew. A weight lifted from her shoulders, the final part of the puzzle fitting together.

When they sat and ate dinner the discussion flowed and she sat back and listened, the sound of the men's voices a soothing, warm sound that enveloped her. Most of her life had been spent in the company of men with only a few women to talk to over the years. She had quickly become attached to Bobby, he was much like she was. He spoke slowly and thought about what he said, his ideas similar to hers about the way to train animals or run stock in the paddocks.

He wanted to work while he was here, and Grandpa's

face lit up as they organised what they would do in the next few days. A truck was picking up a load of cattle at the end of the week, taking them back to Rockhampton. Bobby would get a lift back with the driver and then easily make his way south from there. 'The train's easy enough and quick. I don't want to leave Ruby for too long. The markets are busy even when there are two of us.'

Bobby talked about his life when he'd first arrived on Astral Station as well as the business that Ruby and him now ran. Grandpa was curious about the production of organic produce and he ran his hand across his white beard as he listened. 'There are so many more opportunities for young people on the coast. These properties out here are great when a family is running them, but I worry about Sarah here. She needs to spread her wings.'

Sarah sat up quickly and stopped her daydreaming. 'Now, now Grandpa. This discussion is old and I know what I want, and that's to be here with you.'

The old man muttered under his breath and looked over the rims of his glasses that he used for reading. 'Bobby and I need to talk about what my thoughts are on your future.'

She bristled, a scowl crossing her face, reminding Bobby of his own angry look. 'Don't discuss me and my future. I'm twenty-one years old and I'll decide what I want to do.'

Grandpa leaned back in his chair and she could tell he wanted a cigarette. 'I used to smoke inside but young Sarah laid down some rules a few years ago.'

Bobby stood up. 'Maybe we can sit outside.'

Happy that someone had taken his side, Grandpa stood also. 'Sounds like a good idea. It's that bloody hot the air con's not making much difference anyway. Sometimes you can't tell if it's working or not.'

'Any excuse for a smoke,' Sarah said, leading the way outside and holding the door open for the two men.

Although the sun had long set, the night air was heavy and heat pressed down on the parched land. 'We have to get rain soon,' Grandpa said. 'I feel like there's some coming.' The three of them looked across the paddocks, the glow of the moon lighting up the countryside. There wasn't a sound, the land and its animals still. Grandpa's voice was deep and she soaked in the sound of it. 'You know I've lived on this property my entire life, and my parents before me. That land is in my bones, it's a living part of me. I'll die out here. I don't want to be anywhere else. If I get sick I'll go to the top of that hill there,' he pointed to a small hump in the distance, 'and no one will find me. No hospitals for me.'

'Don't talk like that. You're going to live forever,' Sarah chided him.

Grandpa threw Bobby a knowing look. 'It's a good thing that Sarah tracked you down after all these years. I'm sorry to say—because she's my daughter—but Leila wasn't very good at being a mother. Sara was lucky to have her grandmother and me as family. We brought her up and like us, she's attached to this property. It's interesting that you made a move from working out here.'

Bobby leaned on the verandah rail. 'It's a beautiful part of the country and if it wasn't for Ruby-Rose I'd still be out here. I was a loner though. Happy about it at the time, and it suited me as I didn't want to be amongst people. Now my time is spent on the mountains near the coast.

It's cooler, the air is clean and I've settled into the next part of my life.'

'Hear that Sarah. You can make a change and still be happy.' The old man ignored her glares, continuing to face Bobby and make sure he had his full attention. 'Has Sarah told you she dreams of being a vet?'

Bobby was surprised. 'No, that's the first I've heard of it.'

Grandpa talked over the top of Sarah, who tried hard to stop him from revealing her secrets. 'She's wanted it for a long time, and I tried to find out information for her and ask the local vet. Did you tell Bobby that you talked to Bill only the week before you left? That was, in fact, the day you found out your mother hadn't been telling you the truth about who your father was.'

'Grandpa. Enough. Bobby doesn't need to know all those things.'

Bobby straightened up and gave her a stern look. 'I actually do. I asked you back at our place what had happened to your schooling and why you didn't continue. You didn't mention that there was something you wanted to do.'

'Well, she does want to do something other than working here.' Grandpa took deep puffs of his cigarette, flicking the ash into a tin next to him. 'She needs to find a way to do her senior schooling and then study. It can't be done properly from out here. Someone needs to help her and none of us here know how to.'

'Why didn't you say something when you were at our place. Ruby is great with that sort of thing. She's a social worker and spent years at university. She'll know all the ins and outs and she'd be able to work out how you can do it.'

Sarah smiled at Bobby before glaring at her grandfather. 'Look, it's something I think about from time to time, but it's not really what I want.'

The old man's voice carried a hint of frustration. 'That's bullshit! You dream about it and the only reason you won't go and do it is that you'd have to move away from here and leave me.' He looked squarely at Bobby. 'I want her to go. I want her to do it. She'd make a great vet.'

Bobby crossed his arms. 'You would. I could see you doing that. Why didn't you tell us?'

'It's too hard and you should understand how I feel. You said you didn't want to leave out west, it only worked because you were going to Ruby.'

A dingo howled to the west and Grandpa leaned over and kissed her on the cheek. 'I'm going to bed. It's an early rise in the morning.' He nodded at Bobby. 'You and I will talk tomorrow. Goodnight Sarah.'

CHAPTER 25

The two men rode together through the gates. Sarah had been given a different job that took her in another direction. She squinted at them as they turned and waved. Grandpa was being obstinate and talking behind her back. As she hoisted herself in the saddle and took off through the gate she worked out that if she finished her jobs quickly, she'd be able to ride over to where they were and hopefully not give them enough time to discuss too much. They had hit it off *too* well and now it appeared that they might have the same thoughts on her future.

* * *

Thomas watched Sarah ride out along one of the fence lines. He was pleased to have Bobby's full attention. It had been worth it just to see the sparks in Sarah's eyes when he'd instructed her to head off in the opposite direction. Finally, he had an ally who could help convince his head-strong granddaughter what she needed to do. It was time she stopped worrying about him. He'd survive.

Bobby looked much like Sarah did and it was easy to see that they were father and daughter. Thomas also recognised their similar character traits. Bobby talked and rode very much like she did, even the way he held the reins and swung down from the saddle. It was however his dark eyes that drew Thomas in. They were Sarah's. The same thoughtful gaze, watching and taking in everything. Thank goodness she had followed up Bill's story and looked for him. Thomas sat up straight in his saddle, his knees pressing into the horse's side. Now was the time to talk. Bobby could guide Sarah to where she needed to go. Today's discussions might change all their lives.

* * *

There was a sense of elation to be back in the saddle and out amongst the cattle and dust. Bobby rode most days at home but this was different. Thomas was beside him and he admired his firm seat on his horse, his back straight, his hands relaxed on the reins. You could tell he'd been in the saddle all his life and he admired how he was still fit and riding at his age.

'You still enjoy being on a horse, Thomas?' Bobby asked.

The old man adjusted his hat, his hand flicking away the flies that hung around the horses. 'The trick is not to stop. Keep moving and riding. The day I can't get on the horse will be the day I die. It's been my entire life.'

'It sounds like Sarah wants to make it hers too.'

'She thinks that because she's never been away from

here. I'm telling you, I want her to go. I'm keen to discuss her future with you.' He turned and grinned at Bobby. 'Without her butting in. Imagine how I feel that she's not following what she wants to do because of me. I've been trying for years to get her moving, to do something other than out here. I know she doesn't want to leave me by myself, but I'll be okay. I've got my sons and Josie nearby. I'd miss her like hell but it's easy to get back out here now from the coast. The roads have improved and there are always flights if you had to get here quickly. I need your help. Perhaps it's meant to be that she found you at this time in her life.'

Bobby listened carefully, wishing the topic had been discussed when Ruby was around. 'There's an easy solution to this,' he replied.

Thomas looked at him, waiting for him to continue.

'I'd need to ring Ruby and talk about it, but I think Sarah should come back with me. We can drive back together. I'll wait a few extra days if she needs some more time to pack. Let's talk her into moving back with us. Ruby will sort it out. I'm telling you, this is what she's good at – organising people and talking to them to get them on the right track.'

'I wish I could meet her,' Thomas said. 'She sounds like a great lady. Sarah has taken to both of you very quickly. She's not usually that trusting, but there you go, maybe that's because you're family.' He chuckled, 'Long lost family and no doubt this was a shock to you, but family you are.'

* * *

Ruby nearly jumped down the phone when Bobby rang. He'd waited until they returned to the house and Thomas asked Sarah to go down to the shed with him and check on some machinery. She'd been annoyed that she hadn't met them out in the paddocks and they'd obviously had plenty of time to talk about her.

Now Bobby explained to Ruby everything Thomas had talked about. He knew she would jump at the opportunity to help. The conversation was short and as he expected, she was beside herself, excited at the thought of having Sarah not only come and live with them but also helping her find her way through schooling and then onto university. 'I'll be in my element Bobby. You know I love doing that sort of thing.'

'I just wanted to make sure it's not an intrusion,' he added. 'After all, we were enjoying a very comfortable life with just the two of us.'

The decision was easy. 'Bobby, this is your daughter and I'm going to think of her as mine as well. Good luck with talking to her about moving though, she seems to have that same stubborn streak that you do.'

CHAPTER 26

The three of them sat on the verandah after dinner. Thomas waited until the time was right. He nodded at Bobby, both looking at Sarah who eyed them suspiciously. 'Grandpa, you look like you're about to say something.'

He placed his hand on her shoulder. 'Actually, my dear, I do have something to tell you.' He looked at Bobby for support. 'Both of us do.'

Her eyes narrowed. 'I'm not excited that the two of you are talking about me and my future. I'm twenty-one, I know what I want.'

Bobby took a deep breath. 'We've come up with an idea and your grandpa says he won't take no for an answer. I'm suggesting that you return with me and come and live with Ruby and me.' He held his hand up as she went to speak. 'Hear me out. I've talked to Ruby just before on the phone, and she agrees that if you think that's what you might want to do then you need to come back and we'll help you sort out how to make it happen.'

'I finished school when I was fourteen. I wouldn't even know where to start.'

Grandpa leaned forward in his chair. 'That's where Ruby comes in. Apparently, that's what she's good at, helping people get to where they want to go.'

'She has contacts and knows her way around education processes,' Bobby added. 'She won't sleep tonight with excitement about helping you. I'm sure she'll have it worked out well before we return.'

'It would take too long to get qualified. I'd have to do my senior schooling before even thinking about university. I'm not doing it through Distance Education again.'

'You're only young,' Grandpa waded in again. 'If you don't do it now, you'll always regret it. Think about it. If you study and become a vet you can come back out here and work. There are always jobs for people with those skills.'

The two men continued to discuss all the positives about their plan. 'You'd have support and free accommodation. We have a small cottage that you could have as your own. That way you'd have your own space. You could come back out and visit your grandfather whenever you wanted.'

***

Sarah stomped around the house, returning time and again to argue with them, but they sat calmly talking about anything but her education and moving. It was as if they'd decided what she should do and that was that!

It was annoying that they were similar in their thoughts and now she was up against not one, but two men who wanted to make decisions for her. The idea they'd proposed was exciting but also terrifying. In her heart she knew it was what she'd always wanted but Grandpa was getting old. She didn't want to lose time with him.

She banged the screen door behind her as she returned to them for about the fifth time. 'I'll need to come back every couple of months and stay for a week. I won't be able to go longer than that.'

The two men stole cursory glances at each other and she was sure Grandpa's lips curled up in a smile. But as quick as she noticed, the look was gone, replaced by a serious, commanding stare. 'It might depend on your program or whatever works out with your schooling. Why don't you just see how it goes?'

She turned to go back inside. She wasn't winning on any front.

Bobby's voice was cajoling. 'Let's say that we'll make sure that any chance there is to return for a visit we'll make sure it happens.'

She twirled around. 'I'll not take any charity either. I have my savings and I'll use that when I need. I'll have to pay my way. I'll get a part-time job or something.'

Grandpa went to talk but stopped when Bobby threw him a silent look.

She glared suspiciously at them. 'What's that look for? Don't you two make any other plans for me.'

'Well, Bobby just thought that you might be able to help with their business. On a paid basis, that is.' Grandpa leaned back in his chair, his hands crossed on his lap.

He looked, as Grandma would have said, like the cat that ate the cream.

She thought hard. 'I'll go along with your plans but I'll only give it a few months. I'm telling you both now if it doesn't work out or I miss home too much you won't keep me away.'

'We think six months is a good idea,' Bobby said. 'You must give it a proper chance. It's going to be a big adjustment.'

She scowled, crossing her arms in front of her. Looking from one to the other she shook her head, before pushing her chin out and giving them both a defiant look. 'Okay.'

Grandpa stood up, his face covered with a wide grin as he wrapped his arms around her. 'You've made me very happy.'

She hugged him back. 'Six months. That's all and if I don't like it I'm coming home.'

***

It had taken the rest of the week for her to work out what to bring and what she needed to do before going. Her unease at leaving Grandpa settled a little when she spoke to one of the workers who did regular stock work for them. His name was Clancy and Grandpa thought highly of him. He'd asked if he might rent one of the huts they kept for workers and stay on a permanent contract for the next year as well as this one. 'My girlfriend, Beth, is keen to come and work out here. She's done jillaroo work and she's also a great cook. Your other cook is going soon so I thought you might have some work for her.'

It had been a well-timed arrangement and Sarah talked to Beth over the phone the next day. She agreed to keep an eye on Grandpa and make sure the house was cleaned and he was eating properly. 'I'll let you know what he's up to.'

'Clancy's girlfriend, Beth, sounds nice and she's promised to keep in touch with me,' she told Grandpa. 'I'll know as soon as something's wrong. Don't think I won't find out when you go for a tumble or one of the horses throws you. There are mobile phones these days, you won't be able to keep anything a secret.'

***

Grandpa hugged her for a long time before letting her get in the car to leave. He'd presented her with a pen set, the old quill ink type. The handle was carved from wood and his name was engraved on the metal that made up the top part of it.

'This was my father's and his father's, before that. It came out from England with them. Keep it and remember that we're all counting on you achieving what you want.'

She had choked up and been unable to reply, eventually pulling away from him, giving him one last long hug before taking her seat in the passenger's side of the car.

Leaning out the window, she waved as long as she could still see him, leaning over the gate, his hand held high in the air. A hollow thumping in her chest made her take deep breaths and she wound her window up before looking straight ahead.

Neither she nor Bobby spoke until they reached the intersection where the road met the main road into Boulia. He stopped to give way to a cattle train, the empty carriages clanging noisily behind the truck. Dust billowed up and for a while everything was hidden behind a cloud of brown. When it eventually cleared Bobby looked at her. 'You okay?' he asked.

She looked straight ahead, not wanting any conversation. 'Yep.'

He turned the vehicle slowly onto the main road, putting his foot down to begin the long journey back to the east coast. 'Right then, let's do this.'

*R*uby spent the week that Bobby and Sarah were gone making sure that everything was in place for when they returned. They had discussed living arrangements over the phone and it was agreed that the cabin Bobby had first stayed in when he arrived at Tall Trees, would be a private and comfortable place for Sarah to live.

Ruby cleaned it from top to bottom and had fun arranging some different pieces of furniture she had stored in the shed, as well as fitting it out with new linen and towels. There were two cabins on the property and so far she had only fixed this one up. Maybe in later years they could renovate the other one and rent it out for weekend stays. This one would be perfect for Sarah and give her space of her own.

Bobby and Sarah were going to make the most of the drive back from Boulia and call in at a couple of places along the way. It was exciting that Sarah was going to share their life. Ruby had already made enquiries about what was needed to get started on the appropriate courses and she couldn't wait to tell her that she would be able to begin what was needed to complete her senior schooling in the coming weeks. The Distance Education College ran courses over the holidays, and a summer course would see her begin what was required. After that there were two more semesters of work and if she could manage to pass everything she could then apply for the university course.

It was easy for Ruby to find the information. She still had contacts in the education sector and she knew her way around the websites and application processes. She made a list of other priorities: clothes, shoes, stationery and a computer. There was much to organise and she would also be able to help Sarah with her studies. It was perfect.

For the last couple of months she had felt like something was missing. Although she had told Bobby she didn't want to pursue the path of trying to have a baby, her mothering instincts needed to be fulfilled. For so many years there had been her mother, and then her dad to take care of. After her father died she had spent time helping Bobby get back to a good place in his mind.

It was what she loved, helping people. Now that Bobby had found his place in life and was settled, he no longer needed her help, they were a team. Working with Sarah would fill the gap. It was what she was good at.

PART 2 - CHAPTER 28

ROCKHAMPTON 2004

*S*imon sat on the front step of the timber house where he lived with his mother, Theresa, and younger brother, Liam. He pushed his hands over his ears, trying to block the noise from inside. Liam was, as usual, arguing with their mother, her screeching voice flinging words in a continual flow of anger. It was always the same. Theresa took very little to fly into a tirade of rage. As she told them, she was over it. She'd brought up the two older girls, who had now left home, and she'd put in ten years or more with him and Liam. Enough was enough. 'I'm over it, you hear me. I can't take any more of either of you. Both of you need to leave school and get a job. You're just stuffing around, getting in trouble, and now suspended for smoking again. You're wasting my money.'

Liam's voice had not long broken and he started in a high voice that after a few words sunk to a deeper tone. 'You don't spend any money, Mum. Our uniforms are from the chaplain and the shoes from Vinnie's. The only things you spend money on are your smokes and grog. No wonder the girls left. They were better off out of here.'

'I've given up everything for you kids. My whole bloody life. And this is the thanks I get. You made money last week mowing lawns and you haven't given me a cent. What sort of way is that to treat your mother? My brother, Bobby, went to work when he was your age.'

'Mum, it's against the law for us to leave school now. You're supposed to make sure we get an education.' Liam's voice had found its full force and echoed down the hallway and out through the front door and open windows. The neighbour next door, Fred, lifted his head from the newspaper he was reading and stared at Simon. Fred sat on the small verandah at the front of his house, his fat gut spilling over his shorts as he perched on a white plastic chair. He flicked a cigarette butt over the railings, glaring hard before shaking his fist at a bunch of kids on bikes who rode past, one of them hurling an empty coke can into Fred's front yard.

Simon watched the kids on bikes. They were all a bit older than he was but he knew them all. Everyone knew everyone in these areas.

The homes on their street were all the same. Low-cost public housing, their newly painted picket fences and new roofs not enough to hide the fact that most of the yards were littered with a variety of broken furniture, bits of cars, a multitude of plastic toys, and an array of kid's bikes that lay where the last rider had left them.

Simon looked away from fat Fred. He didn't want to give him the opportunity to yell out an obscenity, or for him to tell Simon to tell Theresa to shut up. He moved his body so it faced away from next door. The only reason

Fred's house was quiet these days was because his wife and son had moved away. Fred didn't even know where they'd gone. They just took off while he was down the pub placing his bets and having his daily dosage of beers.

The kids in the street repeated the gossip from their mothers, who said that Fred's wife had gone for good, a note sticky taped to the fridge door letting Fred know they'd placed a domestic violence order against him and weren't coming back. Simon grimaced as his mother yelled more obscenities at Liam. Fat Fred yelled something out to him also, but he ignored him. He had no place interfering in their home or telling them what to do. An object hit the wall inside and he flinched at the sound of glass breaking. He stood up and made his way cautiously in through the front door.

It was dim inside, his mother always wanted the curtains pulled tight. She told the boys it was how her house had been when she was growing up and that's what she was used to. She was paranoid that the police were watching her and that they'd come and take her away. Simon ducked as a mug flew towards the wall, narrowly missing him as he jumped out of the way. Liam was edging his way towards Simon and the front door. It looked like Theresa had lost the plot again. She stood with a vase in her hand, threatening to hurl it through the air. 'Mum,' Simon yelled as loud as he could. 'Put it down. Smashing things is not going to help anything.'

Theresa stood in front of him, her dark hair straggly, a singlet top and dirty tattered denim shorts hanging on her gaunt body. Silver bracelets dangled on her arms and a smattering of tattoos covered her legs. As usual she had a cigarette in her hand, her lips pressing on it as she pushed it to her mouth and dragged back hard. 'You two aren't grateful for nothing I've done. You're keeping cash from me. I know he's got money. I saw it and he won't even give me half of it.'

He held his hands out, trying to calm her down. No doubt she'd run out of grog and money. 'Mum, we also need money. Liam is trying to save up for the scientific calculator at school. We've given you more than half of what we earned this week. We only have part-time jobs don't forget.'

Liam stood behind him and Simon knew he was mad, his brother's voice shaky when he spoke. 'I told you, Mum, don't go through my stuff. It's my money and I give you more than I keep. I worked all weekend serving food at the club. I've hardly slept and I've got exams at school. I'm not giving you all of it.'

'You're an ungrateful little bastard.' She came towards them and Simon smelt the alcohol on her breath. At least it wasn't drugs anymore, that addiction seemed to have paused for the moment. He wasn't sure that the grog was any better though. She was a different person when she drank and he stood firmly in front of Liam, hoping like crazy that she'd calm down.

Liam had only started high school this year and was a year younger than Simon. They looked like twins, everyone said so. Some of the teachers who remembered their sisters, Gaye and Lola, said that they all looked the same. 'We can tell you Carlon kids a mile off. His sisters had left high school a few years ago, after they completed year ten. They needed to get away from home, out of the way of Theresa and her habits. They'd only recently moved up north and were working for one of the big motels on the islands in the Whitsundays.

Sometimes they sent a postcard or birthday card and they always included photos that showed blue skies and sandy beaches. It looked like paradise and Simon dreamed about visiting them one day. At the rate he and Liam were going though they wouldn't have enough money to buy food for the week. It wasn't the girls' fault that they didn't hang around. It was best to get out when they could. Theresa had made them do so much work around the house that they may as well be working in a motel and getting paid for the same thing.

Simon knew they wouldn't come back. A postcard or phone call at Christmas time was as close as he was going to get until he and Liam could work out a way to also escape.

The teachers at school had told him it was a shame the girls hadn't stayed at school. They were clever and could have been whatever they wanted. Their English teacher had a soft spot for Liam and Simon as did their math teacher. In fact, all the teachers they had were encouraging, insisting that they needed to work hard and go to university.

The Guidance Officer had even had a meeting with Theresa. He'd made sure the boys and most of their teachers were also there. They'd sat around a big round table and he'd tried to impress on Theresa that her sons needed to study hard and continue until year twelve. He didn't want them leaving as their sisters had.

Simon had noticed knowing looks between his teachers. He wasn't embarrassed about his mum, at least she had worn some decent clothes and been sober the day of the meeting. It was just that she didn't understand that both he and Liam actually liked school. They wanted to learn and go to university.

Theresa was quiet and polite during the meeting, nodding in agreement as the teachers spoke. Yes, she would let the school know if they needed help and she'd make sure the boys came to school. She'd shaken their hands at the end, even smiling a little, as always, not showing her teeth which were black or missing.

She didn't talk all the way home in the car, and the boys knew that her silence was building up into a verbal explosion. And it had. As soon as they were back in the house she had let them have it. 'How dare you sit there all smug and posh, agreeing with everything those stupid teachers suggest. We don't need their help! It's okay for them to sit in their fancy jobs and tell you not to work too much and to concentrate on your schoolwork. They don't have to find money like I do to pay the bills. Don't ever make me go up there again. I hate anything to do with schools and teachers. They're all a bunch of hypocrites!

They'd tried to explain to her that it wasn't like when she was at school. There were lots of good people out there who genuinely wanted to help.

'Load of bullshit,' she'd said through her clenched teeth. 'And you aren't that smart so don't get your hopes up for all that crap they're talking about.'

They'd given each other the look, knowing better than to add fuel to the fire. It was best if they stuck together and worked things out themselves or asked at school for advice. There was no other option because they were never going to get her to understand the way they thought. They had dreams, aspirations and hopes for getting out of where they lived. They wanted to be able to buy things like other kids had or go on a holiday to somewhere nice. Just to even have decent beds would be good.

Occasionally they got a taste of what life could be like. On a rare occasion their mother acted as a mother should. If she stayed off the drink and didn't gamble or spend her pension on grog, she could actually cook and would make them a decent meal, even serve ice cream for dessert. But most of the time they had to fend for themselves, feed themselves whatever they could scrape out of the fridge or find in the bins behind the local grocery store.

Now she was about to throw a vase at them. This was not the mother who had served them ice cream the week before or told them she loved them last month. This was the real side of her.

Liam muttered behind him. 'Watch out, he's coming.'

Simon backed up as a man emerged from a room behind their mother. His shoulders stretched from one side of the doorway to the other and his head nearly hit the top. He wore blue work shorts and a navy-blue singlet that barely covered his huge stomach. His head was bald and his round face was ruddy and red. No doubt he was still sporting a hangover from the previous night's drinking. That might also be why their mother was in such a bad mood. They'd probably drunk all the alcohol and were now suffering the after-effects. It was not a good situation.

This was their mother's boyfriend, Boris. He'd been around for a while and at the start had seemed okay. But as he settled into the relationship, his true colours had come through and the boys knew to stay out of his way if he was in one of his moods. By the look of him, that was now. His voice was a deep growl. 'Are you boys giving your mother a hard time? You'll have me to deal with if you are.'

Theresa smirked and straightened up, pushing her chin forward. She had backup now and Boris always took her side. He took a step towards them, pulling his shorts up, his eyes narrowing.

Both Liam and Simon looked at each other, nearly tripping each other up as they hastily turned and fled down the front steps. They stopped at the letterbox and looked back. Boris's huge frame towered like a threatening giant in the front doorway, his massive calf muscles bulging as he stood firmly. 'Give your poor mother some peace. Piss off both of you.'

They didn't need to be told twice. They grabbed their rickety pushbikes, their only means of transport that they'd found in a nearby suburb when kerbside pickup was in swing. That same day they'd carried an old desk all the way home, a lamp and chair balancing on the top of it as they smuggled it in and set it up in their bedroom. It sat in between their mattresses, their beds long broken. 'You only need a mattress. You never make your bed anyway,' their mother said.

They had furnished their bedroom from other people's throwaways, the prize possession a globe that stood on a stand that had been broken when they found it. Liam had fixed it and placed it in the middle of the desk. It was amazing what people in other suburbs threw out. At night they'd rotate the globe and close their eyes. 'Where you stop and point to is where you're going to travel to,' Simon said. 'They'd spin the globe for ages, reading out the names of the different countries and cities that were a distant dream from the run-down house and suburb where they lived.

The globe was like the books that they studied at school. The words and pictures took them to different places. To a world that was vastly different from the one they shared with their mother. They both loved school. It was their safe place, calm and civilised in comparison to the chaos at home. Their mother would never understand it. She told them constantly that she had hated school. Anyone who worked there was a mongrel and all she had wanted was to leave. They should do the same and get jobs and support her.

They tried to tell her that it was illegal. Kids these days had to stay at school until they were a certain age. There was no way they were leaving. They tried to talk to her about what they wanted to do in the years to come.

Theresa scoffed at their ideas. They needed to get their heads out of the clouds and face the facts of life. Her tirade of words and barrage of insults was constant and she made it as hard as possible for them to continue. Now she had Boris on her side. He had left school when he was thirteen and supported his mother and grandmother. They should do the same.

CHAPTER 29

*S*imon stood on the banks of the river, his bare feet thrust into the muddy slope as he hurled rocks out as far as he could. Liam sat higher up the bank, his knees drawn up, his head resting on them as he watched. Life wasn't fair, Simon thought. Most kids they knew didn't want to go to school or learn in class. They were happy to leave as soon as they could and hang around the house or spend their days in the bush near the river, hanging out with other kids, smoking, drinking, and stealing what they could.

He and Liam had tried that but they'd been caught and dragged up to the school office. The guidance officer spent hours talking to them about not wasting their lives. What were they supposed to do though? They couldn't tell anyone at school what life at home was really like. That it was getting harder and harder. Simon threw another rock. It was embarrassing not being able to afford what they needed for school. Last week he'd even let his anger get the better of him and punched one of the older boys who had followed him around at school making fun of his clothes and shoes.

Squeezing his eyes shut he willed back his tears. He didn't want to be like the others on the streets where they lived. He didn't want to be like Theresa or Boris. He dreamt of being like Miss Cooper, the teacher he had for English. He wanted to speak properly and be able to quote the great writers and poets. To be able to rattle off historical facts like his history teacher or to know the technical information that rolled off the tongue of his favourite science teacher.

He wiped his eyes and walked up the bank. Liam was using a stick to carve letters in the dirt. Sitting beside him, he scuffed the dirt with his shoe. 'What are we gonna do?' Simon asked. 'She's going to make us leave school. Well at least me. You're too young, but Boris reckons he has me lined up for a job with one of his mates. Labouring. He said it will build my muscles up.'

Liam's brown eyes were sullen. They both had their mother's dark hair and dark eyes and when Simon looked into his brother's face it was like looking in a mirror. Their skin was tanned and although neither of them remembered their father they knew from photos that he also had dark hair and olive skin. He had left before Liam was born and ended up in jail not long after. Theresa kept track of him for a while, but then he disappeared and as much as she tried to get some child support money from him, she nor Centrelink had been able to find him.

Once Boris came on the scene she stopped looking for him and hadn't even blinked last year when Boris came up with a newspaper article about their father's death. He had been associated with gangs down south and ultimately paid the price for years of crime when he was taken out by members of another gang. 'Good riddance to bad rubbish,' was all Theresa said.

The only other family they knew about was their mother's brother, Bobby. They'd met him once years ago but then their mother had moved further away. When they asked if they could visit him again, she said she didn't have time. They knew he rang her sometimes though, they'd heard her talking to him on the phone. Most times she asked him for money.

Liam reached into his pocket and pulled out a cigarette. It was bent and he carefully straightened it, placing it between his lips.

'Where did you get that?' Simon asked, impressed that Liam had been organised to not only have a smoke on hand but now also pulled a lighter out of his shorts pocket.

'Stole it off Boris,' Liam replied, dragging back as he lit the end.

Simon waited for him to share the cigarette. 'I hate him. I reckon he'd hit us if he got the chance.'

Liam lay back and passed the smoke to Simon. 'I try not to get in arm's reach of him. You know what I don't understand. How come he's nice to Mum. He never yells at her or gets angry with her. He just hates us.'

Simon lay back also, taking another puff before passing it back to Liam. The cigarette made him feel good, even more so because it was Boris's. It stung his throat and the smoke smarted his eyes, but he didn't care, at least they were doing something that would annoy their mother.

'I hate him,' Liam said. 'I don't want to go back there. She loves him more than us.'

Simon looked up at the sky, white puffy clouds sitting directly above. 'I wish we could go to one of those places on the globe. Barcelona, London or an island in the Pacific Ocean, Fiji maybe.'

Liam rolled onto his side, holding his head up with his hand. 'You need money to go there. We aren't ever going to get there if we don't get out of here. The teachers can see that. They would have seen hundreds of kids like us start and not finish. Probably end up right back on the same street. That's why they're pushing for us to keep studying. Who are you going to believe, Miss Cooper, or Mum and Boris? I think the teachers know what they're talking about.'

Simon sat up and crossed his legs. 'We are smart. I don't even have to work at school and my marks are higher than anyone else. In English, I'm so far in front of everyone the teacher reckons he wants to move me up into the older classes. He said I'd fit in easily with the senior kids and that I'm at a higher level than most of them.'

'We are smart.' Liam added. 'But how are we going to keep learning when she keeps telling us we gotta work?'

They sat looking at each other, passing the smoke back and forth until there was hardly anything left. Simon pushed it into the dirt, thinking hard. 'I reckon we should leave, run away.'

Liam's eyes were wide and he sat up straight. 'Where would we go. If we run away we'll never be able to go to school. Where would we get food from?'

They both sat looking at the river, their attention

drawn to four rowing boats that entered their line of vision. Rowers stroked in time as the person at the front called out through a speaker. Liam's eyes followed the movement as they glided across the water. 'See those kids in those boats. They're from the college in town. Look at them doing rowing for sport. Mum won't even get me the proper shoes to play footy. How come some kids have so much and we have nothing?'

Simon stood up and watched the rowers until they rounded the bend of the river further up. 'I have an idea.'

'What? We steal one of those boats and row our way to somewhere else,' Liam said, picking up a rock and pelting it into the river.

'No. I have a good idea.'

'What?'

'We run away to Mum's brother's place. We go and see Bobby. Maybe we can live with him and go to school. He's the only family we've got apart from our sisters.'

Liam laughed. 'That's a stupid idea. He's probably worse than Boris. He'll only send us back to mum anyway. Who's going to want two boys?'

Simon was serious and his body tensed with what he saw as their only solution. 'It's our only option. I'm not staying any longer. I reckon we pack a bag each and leave after they've passed out tonight. They won't wake until late tomorrow and by then we'll be long gone. She won't ring the police because she'll be worried that they'll come and visit the house. She'll think we'll come back after a couple of days.'

Liam was considering the idea, his face serious. 'We could always leave a note.'

'We could.'

'Do you know where he lives? How far is it?'

He lives near a place called the Glasshouse Mountains and I know it's not that far from the ocean. Remember he sent Mum some photos. They're up on the cabinet with the photo of her and him, under some magazines. She doesn't even remember they're there. I looked up where the place was at school once and it's north of Brisbane. The address is on the photo. I reckon it's about ten hours from here by train.'

'Are we going to catch a train?

Simon thought hard. 'Yes, I think that would be best. We could hitch a ride but we don't want to draw attention to ourselves, plus there are crazies out there. I don't want to die escaping.'

'It would be like escaping from Alcatraz,' Liam said, his eyes lighting up. 'No one would know except us. We'd be like the prisoners avoiding the guards, that would be Boris and Mum.'

Simon's spirits surged. They had a plan. Between them they had managed to save some money, keeping it hidden from their mother. They would have enough to buy a train ticket and get some food in case they took a while to find Bobby. His heart sank when he thought about what his reaction might be. Mum had said he didn't have any kids of his own and he was with a woman who they'd grown up with. She spoke about him like he was a nice person. Maybe, just maybe he would help them.

CHAPTER 30

*R*uby sat on the wooden bench seat under the canopy of trees. Sometimes when she was home by herself she liked to walk down and spend time relaxing in the shade under the sprawling branches. When she was in this spot she felt close to her dad, almost as if he was there listening to her thoughts, nodding, or adding advice as she mulled over different situations.

Her Mum and Dad's beautiful faces came to her. She wished they were really here, sitting next to her. There was no use yearning for their real presence though, now it was their memories that kept her company. She sighed as she stood up and walked towards a towering poinciana tree, its rambling branches solid as they reached out, a blanket of bright red flowers covering the ground below. The remnants of a tree house could still be seen in between the branches and she smiled as she remembered the one she and Bobby had spent most of their childhood in. One day she was going to get him to re-build this one.

She would ask him to make shelves and timber boxes for tables just like theirs had. Maybe she'd even get silkworms and they could watch them hatch and grow into white caterpillars that would eventually transform into fluttering moths with black bulging eyes.

Bobby had overcome so much in the last two years. The personality of the boy she had once known had returned and her heart filled when she thought of their life together. Now she also had Sarah to think about. In her mind, she went over the other items she wanted to purchase to make the cabin comfortable. Stretching her arms high she moved away from the trees, making her way back to the track. Rusty ran towards her, he had been busy chasing something in the long grass and now jumped around her, yapping at her to throw him a stick. She bent down to pick one up, watching him as he twirled around and focussed on something further down the long driveway.

His ears pricked forward and the fur on his back stood up as he growled. She looked towards what was bothering him. Two boys were walking towards her, stopping every so often as they stared up at the trees. They hadn't seen her, where she stood underneath the canopy and she grabbed Rusty's collar, telling him to be quiet. They were only young kids and she wondered if they were collecting donations or selling something. Rusty barked sharply and one of them looked up and stopped, speaking to the other boy as he pointed to where she stood.

She let Rusty go as she walked out from under the trees and onto the driveway. The dog bounded towards them and they both stood still. Rusty stopped also, keeping his distance and barking loudly. As she walked toward them she wondered who they were. Most kids in the area visited the local markets so she would probably know them.

The taller one waved and she waved back, adjusting her sunglasses, the western sun bright as it shone in her eyes. When she called Rusty he stopped barking and instead began jumping around, licking the boys' hands and wanting them to play. Some watchdog, she thought.

One of them called out. 'We're looking for Bobby. Does he live here?'

She bent down to settle Rusty before standing up and staring straight at them. Looking from one to the other she took off her sunglasses and cleaned them on her t-shirt, blinking a couple of times before raising her eyes to meet theirs again.

The other boy spoke. 'We're looking for a man called Bobby. Do you know where he lives? Someone in town told us to come this way.'

She closed her eyes and opened them again. Both boys were the image of Bobby when he was that age. Was her mind playing tricks? Her heart lurched. Please don't tell me he has two sons that he doesn't know about, she thought. She went to speak but the words stuck in her throat.

They all stared at each other, the taller boy eventually speaking. 'We're looking for a man named Bobby. He's our mother's brother.'

The words took a moment to register. She laughed out loud, sending Rusty into another barking frenzy. It took a while to get him to be quiet. 'Oh, my goodness. You must be Theresa's boys.'

They nodded as she held out her hand for them to

shake. 'I'm Ruby. Bobby's partner. I guess that makes you my nephews.'

The older boy shook her hand. 'I'm Simon, and this is my brother Liam. We've come to talk to Bobby.'

'Where have you come from? Is your mother with you?'

Liam shook his head and placed his backpack on the ground. He pulled his shoulders back and moved his neck, stretching it from side to side. 'We came by train. It was about ten hours. Mum isn't with us and we really need to talk to Bobby.'

For some reason, she wanted to wrap her arms around Liam. He was only small, his skinny legs sticking out from shorts that were too big for him, a large t-shirt hanging down over them. His face had an anguished look to it, almost like he'd seen and heard plenty in his young life. She looked from him to Simon. They had that same distrusting look in their eyes that Bobby used to get. Simon was also thin, his clothes also hanging loosely on his gaunt frame. 'Bobby isn't here at the moment. He's …' She looked down and thought hard. 'He's coming back from out west. He should be back here by late this afternoon or tomorrow.'

The boy's shoulders sagged and they looked at each other, defeated. Their faces lit up however, when she spoke to them again. 'I tell you what though, I'm just about to have lunch and I'd love it if you'd join me. I see you have backpacks with you. Would you like to stay the night and wait and see your Uncle Bobby when he comes back? There's plenty of room and food, and I know he'd love to see you both.'

Wide smiles crossed their faces and she breathed a sigh of relief when they nodded. 'Follow me,' she said, picking up Liam's backpack and hoisting it onto her back. 'You fellas look like you wouldn't say no to a good feed and a cold drink.'

CHAPTER 31

It was obvious to Ruby that the two boys had probably left home without the consent of their mother. Theresa would have rung to let Bobby know they were coming if this was a planned visit. Theresa hadn't bothered with Bobby for a long while and if he didn't ring her every so often they wouldn't have any contact with her. They hadn't seen the boys since they were little so it was obvious that something was going on to make them turn up on their doorstep. She'd give them something to eat first and then find out the details of their journey. For now, food was the priority.

***

Simon's heart sunk when they were told that Uncle Bobby wasn't around. At least the lady was nice. Ruby reminded him of Miss Cooper, his English teacher. Her voice was calm and kind and he had thought Liam was going to cry when she picked up his backpack and put it on her own back. His mind was blurry and he just wanted to put his head down and sleep, that was after they ate of course. The train ride had been rough and the security guard had kicked them off, not believing their story that they were on their way to visit relatives. 'You look like you're homeless. It's not school holidays. It's the middle of the week and you're too young to be travelling on your own. If you don't get off I'm going to ring your parents or the police. It's called truanting!'

They didn't have time to try and get a refund for their ticket or to go and buy some food. There had been a cargo train parked on the other side of the station and pretending like prisoners from Alcatraz they had crept alongside the carriages until they had found a trailer with cars parked on it. The security was looking the other way when they found one that was unlocked. It made a comfortable bed for the night although they had become too relaxed and been discovered by train staff the next morning, two stops before their final destination.

Nothing was going to stop them though and they'd walked along the tracks, ducking off into the bush when a train passed. Their feet were covered in blisters and Simon cursed the second-hand ill-fitting shoes they wore. His body had ached from being curled up in a small space all night and his legs felt like they might drop off. He'd tried to stay awake and keep an eye on his brother as they'd lay next to each other to feel safer last night. Liam looked like he felt; confused, tired, and lost. It wasn't until they reached the small town near to the address they had for Bobby, that he breathed a bit easier.

Now this beautiful lady called Ruby, who also wanted them to call her Aunty Ruby, had placed plates of food in front of them. Large glasses filled with lemonade and bobbing ice cubes were already worth the journey. He glanced over at Liam, who was also stuffing food in his mouth, almost as if he was scared it would be taken away before he got a chance to eat it all.

Simon tried to warn Liam to slow down but Ruby had noticed and stared hard. Gripping the table his muscles tensed, waiting for her reaction to Liam's bad manners. However, now he felt even more confused because when she spoke she didn't yell or stand up and make Liam cower, instead her voice was gentle and kind. 'There's so much food here and more in the fridge. Please don't rush it so much. You'll get a stomach ache.' She passed him his drink. 'Please stop and take a sip. There is no hurry, you can sit here as long as you want. Please. There is plenty of food. I promise you I have more than we can all eat.'

Liam stopped chewing and took a deep breath as he glanced at Simon. He finished what he was eating before speaking, thankfully remembering his manners. They didn't want to get thrown out when they had just arrived.

'Sorry, Aunty Ruby, I'm really hungry.'

She smiled at them and Simon's heart melted. How come their mum wasn't like her. Why did they have to end up with someone who yelled and screamed and didn't want to listen to what they had to say? Ruby cut up an orange and offered it to them. 'Bobby and I grow a lot of this fruit. It's our business. We grow organic produce and sell it at the local markets. Try these oranges. They're the juiciest ones you'll ever find.'

They both put their hands out. 'Thank you,' Liam said.

'Organic crops are the best way to go. That way you're not polluting the waterways with toxic sprays and fertilisers. It makes for a more sustainable future.'

'Plus, these are the best oranges I've ever tasted.' Simon added. 'Was it easy to get certified as an organic grower? I've read that the ground must be devoid of any pesticides or toxins for a number of years before you grow and there can't even be anyone within a certain radius who uses chemicals on their crops.'

He could tell Ruby was impressed. 'Wow, you two know a bit about it. Do you know someone who grows organic crops?'

Liam shook his head, his eyes closed as he sucked the juice out of the piece of orange he held in his hand. He placed the rind down on the plate in front of him, wiping his mouth with his t-shirt. 'No, we don't know anyone, and I've never seen it growing. Simon and I read a lot and we're both good at geography and science. At school we learn about the environment and the best practices for farming and livestock production. There's so much to be done to improve the way we live, and it needs to be done carefully.' He looked at Ruby. 'Do you know about global warming and the ozone layer?'

She leaned back in her chair, a slight smile on her face. Simon decided then and there that he liked her, maybe even more than Miss Cooper. She was pretty, with green eyes and some freckles on her face. She was also tall and wore neat and clean clothes. Her brown hair was tied back in a pigtail and her eyes were excited as if she was really pleased to see them. Surely if she was nice, Uncle Bobby would be too.

She leaned back in her chair and crossed her legs. He

noticed her painted toenails, they were just like her fingernails. Not bright tacky colours like the girls at school had, but pretty pale colours that looked nice against her tanned skin. When she answered him she spoke slowly, like there wasn't any rush, as if she had plenty of time to talk. 'I do know about climate change, Liam. I read quite a bit and Bobby and I try to live as environmentally friendly as we can. I don't like using plastic and we recycle when possible. I believe one day that perhaps everything will change and maybe we'll even drive around in electric cars.'

Simon groaned. 'Don't start Liam on that. He's crazy about electric cars. Tell him to be quiet right now because he'll give you every fact and statistic on the topic.'

Ruby and Simon laughed as Liam launched into a lengthy information session on the merits of cars that didn't need petrol to function.

***

Ruby watched the two boys. They were like twins. 'Wait here,' she said. 'I have something to show you.' She went inside and returned with an old black and white photo of her and Bobby around the same age as the boys were. 'This is your Uncle Bobby when he was a kid.' She passed it to Simon who peered at it closely, his eyes widening as he recognised the resemblance. 'He looks like me and Simon,' Liam remarked. 'Maybe a bit taller but just as skinny.'

'He's going to be surprised that you're here. Your mother didn't ring. I would have thought she would have let us know you were coming for a visit.'

They looked awkwardly at each other and Liam averted his eyes, peering back at the photo. Neither spoke and she tried again. 'Does your mother know where you are?'

Simon twisted his mouth and bit his lip. 'Maybe.'

She tried to remain serious. 'That is not exactly a yes. If she doesn't know you're here she might be worried.'

Liam stood up and shook himself, a few crumbs falling to the ground as he stretched his legs. She wondered where they had slept last night. It was obvious they hadn't been at home tucked up in bed. Their clothes were crushed and dirty and their hair was unbrushed. It was also clear from the food they had devoured that they hadn't eaten much in the last day or so. They were also avoiding her questions. Eventually, Liam answered. 'Nah, don't worry about it. She'll be right.'

'I think if she's unaware of where you are, it might be good if I give her a quick call and let her know that you're here safe and sound.'

They both turned to her, their eyes wide. Simon put his cap on his head, pulling it down low over his forehead. 'She won't be interested. You can ring her if you like but she won't care.'

Ruby tried to sound as kind as she could. She didn't want them taking off again before Bobby arrived back. 'Be honest with me. It's okay, you're not in trouble with me. I just need to know. Have you run away from home?'

'We need to speak to Bobby,' Liam said, 'he might help us.'

'What do you need help with? Maybe I can help.'

They looked at each other and she knew they would be weighing up the pros and cons of telling her what was going on. She tried to work out their ages. She remembered that they were only a year or so apart and she thought perhaps they were about twelve. From memory, Bobby had only met them once or twice.

Although he rang Theresa every so often, she was cagey about where she was living. A couple of times she'd rung and he'd sent her some money. 'I'm not in trouble,' she said, 'I just need some new tyres on the car. I'll pay you back.' He'd discussed it with Ruby and then decided it was best to leave her alone. He made sure she knew he was there if she needed help, but she assured him she had a partner and didn't want Bobby bothering her. 'I'll ring if I need you. Thanks for the cash,' had been her last words to him.

He'd tried a few times to ring her after that but hadn't been able to get her. It would be interesting to see how he reacted to his two nephews turning up on his doorstep.

Liam moved over next to where Rusty lay in the sun. He patted his head and Rusty reciprocated by pushing his nose into Liam's hand when he stopped. Liam looked up at Ruby. 'We're not going back no matter what. Even if you dob us in to Mum or the police, we'll just run away again. Simon and me are not ever going back there.'

Simon wasn't saying much and she made sure she spoke carefully. They had obviously left for a reason and it sounded like they wanted Bobby's help sorting something out. Once he returned he could talk to them and if needed, he could drive them back home. Perhaps he could talk to Theresa and work out what the problem was. Families often had arguments and kids ran away. The boys would soon change their minds and want to go back.

A few days away would probably cool any argument they'd had and give Theresa and the boys time to think about everything.

She looked at them, speaking slowly to make sure they understood. 'I'd really like you to stay here with me. Bobby should be home today or tomorrow and he'll help you work everything out. I'm hoping he's back here late this afternoon. I do need to give your mother a quick call though. That way she won't ring the police and they won't be out looking for you. Don't worry I'll make sure she knows you're safe here with me and that you're going to stay for a little while. Is that okay?'

Simon nodded. 'Are you sure you're not going to ring the cops?'

'No way. Why would I do that? You're our nephews. I just can't let her worry about you though. That wouldn't be right. Do I have your permission to ring and your word that you will stay here until Bobby comes back?'

'Yes.' They spoke in unison and she felt a wave of sympathy for them. They were only young and it was obvious something was going on at home. 'I tell you what. While I'm ringing your mother how about you grab a towel from the cupboard over there and make the most of the bathroom. There's a shower and a great big tub. Shampoo and soap, everything is in there. Use what you need and take as long as you want. If you sort your clothes into piles, I can wash whatever is dirty. I'm going to ring your mum and then I'll set the bedroom up for you. There are two single beds in there, so I hope that's okay for you to share a room.'

Liam grinned from ear to ear. 'A bathtub! Yay.'

'Thank you, Aunty Ruby. We share a room at home. We like being together.' Simon also grinned at her and she felt a weight lift from her shoulders. Hopefully this problem would be solved with a couple of nights away from home. When Bobby returned they'd work it out and bring the family back together.

CHAPTER 32

*O*nce the boys disappeared into the bathroom Ruby rang the number that Simon had given her. She cleared her throat, going over what she was going to say. At first, the phone rang out and she waited a few minutes before trying again. Hopefully Theresa wasn't out searching for them or distraught with worry. She rang again, the ring tone echoing loudly as she waited. Just as she was about to hang up someone picked up at the other end.

No one spoke and she waited before talking. 'Hello, it's Ruby here.'

It took a while before there was a reply. It was a man's voice, croaky and stilted, almost like he had just woken up. 'Who? What do you want?'

'I'd like to speak to Theresa, please. It's Ruby, Bobby's partner. Could you please put Theresa on the phone?'

'What do you want?'

'I want to talk to her about her sons.'

It sounded like the man on the phone was eating, his

words coming through in between bites of food. 'She won't want to talk to ya. She's asleep. What do you want?'

Ruby tried to be patient. 'Who am I speaking to?'

'Name's Boris. I live here.'

'Okay.' She took a deep breath, hoping she was doing the right thing divulging where the boys were. 'I have Simon and Liam here with me.'

She waited while he chewed, the noises echoing through the phone. 'Well, aren't you the lucky one?' More chewing noises were followed by a loud burp before he cleared his throat and spoke. 'You can bloody well keep them there.'

'I'm concerned that Theresa might be worried about where they are.'

'I can tell you right now, she's glad to see the back of them. Let the little bastards stay there.'

Ruby was taken aback. This was not the response she had anticipated. 'Can I please speak to her?'

The man cleared his throat. 'She's asleep and I'll reckon she'll be that way for a while.'

'When she wakes up can you please tell her that the boys are here with me?'

'You can have 'em.'

'Look, Boris, I'm not sure what's going on but please tell Theresa when she wakes to give me a ring and the boys are here, safe with us.'

It sounded like Boris dropped the phone and Ruby held it away from her ear as crashing noises echoed down the receiver. Eventually he must have picked it up and she could hear him grunting as he moved around before speaking to her. 'Good riddance to bad rubbish.'

With that, the line went dead and Ruby was left

holding the phone to her ear. For goodness sakes. What sort of home was it where Theresa was not worried about her sons? Was the man called Boris telling the truth?

***

She waited on the verandah, going over the events of the day. The boys had looked like they needed a good scrub and she hoped they'd found where everything was. Liam emerged first, his hands full of dirty clothes. Simon soon joined him, his hair washed and face clean. 'I bet you feel better after that,' she said.

'I could live in that bathtub,' Liam said. 'Can we have a look around? I saw some horses behind your house.'

'I'd love to show you around in a moment,' she said. 'First though we need to talk about why you left home. Now, don't look so worried.' The colour drained from Liam's face and she smiled at them trying to put them at ease. 'I rang your mother but she was asleep.' The two boys exchanged a look of indifference. 'I spoke to a man called Boris.'

'That's Mum's boyfriend,' Simon said. 'He lives with us.'

She nodded. 'Do you get on with him?'

Both answered together. 'No.'

'I told him you were here and if he could pass that message onto your mother. I wasn't sure if he would but I didn't have any other option. I don't want her worrying where you are. Do you think he'll tell your mother that you're safe and here with me? He didn't seem worried and he said she wasn't either. Do you think he's telling the truth?'

Both boys grinned at each other. 'Good old Boris,' Liam said. 'He'll be pleased that we're gone. I'm tired of worrying about him and Mum. I want to go and explore.' They both jumped down the stairs, Rusty bounding along behind them, yapping with excitement. It was as if their troubles had left them and they appeared to relax, the worry disappearing from their faces.

Simon turned back to her. 'Yeah, he'll tell her and he wasn't lying, she'll be glad we're out of her way. She might sleep for a while though. I wouldn't hold your breath waiting for her to ring back or anything. Can we have a look around the place? There's so much space.'

Ruby followed them, resigning herself to the fact that she'd tried and Boris knew where they were. The boys raced ahead of her. They'd changed into different clothes but the new ones weren't any different from the ones they'd taken off. It wasn't lost on her that all their clothes were old and faded, their sandshoes barely holding together. At the moment they looked like they'd been let out of jail, their eyes trying to take in everything at once, running back and forth to tell her what they could see.

It wasn't the time to ask too many questions, that would be better left for when Bobby returned. For now, they were safe with her, their mother knew where they were and when Bobby talked to them he'd work out how to take them home.

Liam ran ahead with Rusty hot on his heels. A narrow track led up the grassy slope behind the house and she enjoyed stretching her legs as Simon walked beside her, asking questions about the farm. He stopped every so often to look back at the view in the valley below. His face was a mixture of awe and sadness and Ruby tried to read his thoughts. He reminded her of when Bobby was a kid and had been upset about something that had happened. Even though he'd relaxed since the phone call, Simon's face had the same pinched look, like he was carrying the weight of the world. It made her want to wrap her arm around his skinny shoulders and squeeze him tight.

Soon they caught up to Liam who had stopped at the fence of the horse paddock. The group of horses cantered towards them, a couple of them throwing their heads around and kicking out sideways. The horses picked up speed and Bobby's horse, Astral, bucked, kicking his rear legs high in the air before galloping towards them. He stopped just short of the fence, his ears forward, his coat shiny as he pushed his head over the fence. Both boys jumped backward, and she laughed at the fear on their faces.

Reaching up she stroked the horse's forehead, talking to him and scratching behind his ears. 'He won't hurt you. This is Bobby's horse, Astral, and the other two are Brandy and Tap.

They stood behind her, Simon grabbing onto her arm when Brandy tossed his head and whinnied loudly. 'We've never been up close to a horse.'

'He thinks we have food for him. I should have brought some carrots. They're all friendly and they only want your attention. Mind you it's a different story when you ride them. The chestnut one, Brandy, is mine. He's a lot quieter to ride, not like Astral. That's why he's Bobby's. Your uncle is at one with a horse. When he was a youngster and then a young man, he spent most of his young life out in Western Queensland on the cattle properties.'

Simon came and stood beside her. She took his hand

and put it on Brandy's shoulder. 'Give him a good pat. He'll love it,' she said.

Brandy stood still while Simon stroked his neck. When the horse turned and sniffed his hand, Ruby instructed him to ignore him. 'He won't bite, he's just checking you out.'

Simon's dark eyes stared hard, his gaze never leaving the horse. 'He's beautiful. His coat is so silky and look at him, he's looking straight at me.'

'He seems to like you,' Ruby said, 'Rub your hand up and down his face. Liam why don't you come and pat the other two here. They'd like some attention too.'

'Nope, not me. They have teeth.'

She laughed. 'Come on.' She pulled his arm and made him stand in front of her, holding his hand up to pat the face of Astral. 'See, he loves it.'

The horses pushed their heads further over the fence, relishing the attention. Soon Liam and Simon moved their hands with more confidence and felt the horse's manes. 'I'd like to learn how to ride,' Simon said. 'I reckon you'd feel really free when you're on a horse. Do you think Bobby would teach me?'

'We'll see. Wait until he's back and we work out what's happening with getting you both home. Maybe there will be time for some riding lessons. You could learn on Tap, he's older and quieter.'

'Do you really think we could have a ride?' Liam's eyes lit up and he turned to her. 'Like actually sit on top of one of them.'

She smiled as Brandy pushed him gently with her head. 'First lesson, don't turn your back on Brandy. He's cheeky and that was a gentle shove to say, more pats please.'

It was hard to drag the boys away. They were fascinated and Liam asked continual questions. Simon was also intrigued and she detected a kindness in his soul and a fascination with nature. There was something endearing about them both. She watched as they played with Rusty, taking it in turns to throw a stick for him, her thoughts turning to why they were here.

'We might head back. Bobby could possibly be back today, he wasn't sure. I need to talk to you both before he gets here.'

As they began to walk back toward the house they talked about the cows and other areas of the farm. They hadn't been on a farm before or ventured too far from where they had lived for the last few years. 'Mum doesn't take us anywhere. We just stay around our neighbourhood,' Simon said.

Liam's eyes clouded over when he talked about home and she noticed neither elaborated on their home life, or voluntarily shared further information about why they'd run away. She waited until she had their full attention. 'When Bobby comes back he'll have someone else with him. She's a young girl and her name is Sarah.'

They both looked at her, Liam clinging to her arm as a cow lifted its head to look at them as they walked past. 'Is she the same age as us?' Simon grabbed her other arm as the cow took a step forward. Ruby stopped and made sure she had their full attention. 'Listen to me, both of you. When you walk past a cow, don't let it intimidate you. Don't make eye contact, hold your head high and put your shoulders back. Like you're not scared of it. Don't run, just walk slowly and ignore it.'

They followed her advice until she told them they could turn around. The cow had returned to the lush grass, although as Ruby said, it was still watching them. 'Cows will try and scare you but you have to be the boss. Now getting back to what we were talking about. Sarah is older than you both. She is twenty-one and she is,' she paused, 'Sarah is Bobby's daughter.'

Simon scrunched up his face. 'That means she's our cousin. Mum said we don't have any cousins. She said Bobby is our only relative.'

'You're right. She is your cousin.' She took a deep breath, guiding them up a grassy slope. 'It's a long story but Bobby only found out a few weeks ago that he had a daughter. When he was a young man he lived out west and had a girlfriend called Leila. They were together for a while and then he left for another job. He didn't want to be with her anymore. I guess he fell out of love.'

Liam nodded. 'That happens sometimes. I wish Boris would fall out of love with Mum.'

She continued to explain the situation, pleased to see that they both seemed to understand what had happened. She gestured for them to sit down. 'This is a great place to sit. In front of them the valley stretched wide and like everyone else who saw the view the boys asked continual questions about the peaks that jutted out from the valley floor.

Ruby eventually swung the conversation back to Sarah. 'It's good timing that you're here because you can meet your cousin.'

'Simon shaded his eyes. 'Is she going to stay long?'

'I think she is. She wants to study to be a vet. Bobby and I are going to help her do that.'

Liam sat up straight. 'Wow, that's six years at university and you have to be good at science. I thought about that but I'm going to be a doctor. I reckon that will be more my thing.'

She tried to keep a straight face. For thirteen years old, Liam was wise beyond his years and obviously highly intelligent. Turning to Simon she nodded. 'It sounds like you both like school and learning. What do you want to be Simon?'

He stretched his gangly legs out and kicked his shoes off. 'I'm not sure but I want to go to university. I might become a teacher. The teachers at school say Liam and I are gifted and talented. I'm not sure what that means but we get the best marks in all our classes.'

'Wow. That's so good. Well, you know you can be whatever you want.'

Simon threw a stick to Rusty, the dog bounding away through the long grass. 'That's what the teachers tell us but Mum wants us to leave school. She says we should get a job and pay her the money we earn.' Simon drew his legs up under him, resting his chin on his knees. 'We told her we're too young.'

'You are too young. It's illegal. Besides you need to finish year twelve and then go to university if you want to be a doctor or teacher. We can talk to your mum about that. Bobby will have a chat with her and I'm sure she'll listen to him.'

'She doesn't listen to anyone,' Liam said. 'The teachers at school have tried to talk to her but she thinks she knows it all, but she doesn't. All she knows is her wine and smokes. She doesn't care about us.'

'Don't say that.' Simon's voice was angry. 'She does care about us, she just gets a bit mixed up sometimes.' He turned to Ruby. 'She's a good person and she's our mum. She just goes off track.'

Liam stood up. 'Don't defend her. She's nuts.'

Simon shook his head. 'Liam fights with her all the time. He can't keep his mouth shut and she gets angry with him. It drives her crazy. Like poking a bear.'

Ruby held up her hand, grateful when Liam grabbed it and pulled her to her feet. 'It sounds like you have a lot to talk about with Bobby. Hopefully, he can help you work it out before you go back.

CHAPTER 33

They hadn't gone far when Ruby stopped and sat down. In front of them the hill became a little steeper, its smooth grassy slopes perfect for a race. 'This hill is the best place for tumbling races.' Before long they were all lying down. 'You can't start until I say.' She pushed Rusty away as he tried to lick her face. Twisting her head around she checked they were ready. 'Ready, set, go!'

All three of them rolled down the grassy slope, Ruby's head spinning by the time she reached the bottom. She was ahead of the two boys who had taken a while to work out how to keep going in a straight direction, plus they were having trouble getting Rusty out of the way.

They stood up once they reached Ruby, jumping up and down, cheering as she put in a couple more rolls. Liam did a cartwheel and Simon cheered loudly, their noisy calls echoing over the paddocks. When they finally stopped to get their breath, they realised that someone was calling out from further down the paddock. Ruby waved as Rusty took off at a million miles an hour to Bobby and Sarah, who stood at the gate watching them.

She put her arms around the boys' shoulders. 'Bobby and Sarah are home. I'll race you to the gate.'

*I*t had been a long trip back in the car and Sarah was looking forward to something to eat and drink. She'd relaxed when Bobby drove back through the tunnel of trees and up towards the house. The house was quiet and not even the dog was around when they stepped up onto the verandah. Noises from further up the slopes alerted them to where Ruby and Rusty were.

They leaned on the gate, looking towards where the noise was coming from. 'She's having fun.' Bobby's face lit up as he watched Ruby and a couple of kids rolling down the hill, Rusty jumping all over them as they competed to get to the bottom first. Bobby shaded his eyes trying to get a better look. 'They must be kids from town. I'm not sure who that is with her.'

The smaller boy did a cartwheel and then Ruby finally spotted them. Rusty raced towards them, the others running behind him. Bobby opened the gate, holding out his arms as Ruby threw herself into them. He wrapped his arms around her, both laughing as he spun her around in the air. When he put her down he kissed her on the lips. The two boys stood awkwardly, the taller boy looking at Sarah before averting his gaze. They reminded Sarah of someone and she couldn't work it out. It was almost like she'd seen them somewhere before.

Bobby stood still, staring hard and for a moment no one spoke. Suddenly the smaller boy walked up to Bobby and put his hand out for him to shake. 'Hello. You're our Uncle Bobby. You might not remember us, but I'm Liam and he's Simon.'

Bobby was taken aback and blinked a few times before taking the young boy's hand. 'Liam and Simon. I haven't seen you for years. Has your mum brought you for a visit?'

He looked around before turning to Ruby. 'Is Theresa here?'

Ruby gave Sarah a hug. 'I'm so pleased you've come back to us. Now, a few things have happened since you both left.' She linked her arm through Bobby's and gave him a funny look. 'The boys decided to come and visit us by themselves. They wanted to see you. I've rung Theresa and let her know they're here. Perhaps we should all go and have a cuppa and then we can explain everything.'

Simon stepped forward. 'There's nothing to explain. We ran away from home. You're our only other family apart from Mum, so we came here. We found your address on a photo at home.'

Bobby looked from Simon to Ruby, his eyes questioning. 'Is Theresa coming here also?'

Liam went to answer but Ruby cut in, placing her arm around the boy's shoulder. 'Let's head back to the house.

We all need to sit down and have a long talk. Sarah, meet your cousins, Simon and Liam.'

Sarah's heart pounded hard. In less than a month she had added four more people to her family. No wonder she thought she'd seen them somewhere before. She stared back and forth. They looked much like Bobby and ... just like she did.

***

Simon's nerves rattled in his stomach as Bobby ushered them towards the table. While Ruby and Sarah went back and forth from the kitchen bringing out everything needed for lunch their uncle dusted off his hat then sat next to them. Bobby kept staring at them, running his hand through his hair before speaking. His voice was deep and the fun of the morning was pushed aside as the reality of the situation sunk in.

Simon looked around for Ruby's support. He noticed that Liam was also looking for her. But it was just them and Bobby, and his uncle didn't look happy as he passed them both a cold drink. Liam fidgeted and Simon could tell he was nervous. It was like when they waited for their mother to tell them why she was angry with them. Like when they waited to see what her reaction would be, verbal or physical, or both. This was just as scary. Bobby was bigger than Ruby was and Simon wasn't sure about him. He had a deep voice and didn't talk that much. He hadn't exactly jumped up and down with excitement when he realised who they were.

Simon jumped when Bobby spoke. Some of his lemonade spilled on the tablecloth and he tried to cover it up by wiping his hand over it and pushing the small puddle around so that it wasn't so noticeable. His hand shook and he could feel his face burning. Bobby stared straight at him and he waited to see if he would yell at him for making a mess. But he didn't.

Instead, his uncle passed him a serviette. 'Don't worry about that. It's no big deal. We don't worry about mess around here. Now, let's start at the beginning. Simon, maybe you should tell me what you're both doing here.'

Liam gulped loudly and Simon could tell his brother was relieved not to have to think about what he was going to say. He cleared his throat and put his glass down, right on top of the wet spot on the tablecloth. Maybe that would hide it for a while. 'We ran away.'

Bobby crossed his arms. They were strong and muscly, nothing like his mother's scrawny arms which were often covered in sores. Simon jumped again and stopped looking at his arms when Bobby asked the next question. 'Why?'

He tried to look him in the eye. That was what the teachers at school always told him to do. Trying hard to keep his voice even he looked up but Bobby's gaze was intense and it was making him nervous. Short answers would be best. 'Because we don't want to leave school.'

'Why would you leave school?'

'To get a job.'

'Why?'

'Money.'

'Why do you need money at your age?'

'Food.'

Liam interrupted. 'Mum wants us to leave school and get jobs so she can have money to spend on grog and the races. She's not taking drugs at the moment but she has a stupid boyfriend called Boris who we hate. We remembered about you and didn't know where else to go, so we came here.'

'Liam and I caught the train,' Simon added, 'and then walked. Mum's not a bad person she just doesn't understand how important school is.'

'Your mother had a hard time when she went to school,' Bobby said. 'She never liked it. I didn't either but that was our life, it doesn't mean it has to be yours. You can't leave school anyway, you're too young.' Ruby placed her hand on Bobby's shoulder as if she was trying to calm him down. His voice sounded angry. Of course he would stick up for their mother, Simon thought. Why would an adult take their side?

'Maybe you could talk to her and she might listen.' Liam held his head high. 'We need you to help us, we don't have anyone else.'

Ruby and Sarah sat down, passing the food around and making sure everyone had a full plate. Simon decided he'd eat quickly and make sure to have some of everything. The discussions were not going as well as they had with Ruby and it was only a matter of time before they were either told to leave, or Bobby yelled at them for running away.

'Do you do well at school?' Sarah asked, passing him a plate full of ham and chicken. His mouth watered at the array of food in front of them and he tried to add to his plate slowly as if he ate like this every day. He didn't want to appear like he didn't have manners, but he'd never seen so much yummy food on one table.

Simon passed the plate to Liam, who held out his

hands waiting for it. Simon whispered, 'Remember your manners.' He turned to Bobby. 'We love it and the teachers help us a lot. They've tried to talk to Mum but it doesn't work,' Simon said.

Bobby piled his plate full of food and kept passing Simon different plates full of salad to add to his. 'What's home like. Is it a good place to live?'

Simon looked down at his plate, hoping that Liam didn't open his big mouth and let out all their secrets that he didn't want anyone else to know. He tried to glare at him but it was too late.

Liam started talking and Simon knew there was no way of shutting him up. 'Like I said, Mum doesn't take drugs anymore but she drinks and smokes. That's where all her money goes. We don't have food in the fridge and the house is dirty. We can't ask any kids over to play because mum's usually drunk or asleep. Boris is angry and yells at us, and Mum and I fight all the time. She throws things at me, smashes plates and vases when I drive her nuts and then Simon and I get on our bikes and ride as far away as we can. Basically, it's shit!'

Sarah's eyes were wide and she stopped eating. 'How old are you?'

'I'm thirteen and Simon is fourteen.' Liam answered.

'You sound like an adult.'

Simon looked down at his plate. His stomach churned and he had the urge to get up and run as far away as possible. Down the driveway and back through the tunnel of trees and over to the mountains on the horizon. Maybe if he just kept running he could forget about everything. This was terrible. He didn't even know these people and now they knew all his and Liam's business. They now knew what his mum was like. They would judge him and Liam. Bobby would send them straight back, after all she was his sister.

As she had often told them, 'Think yourself lucky. Your life is like a king's compared to what I had.' They had been stupid to come here for help. It was a bad idea.

Simon stood up. He looked at Bobby who wouldn't even look back at him. Instead, his uncle was staring hard at Ruby. Was he angry with her for letting them stay? She would probably get in trouble now for not sending them straight back to their mother.

He tried to keep his voice steady, but his throat burned and his eyes stung with tears that threatened to come. 'It's okay. We'll get going. We can find our own way home.'

Sarah and Ruby spoke at the same time. 'Sit down.'

Liam stood up. At least he had taken Simon's cue and they shared a look that perhaps this had not been the right decision. Maybe they should have gone somewhere else where no one knew them. Bobby remained silent, his face stony. He was probably getting angrier and angrier and in a moment they'd cop it for running away. It was time to go.

Bobby pushed his chair back and stood up, his large frame towering over Simon who tried not to shrink back in fear. 'You aren't going anywhere.' He cast his eyes around the group. 'We're your family. All of us. Family help each other.' He cleared his throat and Simon thought he saw tears in his eyes. Why would this upset him?

Pulling the chair back, Bobby beckoned for Liam and Simon to sit back down. 'I, I, well I, know what it's like to have problems at home and for things to be so bad that you need to run away.'

Simon sat down, his eyes downcast.

Liam hadn't sat back down and came to stand beside Ruby, her arms wrapping around him. She was the kindest person Simon knew and his chest ached as Liam leaned against her, wiping his nose with a tissue she passed him. It was hard enough to go through everything himself, but it made his entire body ache when he saw Liam get upset. It was worse than when Liam was angry.

Bobby leaned forward on the table, his hands pressed together, his brow furrowed as he looked at Simon. 'Simon, look up mate.' He did what he was told, biting his lip as the angst throbbed in his head. 'You need to know that we're here to help you both. Don't be worried that we'll go mad at you, or not believe what you say. Know right now that we believe what you're telling us. We don't doubt you and we need to help you work this out so that when you go back, your life might improve a bit.'

Simon wanted to answer but the words were stuck in his throat. How was anyone going to work anything out?

Liam spoke up. 'Simon won't tell bad stories about Mum because he says she loves us and does the best she can. I don't care though. I want to go to school and not always be fighting in the house.'

Ruby pulled a chair next to her and Liam sat down. Her words were always so calm and reassuring. 'We can all help you,' she said. 'To do that we need to talk about everything. We need to know what happens at home, how you're looked after and what you would like to happen. We also need to talk about how Boris fits into your life and how he treats you.'

'You have to remember that anything we talk about here we don't want you to talk about with your mum or

Boris. You can tell us anything you like and we won't repeat it,' Bobby said.

Sarah had remained quiet until now and Simon wondered what she thought of everything. She had probably thought she was coming back to her new home and would just be with Ruby and Bobby. But she spoke up also. 'What happens around the table, stays around the table.' She got up and hugged Simon's shoulders. 'I'm your cousin, so I care about you too. You have three adults here to help you.'

***

The sun had dipped behind the towering trees by the time Simon and Liam finished talking. Occasionally someone got up to go inside for a moment or bring out some more food and drinks. Ruby listened as Bobby talked, knowing that the conversation would bring memories back of his own turbulent childhood. She intervened and helped him out when the boys failed to understand some of his questions. At one stage she cleared her throat and placed her hand on Bobby's arm. 'I think what Bobby is trying to find out is if you feel unsafe with Boris.'

Bobby raised his voice. 'I want to know if he belts you or pushes you. Tell me and don't beat around the bush. Is he violent towards you?'

'We also want to know if there is any inappropriate touching or anything else you feel is not right, not just at home but anywhere,' Ruby added.

Simon shook his head. 'He's whacked us a few times and he threatens to bash us all the time.'

'He holds his fist in the air and his eyes nearly bug out

of his face,' Liam imitated what Boris looked like. 'But he's only hit us with his hand and once with a belt. Mum's the one who hits, well mainly me, sometimes. But it's not that bad. We haven't been sexually abused or touched inappropriately if that's what you're trying to find out.'

There was a look of horror on Simon's face. 'Oh no, he's never done anything like that. No way. We learn about that at school and no way, he's not like that.'

'You would tell us if that had happened wouldn't you?' Bobby spoke quietly.

'Yes, we would say so. He has never been like that or anyone else. He just whacks us. The worst part is how he speaks to us, like we're dogs or even worse,' Simon said.

'He doesn't hit Mum, just us.' Liam fidgeted in his chair. They had been talking for hours and Ruby could tell they needed a break. She looked at Bobby. 'Maybe we've sat for long enough. Is there anything else we should know?'

Simon spoke up. He had opened up more once he realised that Bobby wasn't angry with them and that the reason his uncle went quiet at times, was because he was upset about what had been happening. 'Liam and I are not going to leave school. It won't matter if Boris yells at us or Mum gets angry. We want to go to school. It's our safe place and the teachers are nice to us. They want to help.'

'What we need to work out is how to get your mother to think straight and realise that you need to stay at school.' Bobby stood up. 'I reckon I've heard enough now to go and ring her. Remember I won't repeat anything you've said. We're here to help you go back and to get some changes in place. Is it okay if I ring her?'

***

Simon's thoughts about Bobby changed over the afternoon. Although sometimes his face looked cranky and his eyes darkened, he seemed to be on their side. He hadn't yelled and the best thing was that they all listened to him and Liam. And they believed what they said. Sarah didn't add that much but he had seen her eyes go wide and a look of shock on her face when they spoke about how they often didn't have food to eat, or clean clothes to wear. She had shaken her head in amazement when they talked about riding around the streets, for days on end during the holidays, with no one to care where they were or what they were getting up to.

'But you're so young. Someone should be looking after you and making sure you don't get into trouble.'

Simon decided he liked her also. She was different from Ruby and not like anyone he had met before. She had talked a bit about how she had always lived with her grandparents and how her mother hadn't looked after her properly. 'You only need one person to really care about you and make sure you're going okay. Just one.'

A load lifted from his shoulders, and he breathed a sigh of relief when Ruby said they had sat long enough. The four of them went for a walk while Bobby went inside to ring Theresa. Liam skipped ahead. No doubt he thought just because they had talked about everything, it was all going to be solved and life would be right. Simon doubted that though. It wasn't going to be that easy, although he wouldn't like to argue with Bobby. It seemed like he could be stern when he wanted.

For now though, he wanted to enjoy the end of the

day. Ruby led them down to the huge bunya trees that stood guard over the valley.

Slivers of gold filtered across the valley, the rays of light like the fingers of a giant reaching across the valley. His gaze was drawn to the darkened shapes of the Glasshouse Mountain, their formations rising majestically from the plains. He had never seen mountains like these and their jagged outlines were fascinating. 'I'd like to climb to the top of them. You could see the world from up there,' he told Sarah.

Ruby came to stand beside him. 'Bobby and I have climbed two of them. There are tracks that lead to the summit. Some parts are steep and there are chains to hang onto. The view is amazing from the top and we could pick out our house from the top of that one.' She pointed to Mount Tibrogargan, its shape fading in the hazy light.

Simon looked down into the valley, the lights of scattered farms starting to come on. A breeze picked up and leaves from a tree nearby rustled as a flock of birds descended into the boughs, nestling down for the night.

'I could run up that mountain in one go. I bet I could,' Liam said as he jumped around. When he did five cartwheels in a row, Sarah laughed loudly. 'You have so much energy. It reminds me of what I was like when I was a kid. Maybe we should teach you boys how to ride a horse. That would keep you busy.'

Liam stopped and came and stood in front of her, his mouth twisted in a concerned look. 'We don't have any horses where we live. Do you have horses where you're from?'

She reached over and picked some twigs out of his

hair. 'Where I come from life is all about horses and cattle. It's been my entire life. I know nothing else.'

'But now you'll become a vet,' Liam patted down his curly hair which was springing out in all directions. 'Aunt Ruby said you will.'

The four of them stood together, no one talking as the sun disappeared and the night air cooled. When Ruby turned to return to the house, they followed, all with their own separate thoughts.

CHAPTER 35

*B*obby stood on the verandah watching as they walked towards him. His family. It was a strange feeling, in a matter of weeks he now had three other people, besides Ruby that he had a responsibility towards. Even though Sarah was old enough to make her own decisions he still had an overwhelming desire to help her achieve her best and to also back her grandfather in his wish to see her succeed. Now the two boys were also in the mix.

Theresa had sounded groggy and her voice slurred when he rang her. She said she'd just woken up and had the flu. He wasn't convinced though and had asked her if she had been drinking or taking anything.

'You know Bobby, my life isn't easy. If it wasn't for Boris it would be a whole lot worse. I don't know why you're asking about him and how he gets on with the boys. Those boys need discipline. They get away with too much and the teachers at school mollycoddle them. They need to be able to stand up for themselves. In case you don't remember it's a tough old world out there.'

Her words annoyed Bobby but he held his tongue. As if he needed to be told that. 'Just remember Theresa where we've come from. I don't want those boys in a situation where they're endangered. You of all people should relate to that.'

She'd laughed and then spluttered into a coughing fit. Bobby waited until she finished, her words shaky and hard to understand. 'Endangered! Are you joking? They're as safe as houses here with Boris and me. As if I'd let anything bad go on. I look after those kids better than anyone else could. What have they been saying?'

'They haven't said anything. They stick up for you and it's obvious that they love you. They want to stay at school though, they don't want to leave. That's why they ran away.'

'They're wasting their time at school, plus they're getting into trouble. I bet they didn't tell you that. Smoking and wagging. They think they're smart but they're no smarter than you or me. They need to realise that sooner or later they're going to have to work. We weren't born with a silver spoon in our mouth and neither have they.'

'They seem to be very intelligent. Your Liam is like a little adult and Simon reminds me of myself at that age. He's sensitive though and upset about a few things.'

'Like what? What did he say? You know they think they're badly done by, but they don't realise how good they've got it. Kids these days want everything. You wouldn't know because you don't have any. They need to know they have to work to get money and then they can have stuff.'

Bobby listened to Theresa continue to rant about how selfish the two boys were and how they didn't appreciate anything she and Boris did for them. When he was able to get a word in he let her know he was happy to bring them back and they could all sit down and talk together. They could work out the schooling situation and maybe he could help her sort out anything else she needed help with.'

Boris obviously heard the last part of the conversation. He yelled over the top of Theresa. 'Stick em on a bus or train and they can make their own way back. If the little bastards are smart enough to run away they can get back here themselves.' Theresa handed the phone to Boris. 'G'day Bobby, Boris here. We don't need any visitors at the moment. We're both busy and you can put them on a bus if you want to send them back.'

'Thanks Boris. I was hoping to come and talk to you both.'

'Don't bother. That's the last thing Theresa needs. You have no idea how hard those boys are to manage and they give her a bad time. They've probably told you a load of bullshit and that's all it is. They have a good life here and she bends over backward for them and gives them every-thing they need, plus more. They're ungrateful and that little one is a liar. He makes stuff up.'

'I'm concerned about them going back to school. Can I have your word that you'll let them stay at school and help them with what they need? I don't mind sending some money to buy books or anything else. I'm happy to help with that.'

'Well, Theresa could do with some money help. It's expensive to keep kids these days.'

Bobby noticed the change in Boris's tone once money was mentioned. He would have to get Ruby to help him work out how to get money to the boys without giving it to Theresa. Bobby talked to Boris for a bit longer. When he asked to say goodbye to Theresa again, Boris said she had gone back to bed. 'She needs her rest,' he said before hanging up.

CHAPTER 36

*A*t dinner Bobby could feel Simon's eyes on him, no doubt waiting for him to relay the conversation he'd had with Theresa. 'How about we enjoy the meal Ruby and Sarah have cooked before we talk about anything else,' Bobby said. He'd been a bit more careful about his tone of voice. Ruby had mentioned to him that he'd sounded like he was angry with the boys the night before. 'I knew that you were upset about the situation but I could tell they thought you were angry with them. It wouldn't take much to make them run.'

He hadn't realised that his anger had been so obvious. It was hard to listen to what they were putting up with and all sorts of memories of his own were colliding with the boys' experiences.

Tonight, Ruby as always, steered the conversation in the right direction and soon they were all laughing about the funny stories she told. 'You must have had a nice dad,' Simon said.

'He was the best. Bobby will tell you. We lived next

door to each other as kids and spent most of our time up in a mulberry tree. There was a rickety treehouse that was like a palace to us. We had silkworms, lots of them. We kept them in shoeboxes and watched them hatch from eggs to white silkworms that eventually spun cocoons.'

Liam sat upright. 'Then they turn into moths that lay eggs.'

Bobby was intrigued. 'How do you know about silkworms. Have you boys had them?'

Simon shook his head. 'No, never. I haven't ever seen one.'

Liam continued. 'Caterpillars hatch from the eggs. They feed on mulberry leaves and become a pupa. A pupa is an insect when it goes from being a larva to an adult. They weave a net around themselves.' He swung his head around. 'Like this. They do this and spin a silk fibre. That's how they make silk. The pupa turns into a moth and then the life cycle starts all over again.'

'Wow,' Sarah was impressed. 'How long do the moths live for?'

Ruby spoke up. 'Only about five days. They flutter their wings a lot and spend the time mating, in readiness to lay more eggs.'

'How many eggs do they lay,' Sarah asked.

Bobby and Ruby answered together, 'Lots.'

Liam added in, 'The female moths lay three hundred eggs in their lifetime.'

They all stared at him. 'How do you know all that,' Sarah asked. 'I don't know anything about silkworms.'

'Silkworms hatch in July and August and that's when the mulberry trees are starting to regain their leaves. I'm not sure what a mulberry tree looks like because I've never seen one, but I read that they lose their leaves in winter and when the leaves start to come back on, you know that's when the silkworms will hatch.'

Bobby chuckled. 'That's exactly right. You have a good memory.'

The conversation flowed and Bobby soaked in the moment. Even Simon relaxed and opened up about subjects he enjoyed at school. At one stage Ruby caught Bobby's eye and he winked at her, knowing she would also be enjoying the company around the table. No matter what cropped up she accepted it calmly. She hadn't blinked at the fact that Sarah was coming to live with them, and they were now a family of three. She had her mother's accepting ways and her father's organised and calm manner. Bobby was a lucky man. All he had to do now was ensure that Theresa and Boris kept their word and allowed the boys to stay at school. He had an uneasy feeling about putting them on a bus to Rockhampton, but it was clear Theresa did not want him visiting or dropping them home. He would have to make sure he checked on them regularly though and maybe in the holidays they could come and stay.

CHAPTER 37

*T*hree days at Tall Trees had made a difference to Liam and Simon. Their hair was clean and brushed, their clothes ironed and mended and Ruby had managed to slip into town to buy them each a new backpack they could use for school. She also bought some items of clothing and a pencil case packed full of stationery. They had looked at the new items like they were pieces of gold, packing them carefully for the trip back.

Their two small faces peered back through the window of the bus that would take them home. Bobby stood with his arm around Ruby's shoulder, a heavy feeling in his chest as he waved goodbye. 'I'm not sure this is the right thing to do,' he said to Ruby, who held her hand high in the air, waving until the bus was no longer visible.

'Theresa didn't really give you a choice. We'll see how they go and keep in contact. You can always go for a drive up there to check on them in a couple of weeks if you feel uneasy about it.'

They walked back to their car. 'I don't feel like I've talked to Sarah properly since we returned,' Bobby said. 'At least she seems to have settled into the cabin okay.'

'She's so sweet.' Ruby's face lit up. 'Her and I have a lot to get organised. There are phone calls to make and forms to fill in. She should be able to start her senior schooling via Distance Education in the next few weeks.'

She squeezed Bobby's arm. 'Everything will settle down. We'll get back to our normal routine.'

***

Simon rang Bobby the next afternoon. 'I just wanted to let you know that we got home okay. Mum and Boris are out somewhere.'

He breathed a sigh of relief. 'Is everything okay? How is Liam?'

'Liam is here and we're alright. Mum's a bit cranky about it all and Boris is his usual crabby self, so nothing different really. We're getting our stuff ready to go back to school tomorrow. Liam is still so excited about his bag.'

They talked for a bit longer and Bobby felt somewhat better about the situation. He would leave it a week or so and then ring and talk to Theresa. The boys knew they could ring at any time, he'd made it very clear that either he or Ruby would talk to them whenever they needed. Hopefully, everything would settle back down.'

***

Sarah sat at her desk in the cabin, a window behind it giving her a clear view down the valley. Ruby had made sure that she had everything she needed to start her senior year subjects. She shuffled the photos of her grandparents around, pushing the one of them sitting on their horses to the front. Thoughts of Grandpa filled her mind every day and at breakfast she visualised him sitting at the table eating his breakfast alone. She tried to stop the rising anxious feeling she got when she thought of him on the property by himself, but it was always there.

Ruby had taken her to the post office today and they had picked up the large envelopes that contained all her materials for the subjects she was doing. Together they read through the instructions and outlines for each one. There was no way she would have been able to work it all out without Ruby and the day was spent setting up her books and diary and working out assessment and study timelines.

She was well prepared and filled with excitement when she read the information. This was for real. She was going to get her senior pass and then go on to uni. Her path was mapped and she would do it not only for herself but also for Grandpa.

Bobby popped his head in through the front door a couple of times. 'I'm proud of you Sarah. I can't understand anything you are reading out though. Way above my head. Good luck with it.' He smiled at her and her heart filled. Thank goodness she'd found him. She might have gone her entire life without knowing him or Ruby. Everyone had helped and she was determined she'd work hard and not let anyone down. This was her life now. Studying and helping with the business.

hree months had passed since Simon and Liam had been at the farm. Holidays had come and gone and although Bobby tried to get Theresa to let the boys come for a couple of weeks she had refused his offer. Boris had got them jobs in the holidays and they were busy working with him. At least when he spoke to her she sounded sober and rational. When he quizzed Simon on the phone about how everything was going he replied that everything was okay. He didn't say much, and Bobby could tell he wasn't overly excited about working with Boris.

Sarah had settled in well with her schooling and was already receiving top marks for her assignments. They celebrated with a special dinner, and it seemed like everything had fallen into place.

The markets were busy on Sundays and most days Bobby was kept busy with the crops as well as doing the general maintenance that seemed to be never-ending. He had to laugh when he watched Ruby bound out of bed in the morning. 'I know Sarah is quite capable without me but it's nice to check on how she's going and see if she needs help with anything,' she said.

'You're like a mother hen, clucking around and tucking her under your wing.'

Ruby leaned over and kissed him, 'She's lovely and doing so well.'

Bobby pulled her in closer. 'You're lovely.'

She giggled as he kissed her neck. 'I'm not coming back to bed. I have things to do.'

He watched as she straightened up and blew him a kiss. She was wearing a large t-shirt and a pair of pyjama shorts, the sight of her slender body and tanned legs causing his heart to race. There was an elegance in the way she moved, her brown hair tumbling in waves down her back. They stared at each other, Ruby's green eyes holding his gaze. She took his breath away. He leaned on one elbow, his words softly spoken. 'You're beautiful,' I can't believe I get to wake up to you every morning.'

Leaning down she gave him another kiss. 'We're blessed to have each other. I love you.'

***

Bobby had allowed himself the luxury of sleeping in for another hour. He'd worked late the night before, packing tomatoes in the shed, ready for delivery today. The day was planned, the ute was packed and everything was ready to go. He closed his eyes and drifted off to sleep. The sound of the phone ringing woke him and he waited to see if Ruby answered it. She didn't and he surmised that she was probably in the cabin with Sarah.

The two of them liked to have a cup of coffee before Sarah started the day and he left them to it, knowing they liked to chat.

He got to the phone just as it stopped. It was more than likely one of the cafes in town wanting some produce. No doubt they'd ring back. He'd just started to walk away when it rang again. This time he picked it up quickly. Local orders were important and he was heading in that direction today so it would be easy to add to the delivery.

A boy's voice echoed down the line. 'Uncle Bobby, is that you? It's Liam.'

'Yes, it's me. How are you? The line is not great. Where are you?'

'We're in a phone box near a highway. It's noisy.'

'What's up mate. Are you okay?'

There was no reply and he repeated his question. Liam's voice was shaky. 'We're in Gin Gin. We hitched a ride to get here. Simon won't say it but Mum's gone nuts again. She punched me in the face and Boris threw my books in the bin. He said we were spoilt brats.'

Bobby tried to keep his voice even. 'Tell me exactly where you are. I don't want you hitching any rides. Exactly where are you?'

'We're near the Gin Gin Bakery; in a phone box. We need to get away from Mum. Simon's sitting outside the phone box in the gutter. She punched him when he tried to stop her from hitting me. I think he's vomiting.'

'I need to ring the police. You could stay with them until I come and get you.'

'Nope,' Liam said. 'No way. They'll take us straight back to Mum and we'll cop it worse.'

'Okay. Is there somewhere nearby that you can sit until I can come and get you?' Bobby worked out where they were and how long it would take him to get there. 'I could be there in about four hours. You have to give me your word that you'll stay in the one spot. If you're not there when I arrive, then I'll need to go to the police.' He calculated the time to drive there again. 'If I get in my car right now I can be there even quicker, maybe three and a bit hours. Liam are you listening. Will you stay in the one spot?'

Liam's voice was calm. 'There's a park opposite us here. It has swings and flower gardens. We'll go into the park. There are trees at the back. We'll sit under them. No one will see us. We'll wait for you, Uncle Bobby. Even if you're late and it gets dark, we'll stay here. Even if you can't come until tomorrow we'll still be there. We have nowhere to go and Simon's in a bad way.'

'Do you need to call an ambulance or go to a doctor?'

'He's just sick. He'll be okay. We don't need to do any of that.'

'It's okay mate.' Bobby was already moving around the house, grabbing his wallet and keys. 'I'll be there. I'll come and get you, just wait where you are. If for some reason we don't meet up, you come back to that telephone box and ring this number again. Ruby will be here and if worse comes to worst, I'll ring her also and we can work it out. Whatever happens, don't leave there. Either be at the phone box near the pie shop or in the park.'

'I'll do as you say. I promise, and I'll look after Simon. We'll be under the big tree. We've still got the money you gave us. We hid it like you said so I'll get some food from the bakery.'

'Be careful. I'm just about to leave. I'll see you shortly. Please stay there and don't talk to any strangers.'

Liam's voice was small and Bobby could hear the traffic on the main road next to the phone box. 'Thanks. We won't move.'

***

Ruby and Sarah were in the middle of a conversation when Bobby burst into the cabin. 'I have to go and get the boys. They're at Gin Gin, across the road from the bakery in the park. There's been another fight and Theresa has punched them. I think more than that has happened but that's all they've told me. They've run away again. Liam promised that they'll stay in the park or go to the phone box and ring again if they need. Ruby, you or Sarah have to stay by the phone, in case I don't meet up with them. They have some money so they can ring back.'

Ruby stood up, her eyes wide. 'Oh Bobby, that's terrible. Are you sure you don't want me to come with you?'

'No. I'll be fine. Listen you'll have to take the tomatoes into town and there's another delivery for the café on Main Street.'

Sarah stood up also. 'I can bring my study up to your house and sit next to the phone. Or do whatever else you need me to do.'

'We'll work it out here,' Ruby added, 'don't worry about the deliveries. I'll look after that. You get going and drive carefully.'

He kissed Ruby on the cheek. 'I'll take care. If Theresa or Boris rings, which I very much doubt, don't tell them anything. Just say you haven't heard anything. If I can't find the boys I'll ring back here first. This needs to stop. Those boys deserve better. I don't want them running so far away next time we can't find them.'

'Can you make sure to ring us and let us know when you pick them up,' Sarah said. 'We'll be worried sick otherwise.'

Ruby shook her head. 'It's just like what you went through. Thank goodness they're street smart and have the guts to get out. Go and get them Bobby, and bring them back here. We'll work it out from there.'

*B*obby pulled into the small town of Gin Gin just before midday. It wasn't hard to spot the telephone box and he drove slowly into the parking area next to it. The park was empty and he headed towards the large fig trees that formed a border at the back of the manicured lawns and rose gardens. Liam had followed his instructions and it only took Bobby a few minutes to locate them. Both were curled up at the base of a massive fig tree, their heads resting on their backpacks, their eyes closed as they slept.

He knelt down and touched Simon on the arm. When his eyes slowly opened he stared at Bobby for a moment before rubbing his face and sitting up. Then Liam opened his eyes, his reaction different as he quickly jumped up and gave Bobby a long hug. 'I did what you said. We stayed here all day waiting for you.'

Bobby looked at him, his gut lurching when he saw Liam's face. A dark bruise covered one eye, a purple mark stretching down to his cheek. 'Are you okay, mate?'

Liam put a hand to his face. 'It's a bit sore. She hit me hard.' He clenched his teeth. 'Don't make us go back there.'

Simon stared down at his feet, his shoes covered in mud. His eyes came up to meet Bobby's, the sadness in them causing a lump in Bobby's throat. 'It's okay. You're coming back with me,' Bobby said as he picked up Liam's bag, the boy's small hand hanging onto his.

The three of them walked back to the car. Simon hopped in the back and lay down along the seat, using his bag as a pillow. He closed his eyes as Bobby reached over and wrapped the seat belt around him. 'Have a sleep, mate. We'll be back on the farm in no time.'

Liam jumped in the front, his thin legs stretched out in front of him. 'I'm hungry.'

'I'll stop down the road here and get you some food. I'll give Ruby a call and let her know that you're safe. We'll let Simon sleep.'

***

Once Liam had eaten and stretched his legs at the petrol station he admitted he was tired. 'Go to sleep,' Bobby told him. 'It's a long trip back and it looks like the two of you haven't slept much.'

Simon snored lightly in the back seat. 'Boris threw our mattresses out because we ran away, Liam said. 'When we got back from your place they were gone and we've just been on the floor with a blanket under us. We haven't slept very well and the teachers even rang Mum to say we were both falling asleep at school. They even sent around the child safety people which made Boris extremely angry.'

'Didn't they see that things weren't right? You should have told me about the beds, I would have bought you new ones.'

Liam looked at Simon sleeping. 'Mum just lied to the child safety lady and Simon won't say anything against Mum so they just thought that I was a liar when I spoke out. No one believed me and they talked to us for a while, then Mum, and then they just left. It was a waste of time me saying anything.'

Liam lay back in the seat, his eyes eventually closing. Bobby watched him as he slept, sneaking a look at Simon who was still fast asleep. They both had lost weight since he'd seen them last and it was more than he could bear to see the bruise on Liam's face. He had also noticed bruises on Simon's arm.

How could Theresa hit them when she knew what it felt like. Hadn't their childhood, full of abuse, years of suffering and finally a court case, been enough to teach her something. He gripped the steering wheel tightly, anger filling him at the thought of how his sister could let this happen. The boys were only young. Simon was about the same age he had been when he'd run away. He wasn't going to let that happen. They needed a break, a loving home and a place that was safe.

***

The sun had set by the time Bobby returned to the farm. Ruby and Sarah were waiting and helped him guide the boys into their room. They'd given the girls a quick hug before falling asleep in their beds.

CHAPTER 40

The first light of the morning filtered over the yard as Bobby stood on the verandah, a coffee in his hand. He sipped it slowly, his eyes cast to the valley floor where heavy mist concealed everything that lay beneath. A slight movement under the bunya trees caught his eye and he noticed Simon standing in front of them, his position nearly concealed by their thick trunks.

Making his way towards him, Bobby ran over the events of the day before, in his mind. It had been a long day by the time they returned to the farm and the boys had barely opened their eyes as they said hello to Ruby and Sarah. Ruby had guided them to their rooms, and both had fallen straight into their freshly made beds. It had not been the right time to talk, however Bobby knew there were important discussions to be had today.

He walked slowly towards Simon, whistling as he went to let him know he was coming. When Simon turned to look at him, Bobby's heart ached, the pain in the boy's eyes a reflection of his own childhood experiences. They looked at each other, the same dark eyes and unruly dark hair, almost as if they could be father and son.

'That's a heavy fog this morning,' Bobby said. 'It will be a hot day.'

Simon nodded, his eyes drawn back to the valley.

'Did you sleep alright?'

Simon nodded again.

'Do you feel like talking?'

Simon shook his head, his eyes downcast.

They stood together looking out over the view. A flock of cockatoos squawked as they flew in front of them and a kookaburra began its morning call. Bobby looked up into the trees to try and see it. Simon looked also, his shoulders slumped, his baggy clothes hanging loosely on his gaunt body.

'How about we go up and I'll make you breakfast. I've got some of that local smoked bacon and fresh eggs and mushrooms to go with it,' Bobby offered. 'The coffee pot is on and you can eat and drink as much as you want.' Simon turned and followed Bobby back up to the house. If there was one way to get a boy's attention it was to talk about food.

By the time Bobby finished cooking, the rest of the household was up. Having Sarah with them was like having another Ruby around. She bounded out of the cabin wearing denim shorts and a baggy t-shirt, her hair shiny and brushed.

When she wrapped her arms around Simon's shoulders, he pressed his head against her, no words from him either, but a signal that he appreciated her hug. Ruby and Liam soon joined them and Bobby held his tongue, noticing that Liam, like Simon, still had on the dirty baggy clothes from yesterday. A look from Ruby let him know that now wasn't the time to bother about that. There were bigger issues at hand and the arrival of the boys last night was different from last time. Both seemed defeated, as if they had come to the end of the trail. Even Liam was quiet, his eyes sad, his movements slow.

Ruby broke the ice. 'I have some clean clothes here for you both. I picked up a couple of shirts and shorts at the shop yesterday. There're even some new jocks,' she said.

Bobby tried to sound upbeat. 'When you're finished, maybe both have a scrub in the tub and when you feel like it we can all sit and talk.'

Liam nodded.

Silence hung in the air and Bobby took deep breaths. He wanted to make sure this was handled right. Both boys were obviously traumatised by the latest incident and he knew from his own experiences, that particularly Simon, might not stick around if he had an inkling they were contemplating sending them back home. There was no way Simon would leave Liam though and Bobby wanted to let them know that once they were cleaned up they'd all sit down and discuss what had happened.

Bobby sipped his third cup of coffee while Ruby bustled around the table, filling up cups and piling more food onto plates. As they finished eating she appeared with clean towels. 'Your clothes are in the bathroom. Can you please put any dirty clothes in the laundry basket? Get whatever needs washing out of your backpacks and I'll put on a load this morning.'

As they took the towels and disappeared into the house Bobby went to get up. Ruby placed her hand on his arm. 'Leave them be. Let them clean up and get dressed. You know yourself how a shower and change of clothes makes you feel a bit better.' She looked at Sarah. 'We all need to give them some space. They're traumatised.'

He sat back down. 'I just feel so damn helpless and guilty. I shouldn't have taken them back there.'

Sarah reached over and put her hand on his where it rested on the table. 'Your sister said she'd treat them right. Plus, they were okay about going back. They wanted to be with their mother and she said she'd change her ways. You can't blame yourself, plus you kept in contact with them.'

'Thanks, Sarah. Theresa is obviously never going to change. I need to talk to her and Boris about this. I may have to report them to child services or ring the police. Those two have bruises all over them.'

Ruby spoke quietly. 'We're going to have to take photos of those bruises and how thin they are. We might need it down the track for one reason or another.'

Bobby nodded. 'I'll do that.' He ran his hand through his hair. 'Nothing I said to Theresa has made any difference.'

Ruby stood up and came and stood beside him. 'This shows that their situation won't change in that house. She's had her chance. She might improve for a week or so and do everything right so everyone will be happy. Then she'll go on another bender, or something will annoy her. It's a vicious cycle, Bobby, you know that. Nothing will be any different. The only reason that Simon has stuck around is because he won't leave Liam.'

'I should have been harsher with her last time. I should … I …' He faltered, his hands twisting together as he looked from Sarah to Ruby. 'It's hard. She's my sister and it isn't her fault she's the way she is.'

'We know that, but those boys have to come first.' Ruby crossed her arms, a sure sign that whatever she was about to say would be the rule. 'There's no question about it, Bobby, and you and I discussed this last night. Those boys are coming to live with us.'

He could feel the colour drain from his face. 'That all sounds very good however you're talking about years of child-rearing, bringing up teenage boys who have already got a heap of problems.'

'There's not really a choice. You can't let them go back. It will only happen again,' Sarah said, her voice a whisper. 'You've taken me in. What's the difference? They're your nephews.'

'This is a bit different. You're self-sufficient, plus we have the cabin for you to live in.'

Ruby stared at him, her face set. 'We have spare rooms and there's the other cabin you could renovate for them when they get a bit older.'

Waves of panic hit Bobby. Ruby had already made her mind up, he could tell from the look on her face. 'Have you really thought about this with a clear mind this morning?'

She put her hands on her hips, her words clear and firm. 'There's nothing to discuss. There are no other options. The boys don't have anyone else.'

'It's not just a matter of letting them sleep here and feeding them. Where would they go to school, who is going to help them through all their problems, drive them where they need to go. Liam is just about to start high school. We've never raised kids.'

'I know all that. I thought long and hard about it last night. Actually, I thought about it last time they were here, but Theresa was so adamant things would improve. Nothing is going to change and if we don't take them in it will be another cycle of abuse and family violence. You and I aren't going to let that happen.'

Bobby grabbed her hand. 'I know you want to help everyone, Ruby, but this is different. There are still many years ahead.'

She smiled and his heart warmed as he looked at her. Her green eyes were vivid, her face glowing with the excitement of her idea. She spoke with candour. 'I want them as my family, as our family. We can do it.'

Bobby turned to Sarah. 'What do you think. We are a family of three already. This will impact you too.'

Sarah replied. 'I'm with Ruby. I care about them also and I'll help as much as I can. I don't think we have a choice. We can do it.'

***

They'd spent the morning walking through the paddocks and feeding the horses. The boys were still quiet although Liam smiled when a hare popped up in the long grass and Rusty took off in rapid pursuit. The dog had jumped over obstacles and the long grass, looking much like a hare himself, his noisy yapping echoing over the paddocks.

When he bounded back to them he attached himself to Simon. Bobby chatted about the horses and how the business was going and what needed to be packed and ready for the markets. There were no questions and no expectations for them to say anything. Ruby had commented to Bobby earlier that neither boy had emptied their backpack and no dirty clothes had been put out to wash. 'Just leave them for the moment. We'll talk this afternoon,' he said.

Bobby walked ahead with her, placing his arm around her shoulder and kissing the top of her head. 'You're amazing. I need you to be sure about us offering for the boys to stay though. It's for a lifetime.'

He could tell she was excited at the idea. 'I know. I want to take them on like they are our own. I'll deal with all the schooling and anything else they need. They relate well to you and especially Simon is going to need you to guide him. It's going to take both of us but we can give them a good life here. We'll be their adoptive parents.'

'We have to make sure it's what they want and that Theresa will let them live here. I don't want any back and forth once they're here unless it's for a short visit. I'm not sure that Simon is going to agree to this so easily. He's hardly spoken since I picked them up. You know he always sticks up for his mother.'

Ruby squeezed Bobby's hand. 'I know. It's like he's broken. We're going to have to be careful how we handle this.'

***

When they returned from the walk, Simon walked straight inside and went back to bed. If he closed his eyes the pain went away. Not the pain from his bruises, that was nothing. It was the pain in his heart. If it hadn't been for Liam he would have left the park in Gin Gin and walked somewhere else so that Bobby couldn't find them. He wasn't sure where he would have gone but it would have been a long way from anywhere. Or maybe he would have just stayed away for a while and then gone back home. Mum might be sober by then and life would go on as normal.

Scrunching his eyes shut he tried not to think of her. Not to remember how her face had crumbled up like a woman possessed by the devil. So angry and violent that even Boris had moved out of her reach. When Boris had thrown Liam's books in the bin, something had snapped inside Simon; like a knife cutting across his gut. He'd lunged at Boris, punching and hitting whatever he could reach. Like a giant, Boris had picked him up and thrown him out the front door. He'd hit his shoulder on the door frame but there had been no pain, only a numbness that increased as his mother came to the doorway and screeched further profanities at him.

Theresa had been drunk, rotten drunk. She'd stumbled and had to hold onto the furniture to stay upright as she screamed at him. Although he'd tried to talk calmly his words had enraged her further and when she lunged at him her fist found its mark on his eye. Blinded and in pain he'd fallen backward, hitting his head on the table and sending her favourite vase and photo of her and Boris, smashing onto the ground. Liam had picked himself up and gone back for more. His words had flowed, railing against his mother and the way she treated them. 'You're drunk. Why can't you stay sober and be a real mum.' It was unusual for Liam to cry. Usually, he was so angry that his words flowed like venom, the barbs from what he said always managing to send Theresa into a further rage.

This time though he sobbed as he spoke, one hand pressed against his eye, the other arm tucked up as if it was injured. Simon had grabbed him from behind as Theresa once again lifted her arm to strike him. That was when Boris had picked up the pile of books and tossed them out. Theresa had marched in and grabbed the globe from their room and thrown it out the window. All his dreams went with it. He had nothing left.

When Boris returned from the bins, Liam flew for him like a crazy person, words of hatred and pent-up frustration flowing from his mouth. His words were cutting and Simon wished he could think of responses so quickly. That seemed to push Boris and Theresa over the edge.

He had thought he was going to die when Boris lifted both of them up and threw them through the air. The door had slammed shut behind them and he lay next to Liam writhing on the verandah floorboards, his hand clutching Liam's shirt. At least he could no longer see the contorted face of his mother and he curled up in a ball, the pain in his heart overwhelming.

When everything went quiet inside, the two of them climbed in through their bedroom window and again packed their backpacks. As they walked out through their front gate and up the road, Simon's mind was numb. He didn't think of his mother or Boris, just concentrated on putting one foot in front of the other.

Liam had taken charge and after hearing a conversation between an older man and the attendant at the petrol station, he approached the man for a lift. He'd heard the man saying he was going as far as Bundaberg and remembered that there was a town near there on the highway. 'Excuse me. My brother and I need to return home to Gin Gin. Do you think you could give us a lift?'

'The man looked suspiciously at them. 'What happened to your eye?'

'We came up to play football and we've missed the bus back. Just a bit bruised from the game.'

'Did you win?'

'No, we got thrashed.' Liam attempted a smile. 'That's how I got this. Our mum will have our guts for garters seeing we've missed the bus. We'd really appreciate a lift.'

The man hesitated before answering. 'Okay, jump in both of you. No trouble though and I'm only taking you that far.' Liam could tell from the look on the man's face that he didn't believe the story for one minute. 'I was a bit of a troubled youth back in the day. You seem like nice kids. Jump in. You're just lucky the wife's not in the car because she'd talk your ear off and ask you a hundred questions.'

Liam had sat in the front and talked to the man the entire way. His name was Ted and he'd spent time working on cargo ships that sailed between Australia and Europe. He had a load of stories and Liam kept him busy talking, questioning him and, he couldn't help himself, adding his own expert information and opinion on everything.'

'You're a smart kid. Don't waste it. Make sure you do what you're supposed to at school. Your mum must be proud of you.'

'Oh, she is. She tells everyone how I'm going to go to uni to study medicine or law. She says not to waste time playing football, but you know what it's like. I love being part of a team.'

Ted looked in his rear vision mirror at Simon, who had spent most of the time staring out of the window. 'You that clever too?' Ted asked.

'No one is as smart as Liam. But I do well at school. I want to be a teacher.'

Ted nodded. 'You two have your heads screwed on right. It's good to meet young people who are going to do well. Make sure you stay that way.'

When he dropped them at the phone box on the side of the highway he had got out and shook their hands. 'You made a boring drive interesting. Usually, the wife does all the talking. It was good to meet you.'

They thanked him. 'We'll ring our mum and she'll come and pick us up. Thanks for the offer to drop us off at home but it's a bit out of town. She'll be happy we're back early. The bus won't be here yet as it would have gone out to a couple of smaller towns to drop kids off. Thanks, Ted. Mum will be really pleased.'

***

What Liam had said about their mother being pleased was the first thing Simon thought of when he woke up that first morning back at Bobby's. Mum was never pleased about anything. He tried to remember when she had liked anything they did, or when she had ever been happy about their marks at school. Liam was dreaming, making up stuff like he always did. Proud? What did that word mean? Liam had used what he wished was the truth.

Simon stretched, enjoying the luxury of a thick

mattress, the clean linen and blanket Aunt Ruby had put on for them, soft against his bruises. When they had left Ted's car, Simon had argued with Liam. He didn't want him to ring Bobby. 'We're not going there again. He'll just ring Mum. They might let us stay for a week or so but then we'll have to go back, and nothing will change. Why don't we hang out here for a while and by then Mum might have cooled off?'

'She's not going to change.' Liam's voice was high-pitched and panicky. It had been easy to get this far, but where to from here. 'I'm going to ring him,' Liam insisted.

Simon's head had started to spin and he hung onto Liam to steady himself. His brother propelled him onto the grass, talking to him as he placed his head between his hands. The words were lost though, as Simon's stomach lurched, the bile rising in his throat.

He concentrated hard on sitting upright. He hadn't eaten properly for days. Theresa had been on a bender and the only food he had was what he could scavenge at school. The teachers had noticed something was wrong and tried to give him money for the tuckshop. But he assured them he was fine. Drawing attention to the fact that there was no food in the house would only bring on the attention of child safety again. They hadn't done anything last time and the repercussions from Theresa and Boris after the visit from them had been ongoing.

By the time he stopped vomiting, Liam was off the phone and guiding him to the park across the road. He had barely been able to carry his backpack and Liam had taken it from him, lugging both bags as well as supporting him until they reached the trees at the back of the park. The leaves were soft and warm under the trees and he curled up into a ball, closing his eyes and falling into a deep sleep.

Now they were back at Bobby's, Tall Trees, right where they had been months earlier. It was just going to be the same. At least a break from Theresa and Boris would let him start to feel better and the food Bobby had given them today had gone a long way in restoring some of his energy. He was no longer hungry and clean clothes and a shower had made him feel better. The last thing he wanted to do was talk though. The words weren't there. There was no use. Bobby and Ruby were good people and it was obvious they cared about him and Liam. They had their own lives though. He closed his eyes again. At least a few days with them would be restful. No arguing, no violence and no Boris.

He hated Boris. If he wasn't there, his mum would be different. Boris backed her up when she was angry with them. The two of them were like a team and together they couldn't be defeated. It was no use wishing that Boris would leave. He was there forever.

CHAPTER 41

*T*he smell of the barbeque drew Simon outside. Bobby was cooking and Ruby and Sarah were setting the table, bowls with salads and bread rolls out ready. He rubbed his eyes, noticing Liam sleeping in the hammock at the end of the verandah. 'You slept for a long while,' Ruby smiled at him. 'It's nearly dinner time.'

He forced a slight smile. It wasn't Aunt Ruby's fault that any of this happened. In fact, it wasn't anyone's fault.

'Hamburgers for dinner.' Sarah's cheery voice woke Liam, who sat up and stretched. The marks around his eye had darkened and Simon stared hard, the sight of the bruises sending waves of anxiety washing over him. When Aunt Ruby asked him to help her he followed her into the kitchen, following her instructions and bringing out more food. He loved the kitchen. There was always a smell of something cooking and the shelves on the wall were lined with jars of olives, jams and chutneys. The pantry was full and his eyes roved over the contents when he searched for the sauces Aunt Ruby wanted. 'That's it, third shelf on the left. Next to the flour.'

It was good to do something useful and he walked back and forth, bringing out what was needed. He noticed Sarah swinging Liam in the hammock, the look on his brother's face bringing some pleasure to him. Liam had really copped it this time and hopefully his eye hadn't been damaged. Aunt Ruby would probably take him to a doctor if they were going to stay long enough for that. He busied himself, washing up the few dishes in the sink, trying to ward off the questions in his mind about whether his mother was thinking about what she had done. There was no use wondering. Boris and her would have slept off the binge and then got straight back into it. Hair of the dog, as his mother liked to say.

Boris was probably bragging about throwing them out. It was almost like he could hear his words. 'Fixed those brats this time. Next time they won't be so bloody cocky.'

Simon had heard it all before. Time and time again. It was always the same.

***

The burgers were delicious and Ruby watched the boys devour three each. They were still quiet although Liam had talked to Rusty when he stood next to him, hoping for some scraps. 'No Rusty. Not at the table.' Liam got up and Rusty followed him onto the grass. He made the dog sit, before feeding him a small piece of his burger.

Bobby cleared his throat as they all finished their meal

and Liam returned to the table. 'Okay, I know you boys probably don't feel like this, but we need to talk. All of us.'

Liam and Simon looked at each other.

Sarah spoke first. 'You're my family too so I'm going to be part of this.'

'We thought it best if we all talk together,' Ruby added. 'There's a fair bit to discuss.'

'Firstly,' Bobby said. 'Do you want to tell us anything first? You can say anything, you know we've told you before it never goes past us.'

They both shook their head.

Ruby passed them both a glass of cold water. 'We need you to be honest with us. We will be the same with you.' She nodded towards Bobby giving him the go-ahead. As he spoke her soul warmed. Her love for him strengthened every day. His rugged face and caring nature imbued a warmth and love that made her heart skip whenever they were with each other. Now he faced more hurdles. The previous months had thrown some unexpected changes in their life but turning them into positives had been easy. She hoped this time her gut feeling would be right again. The boys would become their own family.

Bobby cleared his throat, his eyes on the two boys. 'Ruby, Sarah and I have talked about what has happened and what is likely to occur in the future. We've given this a lot of thought. If you return to your Mum and Boris, you might imagine that life will change. Speaking from experience,' he took a deep breath, 'I know from my own childhood that you tell yourself they won't do it again. That they won't hit you or hurt you. It was just a mistake, their anger got the better of them and next time it won't be so bad, or they'll stop before they hurt you.'

Ruby could see he was struggling with his words, and she watched as he re-gathered his thoughts. 'The trouble is, your mum or Boris aren't going to change.'

Simon sat up, his face fixed in a glare.

Bobby turned to him. 'I'm not criticising Theresa, the alcohol and her own childhood has made her the way she is. I've tried to help her many times over the last few years, but she doesn't want help.' He looked down. 'Ruby has tried too, and we can't do any more when she won't accept it or try and help herself.'

Simon wiped his hand over his eyes.

Ruby passed him a tissue. 'We can help you boys though.'

Liam finally spoke. 'She doesn't listen to you. She says she won't hit us and that she'll do the right thing, but as soon as you hang up the phone she does the opposite. That's why our sisters left when they could.'

'When I sent you back last time, Ruby and I hoped that because it was the first time you'd run away for a length of time, the situation might change. But it hasn't and it seems that it's become worse.'

'Mum's drinking more now and so is Boris,' Liam said.

Bobby's voice was gentle. 'Simon, what do you think about everything?'

Simon's hands were clenched together, his face set in a frown.

'We can't help you if you won't talk. Listen to me, I know how you feel but we need to work this out.'

When Simon finally spoke, his words were barely audible. 'We're okay. We shouldn't have called you. I told Liam not to.'

'It's too big for you two to work out,' Ruby said. 'I

know you've had to look after yourselves like adults but these problems are too large for you to solve, and no one has the right to hurt anyone.'

Simon glowered at Liam. 'We're okay. She'll calm down. Maybe our older sisters can help us.'

Bobby sat upright. 'Theresa won't calm down. Nothing will change and your older sisters are only young themselves and trying to get on with their lives. You need to be cared for.'

Simon's voice was angry. 'We aren't going to any of those halfway houses or foster carers. That's what the child safety people said would happen. We need to go back to Mum.'

Bobby looked around the table. 'We would never let child safety take control. Ruby, Sarah, and I, have come up with an idea and we all know it will be the best for you.' He leaned forward, his hands gripped together. 'We want you to come and live with us.'

Simon blinked hard and Liam look confused.

Bobby continued. 'The three of us want you to come and live here permanently. We want you to live in the house with us and go to school in town. We want to take you on like you are our own kids and we'd treat you just the same as Sarah. We're talking long-term. Not weeks or years but forever. As long as you want.'

Liam's voice was a squeak. 'Like, forever more?'

Bobby struggled to keep his voice even, tears threatening to come. 'Yes.'

'What about Mum?' Simon fixed Ruby with a hard stare.

She explained carefully. 'We'd talk to your mum and explain what we want. There are papers we can get her to sign to say we are your guardians.' Ruby made sure she had their full attention and they understood what she was saying. 'That way you would have to stay here though and as your legal guardians we would have full say over what you did. It just makes it that your mum can't make you go back to her and upset schooling here or living with us. It doesn't mean that you wouldn't see her, it's just that you'd live here with us. We would arrange it that you saw her in the holidays or Bobby could drive you back for a visit any time you wanted.'

'Did Mum say she'd do this?' Liam asked.

'We haven't spoken to her yet,' Bobby said. 'We wanted to see what you thought first.'

Simon's eyes narrowed. 'Why would you want to do that? We're only thirteen and fourteen. We still have a few years of going to school left.'

'The three of us have talked about it,' Bobby continued. 'We all think the same. The best thing would be for you to come and live with us here. You'd be safe.'

Simon bristled, his brow furrowed. 'We're safe with Mum. She's not that bad.'

Sarah leaned forward, her dark eyes troubled and concerned. 'Look at your brother's face. What about the bruises on you? Maybe next time it won't just be one hit or throw. Look at Liam's eye and honestly tell us that you or your brother are safe with your mum.'

Simon sniffled and bit his lip, his words coming out slowly. 'I love Mum. I know she hurts us, but I love her.'

Liam was thinking hard, and Ruby wondered if he was weighing up whether he loved his mum or not. 'Do you really think we could live here?' he asked.

'We need to talk to your mum about it, and of course

make sure that you both want to do that.' Bobby looked around the table. 'Sarah made a huge decision to come and live here. By doing that she had to give up being near her Grandpa.'

Sarah explained gently. 'But I know that if I live here and study, I can set myself up for life and do the job I have always wanted to do. It's not easy being without someone you love, but Bobby and Ruby will make it work for you both.'

'Why would you want us?' Simon repeated. 'We can't pay for anything, we eat a lot and that would be five of us living here. Wasn't it always just the two of you?'

'I know,' Ruby was beaming. 'This is a family like I never dreamt of. Of course, no one can take the place of your mum, Simon. We're not trying to do that, but sometimes all you need is one person or a family to help you and it will make a difference to your entire life.'

'That's what I had out west,' Bobby said. 'Good people around me and I was only your age. That was your Mum's problem, she never had anyone good around to help her.'

'Maybe she could come and live here as well.' Liam said.

'Ruby and I have asked if we can help several times over the years, but she won't take any. Now she's with Boris.'

'If Mum agrees, then I would come and live here.' Liam said as he looked toward Simon, waiting for his response. 'That's if Simon says he will. We stay together.'

'Of course, both of you would have to agree. What do you think Simon?' Ruby knew that both boys would have to agree to the arrangement and they still had Theresa to contend with.

Simon looked around the table. 'I still can't believe you would want to take both of us in.' His eyes rested on Sarah. 'I reckon what Sarah is doing is a good thing. She could have stayed out west and kept doing what she was. If she made the decision, then maybe I could too. As long as we could still see Mum in the holidays and maybe ring her every week.'

There was an audible sigh of relief around the table and Ruby thought that Bobby's face would split from the wide grin that crossed it. 'You boys will never regret this decision. One day we'll all look back and talk about this time. We'll make sure that we try and help your mum too. It's not like we'd be deserting her, we just want to make sure you're safe first.'

'Would Mum have to pay you money for us to live here because I don't think she'll do that?' Liam was thinking ahead. 'I could help at the markets or pick vegies and pack for you. I wouldn't want to get paid but I could help like that.'

'I could get a weekend job in town and pay you some money,' Simon said. 'I could ride a pushbike there.'

'Will we need our stuff from home?' Liam asked.

'Firstly, let's talk to your mum,' Bobby said. 'We can work everything else out from there. Money isn't a concern. You'd be our family and we'd take care of all of that. I just want to hear from both of you that this is a good idea. You can't keep running away and you're both clever kids. The schools in town are good and we'd make sure you get the education you need. Ruby knows all about that stuff. We'd also be here for later on if you wanted to go to university.'

'Look how's Ruby's helped me.' Sarah stood up. 'I'm

going to leave you all to work the rest out. I've got an assignment due.' She walked around the table and hugged first Liam and then Simon. 'I can teach you both to ride.'

***

The four of them sat and talked further. Heavy guilt pressed down on Simon. They would be leaving their mum. Even though she was usually drunk, she was always there, even if she was in bed sleeping. He glimpsed Liam, his little face lit up, his eyes excited at the prospect of a new life. He deserved the best. He was brave, standing up to both Mum and Boris. Simon's attention was drawn to Liam's black eye. If they returned home, that and probably more would happen again and again. There was no surer thing. Mum wasn't going to change overnight, and Boris wasn't going anywhere. They had been thrown a lifeline. A life with people who were good and cared about them.

It was confusing though. How could Bobby and Mum come from the same home yet be so different? Bobby didn't have a mean bone in his body and when he spoke his words were calm and reassuring. Ruby had told him that Theresa had suffered badly when she was a kid and that had made her turn to drugs and alcohol.

He put his shoulders back, he didn't want that for Liam or him. They needed to get off that cycle. He would agree. They would both come and live at Tall Trees. 'Just like going away to boarding school really,' as Sarah had said, 'Plus you can see your mum on holidays. Sounds like a perfect arrangement to me.'

***

It took Bobby three days to get Theresa to answer the phone. 'She knows,' he told Ruby and Sarah. 'She knows that it's me trying to ring.'

'Wouldn't she worry where the boys are?' Sarah asked.

'She's that affected by alcohol and obsessed with Boris, she's forgotten what's important. The boys tell me their older sisters never contact her and she barely talks about them. They haven't spoken to them since they left. The family has disintegrated.'

'Maybe they could come and join our family also.' Sarah laughed. 'I'm joking,' she said to Bobby, pointing to the frown on his face. 'You should see the look on your face.'

'Five of us is plenty,' he laughed also. 'It's going to be a different household with two energetic boys added to the mix.'

He shook his head as he spotted Ruby adding to her list of things to do. 'You're in your element,' he said.

'I'm just making sure I have everything organised for when we enrol the boys. There are uniforms to get, books and Bobby you'll need to set up that other bedroom for Simon. He'll need a desk and ...'

'Hang on Ruby. I haven't talked to Theresa yet. This may not be that easy.'

She raised her eyebrows. 'I'm not worried. This will be an out for her and Boris. I have no doubt it will suit them perfectly, plus they won't want the authorities coming around there and checking if you report them.'

***

Ruby had been right. When he eventually spoke to Theresa the conversation was not as difficult as he imagined. 'They're sneaky those two,' she said, at least her voice sounding sober. 'You know they're feeding you two a load of lies.'

Bobby did not beat around the bush. 'Liam has a black eye and Simon has bruises on him. We've taken photos of them and if I have to I will report the incident.'

'Jees, Bobby, when did you become the expert parent. You try it for a while and see how you go. Those two are lazy and dishonest. Boris has had a gutful of them.'

Boris grabbed the phone. 'See how you go mate. Just don't bring them back here when it gets too hard. Theresa will sign forms to give you guardianship. We're thinking of going on a holiday. I bought a caravan, so it suits us.'

Bobby wanted to say so much but the main aim was to get the paperwork signed so it was all official. He kept his voice even. 'I'm telling you now Boris, if you lay one hand on my sister in anger I will not only get the police onto you about the illegal work you do up there, but I'll hunt you down myself.'

'I ain't never laid a hand on her. It's only those two that push my buttons. She's a good mother but if you think you can do better then go ahead. And you can tell them to keep their mouth shut about my work. That's nobody's business except mine.'

Theresa came back on the phone. 'Boris is going to take me away from here for a while so the timing is good.'

A weight lifted from Bobby's shoulders. They weren't going to fight it. 'Did you want to speak to them before I hang up? Don't leave for holidays until that paperwork is signed. You need to go into the solicitors in town,

McGees, tomorrow. Ruby has it all organised. The boys can come and see you on the holidays.'

'You've already told me where to go to sign the papers. I'm not stupid. I'll talk to them next time. I'm still angry with them, besides we're just about to go down the pub.'

'Ring any time Theresa. Don't become a stranger to them. We're not trying to take them away from you, we just think they'll be better at school down here.'

'Yeah, Yeah, I know. I wouldn't let them go and live with you if I didn't think they'd be well looked after. I know I'm not that easy to live with and Boris aint' great with kids.' She sighed. 'It's for the best Bobby. They'll do well with you and Ruby.'

***

By the time he hung up the original feeling of relief changed into a deep sadness that hung over him. How had she become so cold and disconnected from her kids? Why would she hurt them when she knew the effects?'

He went and sat on the front steps, his mind whirling as childhood memories re-surfaced. Simon appeared in front of him. He had been down under the trees, looking across the valley. His face was pinched, his eyes downcast. 'She didn't agree did she. I can tell from your face,' he said to Bobby. 'What are you going to tell Liam. He's got his heart set on living here now.'

Bobby cheered up a little. 'Sorry if you got the wrong impression. It wasn't an easy thing to tell her. Don't forget she's my sister, just like you two are brothers, there is a deep connection no matter what happens.'

'What did she say? When do we have to go back?'

'No, Simon, you're not going back. She agreed.' Simon's face fell and Bobby was careful how he used his words. 'At first she said it would be too hard for her, but after a while she also said it's for the best. She's okay with it because she knows it's better for you both in the long run.'

'Are you sure? Won't she miss us? We're her sons. I keep wondering if we should go back and just see how it goes.'

'Her and Boris are going on a holiday, in a caravan. They're leaving once the guardianship papers are signed.'

Simon blinked several times. 'What? A holiday. We've never been on a holiday in our life.'

Liam came running around the corner, Rusty hot on his heels. He stopped when he got to them, his eyes questioning.

Simon put his arm around his shoulders, a gentle movement with an affectionate squeeze.

'Guess what, Liam. She said yes. Mum said she's okay with us living here.'

Liam jumped in the air and yelled. 'She said yes!'

Rusty barked excitedly and jumped on Liam as Simon looked at Bobby. 'Thanks, Uncle Bobby.'

***

It took ten days for the signed papers that would start the process, to be returned. Ruby picked them up from the post office and made a big deal about opening the envelope in front of everyone at home. 'I now pronounce that we are officially on the road to becoming your guardians.'

They celebrated that night with a special dinner and Bobby's heart was full as he looked around the table. His voice was tinged with emotion as he raised his glass for a toast. 'Out of childhood problems comes solutions and happiness. These are the next steps in our new lives.' They had all clinked glasses. It was a new beginning.

CHAPTER 42

Simon's stomach fluttered with nerves as he and Liam walked with Aunt Ruby up the front steps of the school administration office. He was in year nine and Liam was enrolled in year eight. They had already met the principal, Mr Ronald, and office ladies, and everyone had been friendly so far. It sounded like it was stricter than their last school and the principal had been stern when explaining the rules and consequences for the type of offences that boys their age sometimes engaged in.

He relaxed a little when he stood to see them out of their office, shaking hands with Bobby and Ruby and then the two of them. Liam of course had asked a million questions about who the teachers were, what subjects he would be doing and where the library was. Mr Ronald had been patient and had spoken to Liam like he was an adult. He reminded Simon of the teachers at their last school and he hoped that everyone would be as nice.

Simon had written to two of his teachers to let them know where they would be going to school and what the living arrangements were. He had also given them his new address, hoping that maybe one of them would write back. They were busy people though and he was just one student amongst many.

***

Now on their first day at school he was about to be thrown amongst a crowd of a thousand kids and teachers, none of who he knew. At the old school they knew everyone and everyone knew them. Now it was different. They were the new kids on the block and everyone would be looking at them. He stared down at his shiny black shoes and new uniforms. 'Thanks for buying us uniforms, Aunt Ruby, we've never had new ones before.'

She beamed at them both. Bobby was right, she was like a mother hen with a brood of chickens. She leaned over and straightened Liam's collar. 'I'm so proud of you both. You look so grown up.' He gave her a kiss on the cheek as they said goodbye. She had taken a million photos of them this morning and had nearly cried when Simon said he wanted one taken with just her and then Bobby. He also wanted one with Sarah and there had been lots of jostling and swapping as they all made sure that they had group, and separate photos. Liam had been quieter this morning. He also was nervous and sat silently in the car on the way into town. Ruby hugged them both and waved them off at the gate. 'It's high school, Aunt Ruby. Parents don't come in unless their kid is in trouble. We'll be fine,' Liam said.

Simon was sure she had tears in her eyes as she

hugged them again. A surge of belonging came over him and he called out, not caring who heard. 'We love you.'

She turned and this time he could see she was crying, standing on the stairs up to the car park, wiping her eyes with a tissue. She stood and watched them until they entered the admin building. It was time to get their timetables and begin their first day.

***

Liam found Simon at lunchtime. Both had new lunch boxes and Ruby had filled them with the best sort of lunch any kid would want. They sat together, watching everyone walk past, both concentrating on eating the contents of their lunch box. 'I think she said to leave half for the second break,' Liam said in between mouthfuls, 'but I'm starving now. It's hard work being new in a class. You feel like everyone is staring, checking you out. Thank goodness we have new uniforms.'

Simon stood up and tucked his shirt in and straightened his shorts. 'We've never had clothes like this before. Uncle Bobby said he knew Aunt Ruby would make sure everything was the way she wanted it to be.'

Liam packed his lunch box back in his bag. 'Do you think it's bad not to miss Mum? She must be wondering how we're going. Maybe we should ring her tonight.'

Simon sat back down. 'They've gone away.'

'What do you mean they've gone away?'

'On holidays.'

'You're making that up. We've never been anywhere in our lives.'

'I'm not making it up. Boris told Bobby. They've gone in a caravan on holidays.'

Liam crossed his arms and Simon could tell he was angry. 'I know. I feel the same.' Simon kept his voice low as two girls approached them. 'They never took us anywhere.'

One of the girls came up to them. She had been in Simon's last class and had moved over and let him sit next to her. When she smiled, he smiled back. Her hair was long and blonde and she pushed it back behind her ears as she spoke. 'Hi, I'm Pia and this is Polly. You're new aren't you? Is this your brother?'

Polly had brown hair and wore glasses that made her look smart, like a teacher. He had noticed her in class, her hand always up and her answers correct. The first class had been English and he had listened carefully, staying quiet and not making eye contact with anyone. The best way to not draw attention to yourself was to keep your eyes down.

'I'm Simon, and this is my brother, Liam.' The girls stood in front of them, their arms linked, both sucking on icy poles as they talked.

'I've got a sister in your year level,' Polly said to Liam. 'Her name's Patty.'

'I think I know who she is. There was a Patty in my science class. She knew all the answers.'

'That would be her.'

The girls stood talking until the bell went. Pia was curious about where they were living. She was excited when they told her. 'Oh, I know Bobby and Ruby. They do the markets on a Sunday. So does my mum and dad. Dad's an artist and Mum's a potter. I might see you there on the weekend.'

The girls showed them to their next classes. 'Wow', Liam said before parting ways with Simon. 'The kids here are friendly.'

***

It hadn't been hard to explain why they were living with their uncle and aunt. When anyone asked, they just said their mother lived a long way out of town so it made sense to live at Tall Trees Farm and go to school here in town.

Starting school with everything they needed, new books and stationery as well as looking like everyone else with decent uniforms and food in their lunch boxes went a long way in helping them settle in. The teachers were strict but nice and it didn't take them long to realise the boys were keen to learn and well-behaved. By the end of their first week they already felt they had been accepted. Liam had joined the chess club and been asked to become part of the extended Science group. Polly's sister Patty had befriended him and asked him to sit with her group of friends at lunchtime; an even mix of boys and girls who took him under their wing and showed him around.

Pia happened to be in nearly all of Simon's classes and she always made sure there was a seat for him next to her. On Sunday they'd both be at the markets. 'I'll find you. She told him. Our stall isn't far from yours.'

On Friday night they sat around the dinner table. Ruby and Sarah cooked a lasagne, with crusty bread and a dessert they called Tiramasu. Rusty lay at their feet and Bobby took out his guitar and sang a song. A love song that he said was for Ruby. The stars stretched across the heavens and when a full moon appeared behind them and made its way higher in the sky, Simon thought that life couldn't get any better.

Every now and again he had a pang of guilt, a thought that maybe their mum was thinking about them and missing them. But the phone hadn't rung since they'd been here. She hadn't asked about them or tried to find out how they were. Instead of guilt, a sliver of anger was starting to build and he wondered if he was going to become more like Liam was, angry, disheartened, and not missing Mum at all.

Sometimes he worried that he already loved Bobby and Ruby more than Mum. When that happened, he pulled back a bit from them, didn't talk as much or act as enthusiastic about something as he should have.

One day he had even kept walking past the tunnel of trees and followed the driveway down to the main road. He'd sat on a stump and let the tears run down his face. Where was Mum now? Was she missing him? What if he just kept walking and caught a train back to Rockhampton. Back to his old home and bedroom. Would it still be the same or had she thrown everything out? He wrinkled his nose, remembering the musty smell of their bedroom, the stench from the rubbish bins outside their window that were never emptied, because no one remembered to put them out on bin day.

He imagined his mother's face when she was happy, her thin arms and legs covered in tattoos, the look on her gaunt face when she sometimes smiled. Trying hard to remember, he squeezed his eyes shut. Had she cuddled them when they were little or sat and played with them? Nothing came into his mind. Occasionally his older sisters had pushed him and Liam on a swing in the park down the road or walked with them to the shop to get milk for Mum's coffee. Apart from that he had nothing.

He opened his eyes. A large frill-necked lizard lay not far in front of him, its head swivelling around, trying to work out whether to go past him or not. He felt like taking his anger out on it and throwing a stone at it. Maybe if he threw something as hard as he could the muddled thoughts about returning to Mum would go. Why did he keep feeling like he should return? Would it be better now she'd had a holiday. Perhaps that's what she needed.

The lizard flicked its yellow tongue back and forth and Simon remembered Ruby telling him that they loved to lie under the fallen spiky branches of the bunya trees and that they wouldn't bite you unless you got in their way. He watched it push it face upwards, its long claws entrenched in the dust of the driveway.

They stared at each other for a while before the lizard took one last look and scurried off towards the nearby bushes. Another larger lizard appeared, blocking its way. The two had a stand-off, neither moving, both their tongues flicking in and out. The larger one lunged forward but the other one was quicker and twirled, bolting back the way it had come. The winner turned and scurried back to the shrubs. Protecting its space, Liam thought, as he looked up at a hawk circling above, the blue of the sky vivid behind it. Two small sunbirds flitted in and out of a shrub next to him and he smiled at their speedy actions and long beaks. He watched for a bit longer, standing up and waving when a car approached and slowed down. It was their neighbour, Pete, from further up the hill and he stuck his head out the window and called out. 'G'day, Simon. It's a grand day isn't it.'

Simon pulled his shoulders up and automatically smiled back, his anger dissipating at the sight of a friendly face. 'It is. I just saw two lizards have a fight. The bigger one won.'

'There's always something to watch here. You know I moved here when I was a kid. A bit like you really, I came to live with my uncle and aunt,' Pete said.

'Oh, I never knew that.' Simon was curious why, but thought it impolite to ask.

'They took me in, gave me a break. They're long gone, passed on that is. They were elderly when they took me on. You know I never left. This area is magical. It gets into your blood and you'll soon work out there's nowhere as good.'

'It is a beautiful area.'

'Going for a walk?' Pete asked.

Simon took a while to answer. 'Just this far. I'll head back up now.'

Pete waved as he drove off, the sound of his car fading into the distance. Silence surrounded him and he looked up and down the road again. This was a good place. What would happen to him if he went back to Mum's? Liam wouldn't follow. Nothing would change. Clenching his jaw, he noticed the larger lizard had come back out into the sunshine and was now looking at him, almost as if it was waiting for his decision.

He spoke out loud to it. 'I'm going home. Home to Tall

Trees. No more doubts. Just going home.' With that he turned, his movements causing the lizard to scuttle back into the cover of the shade. Instead of anger now he had a feeling of excitement. He had been handed an opportunity. He was going to take it.

CHAPTER 43

On the weekend Bobby asked Simon to help unload his trailer. He'd picked up an old silky oak desk for Simon's bedroom. Ruby came in as they set it up, placing a lamp and pen set on it. A matching timber chair completed his new study area and he ran his hand over the timber, the smooth sheen of the golden wood a pleasure to touch. He'd held back the words and the over-whelming desire to throw his arms around them and tell them they were the best people in the world.

Sarah stared hard at him when he only replied with, 'Thank you.'

She pulled him aside later that day. 'C'mon check the horses with me, Simon.'

They'd walked together across the paddocks, stopping to watch a couple of wallabies that pushed their heads up from the long grass to watch them go past.

'You know it's normal to feel like you're betraying your mum,' she said, pushing her hands down in her jacket pockets.

He stopped to watch the wallabies. 'What do you mean?'

'I know how it feels when you're given things and people are kind to you. It doesn't mean that you don't love your mum because you accept things from Ruby and Bobby. No-one will ever take her place and even though she might not contact you, you'll still have love for her in your heart. Sometimes though, you have to let go and let others in.'

He scowled at her. 'She hasn't even rung us. What sort of mother doesn't ring and check their kids are okay?'

Sarah laughed and strode out ahead, turning to make sure he was following and keeping up. 'Don't think you're the only one. What do you think happened to me? Mum left me with Grandpa and Grandma when I was only six. She turned her back, packed her bag and left with Lyle. They went as far away as they could. She hardly ever rang. I think the second birthday I had with Grandpa, he rang her. Somehow he found out where they were working and got hold of the number. He talked to her and then she talked to me for a while.'

'That's tough.'

'It was and sometimes I still think about it. But you and I, and Liam, we're the lucky ones. The unlucky ones are those who don't have a grandpa, or a grandma, or a Bobby or Ruby. They're the ones who suffer. You and I, we can get out of the mess. Make our own lives and make sure we don't stuff up like they did.'

'I bet if Ruby ever had had kids she wouldn't have ever left them.'

'Of course she wouldn't. She's a good person but don't

forget she had a stable childhood with a mum and dad who did everything the way parents should.'

'Do you think that Liam, you and I, will live here for a long time?'

Sarah stopped, her dark eyes fixed on his. It was strange sometimes when they locked eyes. Like looking in the mirror. She obviously felt the same. 'Our eyes are the same,' she said. 'You, me and Bobby.'

He stared back hard. 'You haven't answered my question. I'm worried because the other day I walked down the driveway. I was going to leave and go back to Mum. I thought for a while though and well, things change. A lizard I was watching sort of made me realise about the good things in life and how the world was a much bigger place than Mum and Rockhampton.' He looked around. 'This is a beautiful place to live. The other day I realised the chance Liam and I have been given. It was the lizard. It sounds weird, but I turned and came back. I made a decision that this is my home now.'

Sarah wrapped her arm around his shoulders, squeezing him tight. 'Of course, you will live here for however long you want. They've taken you on as their own kids. They think of you two and me as their own.'

He pulled away from her. 'It's a different sort of family, but I think I like it. I'll remember what you said about letting people in.'

'Well, don't forget it.' She stopped walking, a mischievous glint in her eyes. All of a sudden she walked quicker, glancing back at him. 'Race you to the gate.' With that she took off, Simon running as fast as he could behind her.

A group of wallabies bounded off in the other direction and a flock of galahs feeding on grass seeds also took flight, their noisy calls echoing across the hills.

CHAPTER 44

The first few months flew past and Simon felt like he had been at the new school all his life. He had a few good friends, his bestie, as she like to call herself, was of course, Pia. The others, a mixture of boys and girls, were fun to be around and lunchtimes were spent kicking a ball around the oval or sitting together talking about what they were going to do on the weekend.

He was surprised to find out that two of the other boys in his group were in similar situations as he was. Jake lived with his grandparents and Joseph was with foster carers. Both came from similar situations and after a while he opened up and confided in them a little of what his situation had been when he'd lived with his mum.

'Shitty parents. Fathers and step-fathers that beat you up and mothers who live in a world of drugs.' Jake was tall and thin and didn't try and hide anything that had happened to him. 'When I was with Mum I was always hungry. She'd come good for a while but then she'd get a new boyfriend and I'd be forgotten. She didn't have a clue what I was up to.'

'What happened that you moved?' Simon asked.

'Our neighbours rang Nan. They got her number and let her know what was going on. You ever met my nan?'

Simon shook his head.

'Well, if you ever do, be afraid. Be very afraid.'

'Why?'

'Because you don't want to mess with her. She's built like a front row footballer, that's what Pop says, and no-one messes with her. I'll never forget the day she came and got me. She marched in through the front door without knocking, or letting Mum know she was coming. Mum was on the lounge, stoned out of her head, watching television. When I came out of my room, Nan took one look at me and burst into tears. It's the only time I've ever seen her cry. She wiped her face real quick and then started barking out orders. She's good at that.'

'What did your mum do?'

'Nothing, she was out of it.'

Nan gave me no option. 'Get your stuff together, Jake,' she said. 'I'll send Pop back for anything else you might need. Get what you need for school and what you and I can carry. You're out of here and you're living with us. End of story.'

Jake paused. 'And, the rest as they say, is history.'

'What happened to your mum?'

Nan and Pop paid heaps of money for rehab for her. They tried a lot of times but it hasn't worked. She's with some other shithead and living somewhere in New South Wales. I don't see her.'

Joseph added in. 'It's best not to. It screws with your head when they come and go. I haven't seen my mum since I was in grade three. Every time we'd meet up with her she'd cry and tell me she loved me. Then she'd leave and I wouldn't hear from her for another year.'

'What's being a foster kid like?' Simon was curious.

'I've been with my parents, Kim and Bill, since I was six, so they're really like my real parents. There are two other foster kids with us and occasionally they take in an emergency kid for a short while. They're trouble though and they don't usually last. The five of us are tight though. We've all been with them since we were little kids. We're a family. I feel lucky to be where I am. One day I'm going to be a famous singer and earn lots of money. Then I'm going to buy them a huge house and whatever they want.'

'How cool would that be,' Jake said. 'I'd do that for my grandies if I earn a lot of money.'

Simon thought about it. 'I would to, except I think Bobby and Ruby are happy where they are. They have everything and now they have all of us.' He pondered on that. 'I don't think they want anything else.'

***

When he had asked the question at dinner time it had started a full conversation. Liam of course had been quick to add what he would buy if he had millions of dollars. 'They say one day there are going to be electric cars and cars that hover, you know like in that old seventies show, the Jetsons.'

Bobby thought long and hard. 'There is nothing more

that I want.' He looked around the table. 'How could I want more than this.'

Ruby leaned over and kissed him on the cheek. They were always so romantic and Simon had stopped blushing and looking away when they cuddled or kissed. Now, instead of it making him feel uncomfortable it made him feel secure and he loved watching how they treated each other. Maybe one day he would meet a girl like Ruby and fall in love. It was what happened in the movies he watched on television. Sarah always made him watch those silly romance movies. He pretended he thought they were silly but really he loved movies that had a happy ending.

Bobby asked Ruby what she would do with millions of dollars. 'Hmmm. Let me think. Maybe a new car or a new hat.'

They'd laughed. 'Aunty Ruby, Liam said. 'We're talking millions of dollars.'

'I know, she said, but I saw a red hat at the markets last week and I talked myself out of buying it. I don't need it.'

Talking about things we want to do,' Bobby said. 'I have an idea.'

They all turned to him. 'Sarah hasn't seen her grandpa for a while and when I talked to him last week I mentioned school holidays were coming up. He's invited us all to come out and stay.'

'Wow,' Simon said. 'He wants all of us? Liam and me too?'

'Of course, you and Liam!' Sarah said. 'He's keen to meet you both. Mind you I haven't told him how much you eat.'

Liam was excited, his head turning from one person to

the other. 'Where would we sleep? How would we get there? How long does it take?'

They all laughed. Simon was also enthusiastic about the trip. He hadn't been on a holiday before and going out west where Sarah was from and Bobby had also once lived, was the best present ever.

CHAPTER 45

*S*arah was the first one to jump out of the car when they arrived at Western Downs.

It had been months since she had seen Grandpa and she threw herself into his arms as he came down the stairs. He held her at arm's length, his face in a wide smile. 'You look so grown up. I don't think I've ever seen you in a dress.'

She twirled around. 'I've learned to love skirts and dresses. They won't last out here though. My jeans and boots will be on by lunch time.' She looked him up and down. 'You look good. You've had a haircut and are they new clothes?'

He gave her a small nod before holding out his hand to Bobby. The men shook hands and Bobby introduced the others. Simon and Liam shook hands with Grandpa who insisted they call him Grandpa, the same as Sarah did. 'Who would think at this age I'd get to add another two grandsons to my family.'

He held out his arms to Ruby who gave him a long hug. 'So, this is the amazing Ruby?' Grandpa said. 'I've heard so much about you, and what you and Bobby have done to help my girl.'

'She does most of it herself. We love her and now look, this is our family,' Ruby replied, holding her arms out towards the boys.

Sarah put her arms around Simon's and Liam's shoulders. 'Instant family, Grandpa. How good is this.'

They followed the old man up onto the verandah, a spread of food and drinks already laid out on the table. A large tablecloth covered the food and Sarah looked at it. It wasn't one she'd seen before. 'We just put this out. Figured you weren't far off,' Grandpa said.

She stopped in her tracks and turned to him. 'Who is, *we?*'

He twisted his mouth to the side and looked bashful. 'Do you remember Beth Cusack from in town? Her and Robert owned the produce store.'

Sarah thought hard. 'Sure, yes. I remember them. I went to school with Peter Cusack, their grandson.'

'Beth has been by herself for a while and well …' he paused and looked around the group who were all listening to him talk. 'Well, her and I, well ..'

Sarah knew her mouth was wide open, and she kept blinking. 'No way, Grandpa. Have you found a friend?'

He scuffed his boot on the timber floorboards. 'You might say that.'

A cheery voice called out from the kitchen. 'Is that them, Thomas?' I knew as soon as I went for a shower someone would arrive.'

Everyone was silent as Beth walked out to them. She was around the same age as Grandpa and had a round friendly face. She had obviously dressed for the occasion and wore a floral dress that came to just below her knees, her white hair curled and neat, and a touch of lipstick on her lips. The sight of someone else in Grandpa's house was a shock for Sarah and for once she was lost for words.

Grandpa walked over to Beth and took her hand. 'Beth, meet my family.'

They all started talking at once, trying to explain who was who. Liam's voice was of course the loudest and he won in the end, everyone leaving the introductions up to him. Sarah shook her head and gave Beth the warmest hug she could. Beth grabbed her hands and looked at her, her aged wise eyes, blue and deep set. 'I remember you when you were a little girl. You used to come into the shop with your grandma. You're in the same year at school as our Peter. Goodness me, you've grown into a beautiful young woman.'

Sarah blushed. 'This is my father, Bobby, and his partner, Ruby.'

'Pleased to meet you both. I can't believe how much you look like your father.'

Liam broke into the conversation. 'How come Ruby is a partner and not your wife?' he asked Bobby.

Ruby answered, 'We're not married.'

'How come?' Liam scrunched his face up. 'I thought you were.'

'We just haven't got around to it,' Bobby said, 'but we're the same as a married couple. Committed for life to each other. We just don't need a big fancy ring to prove we love each other. I think that's enough questions, Liam.'

They all laughed and Sarah linked her arm through Grandpa's. 'You sneaky man,' she said. 'Why didn't you tell me.'

'I wanted you to meet Beth first. She only moved in a couple of weeks ago, although we've been seeing each other since not long after you left. I went into the produce to get dog food and I was telling her that I'd lost my soul-mate, my granddaughter. She remembered you and asked what you were doing. We talked for ages and before I left she asked me to dinner at the Royal the next night. What was I supposed to do? We just hit it off. We have so much in common and Beth also still rides.'

'So me leaving, might have assisted in you finding a new friend in your life.'

Grandpa was bashful and kept running his hand across his beard. 'Well, um, yes, you could say that.'

***

Simon and Liam were interested in every part of the property. Sarah had started teaching them to ride and both had taken to it, helped along by more lessons from Bobby in the afternoons.

Grandpa had prepared some of the horses, knowing they were coming. The boys were given the use of two older mares while Sarah rode her usual horse. Ruby and Bobby were on bay geldings, Ruby making sure she stayed with Bobby as they rode. She wasn't quite as experienced as he was and they made sure to give her one of the quieter steeds.

Sarah's heart felt like it was going to burst as she watched Grandpa and Beth lead the way. Beth had a natural seat on her chestnut horse and it hadn't escaped Sarah that they had matching Akubra hats. The group rode out through the gate and towards the low hills in the distance. It was early morning and flocks of birds flew overhead. 'They'll be looking for water,' Sarah told the boys. 'It's dry and they're all waiting for the rain to come.'

Mobs of kangaroos took off in the other direction as the group came towards them, the dust flying up in a cloud as they bounded over the small shrubs and tufts of grass. As the sky lightened the heat started to press down. Simon rode beside her. 'It's so hot already. I thought Rocky was hot, but this is way worse.'

'It can get up over forty degrees out here. It's a dry heat.'

'There's nothing as far as you can see. Just dust and those hills on the horizon. It must be eerie out here at night.'

Sarah pointed to the south. 'There are some boulder ranges over there and a waterhole that usually has some water in it. I love it out here. It's all I knew before I came to Tall Trees.'

'But there's nothing here.' Simon looked around.

'That's the beauty of it. The isolation. In summer that sky will light up with the most incredible electrical storms you could ever see. The lightning stretches across the sky and lights up the plains. It rarely rains though, but when it does the Bourke River fills up and waterholes overflow and the water stretches for miles. The entire landscape changes and the land comes to life.'

Simon looked around. 'I can't imagine that, looking at it now.'

'Hard to believe, I know. Most of the time this is what

it looks like. You can go years sometimes without decent rain out here. We get massive dust storms that block out the sun. You don't want to be in one of those. You have to be inside.'

Liam rode up beside them. 'Have you ever seen the Min Min light, Sarah?'

'What's that, Simon asked.'

'This area is famous for the Min Min Light,' Sarah explained. 'I've never seen it but I've talked to some locals who have. It's like a fuzzy white light that hovers just above the earth. They say that the lights follow you but if you chase them you will never return to talk about it.'

'That's not the scientific evidence.' Liam sat upright, patting his horse's neck.

'The Aboriginal people believe they are lights of their ancestors. I like that explanation but scientists conclude that the lights happen when warm and cold air come together.'

Sarah never ceased to be amazed by the knowledge that Liam carried in his head. It didn't matter what topic it was, he usually knew some facts about it. He was a sponge, taking in everything he came across and more importantly remembering even the smallest details.

When they came back from their ride he stood with Grandpa in the shed for over an hour, plying him with questions about the weather, the ground and the Indigenous people who lived in the area. Both boys were obsessed with her grandfather, even Simon, who was usually more reserved than the inquisitive Liam.

'Jees, you and I aren't getting a look in with those two boys here,' Beth said to Sarah. 'They keep disappearing, Bobby with them.'

The women were in the kitchen, Beth making cakes and biscuits while the other two sat and talked. It was Sarah's favourite place and it made her happy to see Beth there cooking food for Grandpa.

'I'm surprised you and Bobby aren't married,' Sarah said, using a large spoon to eat the excess cake mixture from the bowl.

Ruby had thrown on a summer dress today, the heat inside almost unbearable even with the air-conditioning on. It came to just above her knees, a thin leather belt drawing in at the waist accentuating her slim figure. She held her hair up and tied it up, wiping the sweat from her neck. 'I'm not sure I could live out here. It's so hot even in here.'

Beth moved around the kitchen. 'We're used to it, aren't we Sarah. When you're born and bred out here it's normal. Mind you, some rain would be welcome.'

Ruby turned to Sarah. 'Bobby has never asked me to marry him.'

'What? So, you want to get married but he doesn't.'

'Sort of. He said he would but he's scared. Frightened because of everything that happened in his past.'

'Does it worry you.'

'Not really. I mean we're both in the relationship for ever, but sometimes I think it would be nice. I was married before I met Bobby. It was good for a while but then we parted ways. I wanted babies and he didn't. By the time we tried it was too late and I can't have them anyway. It's a hereditary problem. That's why I'm an only child. The annoying thing was that as soon as my husband and I parted ways he re-married and had a family.'

'Oh, that is annoying.' Sarah said. 'I don't think I ever want to have kids.'

'Don't say that.' Beth was shocked. 'Why not? Having a family is one of the greatest joys of life.' She looked at Ruby. 'I mean it's different if you can't, but you shouldn't make your mind up before you even start.'

'I'm going to stay single and have a career. I'm going to finish studying and find a job. I don't want any husband or kids getting in my way.'

'You can do both,' Ruby said. 'You just have to get the right balance.'

***

Sarah thought about the conversation later that night. She'd never even dated much so why would she want a husband. Never, she thought. I like being by myself. I don't want any man telling me what I can and can't do.

Ruby had often tried to talk her into trying to meet young people her own age or even going on a date with one of the locals she met at the markets. But she wasn't interested. Bobby and Ruby were different. They were meant to be together. Strange how he didn't want to get married though. She could tell Ruby was annoyed when she talked about it. That was men though, letting things from the past rule their life and being the one who had to propose. How antiquated was that idea. Another reason not to date.

She rolled over, listening to the silence outside. This place had been her entire life before she found Bobby. Now there were other places where she was comfortable, people who spoke a different language other than cattle and weather, and a world of education and opportunity at her fingertips. This would always be her first home but she was no longer scared to go further, to put herself out there and try things outside her comfort zone. Grandpa had also found other interests and she loved that he was happy.

CHAPTER 46

*O*n the last morning before they left, Sarah rode out to one of the far paddocks with Grandpa. He wanted to check one of the fences and she took the opportunity to spend some time alone with him. A hazy mirage wavered on the horizon and a hawk soared overhead, its eyes fixed on them far below as they walked the horses slowly across the plain.

No doubt the bird was short on prey. When it was dry everyone suffered, and the rodents that usually scurried around had disappeared. Dust kicked out from the horses' hooves and heat radiated from the barren earth. Every now and then dry tufts of grass hanging onto the loose surface dotted the landscape, a few shrubs casting lifeless shadows.

'It's only a matter of time before the rain comes,' Grandpa said, pointing to three cattle that stood silently watching them. 'They're waiting. Sooner or later the clouds will appear and the land will flow with water. You know what it's like. A waiting game. Always a waiting game.'

She reined her horse over closer to his. 'I'm pleased you're with Beth. She's lovely.'

He straightened his hat before turning to her. 'You know I thought I would never love another woman after your grandma. To tell you the truth I never even thought about it, not all these years. But then Beth came along and suddenly I feel like a young man again. Life is a strange thing, Sarah, because if you hadn't left I may not have met her.'

'I'm really happy for you both. It makes my heart sing.'

He laughed. 'What about you? Met any fellas?'

'I've been busying studying and I don't really go out anywhere. Ruby has tried to set me up on dates with a couple of the local boys and she invited some friends over for dinner who are around my age and single. They've all been nice but I'm happy the way I am. I don't want to have a relationship. It's okay being by myself.'

'As long as you're happy, that's the main thing. But don't shy away from meeting a young man. A love for someone is a special thing.'

She raised her eyebrows and smiled. 'I know. You look ten years younger.'

***

Everyone dressed up for the last night. Fresh jeans, with ironed shirts and clean boots was the attire. They'd stood together while Ruby set up her camera for a positioned photo. Loud laughter and raucous jokes flew back and forth when the camera timer didn't go off when it should have. Eventually they managed to get a group shot, even Rusty sneaking in on the side.

As they sat around the table, Bobby's heart was full. In fact, he thought to himself, it was brimming over. Who would have thought all those years ago that he would be surrounded by good people who cared for each other. He never dreamt he would have a family, or a partner like Ruby to share his life. Most of all, who could ever imagine so much love. It was in the air. A closeness and warmth that swirled around him and clung to his soul. He was a lucky man.

He stood and clinked his fork on a glass. Simon and Liam copied him and they all exploded with laughter as the boys stood up, bowing before taking their seats. They had settled into life with him and Ruby, and now their real personalities radiated with no fear of being made fun of, or recrimination about their ideas. He looked around the table before speaking again. 'I wanted to make a toast to our family. All of us here.' Everyone raised their glasses and toasted each other. Bobby turned towards Grandpa. 'Grandpa, did you have that note you wanted to read out. Someone gave Grandpa a note and he wants me to read it out while we're all here.'

Grandpa made a great fuss of looking in all his pockets, even standing up and searching in his trouser pockets. Eventually he found what he was looking for and handed it over. They all leaned forward, waiting for Bobby to read the words.

Bobby's eyes met Ruby's and she smiled at him. She would know that he would be thinking how lucky he was.

He winked at her and cast his eyes around the group. 'I was going to make a speech about how lucky I am to have such a wonderful family and how amazing it is that we have all come together. Now I want to add something to that.'

Bobby opened the envelope that Grandpa had given him and walked around the table. He stood beside Ruby. As he bent down on one knee, Ruby's hand came up over her mouth and she turned in her chair to face him.

Taking a deep breath, Bobby kept his voice even, his eyes locked with Ruby's. 'Ruby-Rose. We have known each other for many years, through thick and thin we survived and came back together. I love you more than life itself. Now, I want to ask you,' he paused and took a deep breath, 'will you be my wife?'

Rusty barked and Grandpa patted the dog's head. 'Shush, Rusty. We need to hear the answer.'

Ruby stood up, leaned over and kissed Bobby as she held out her hand. 'I will Bobby. I would love to be your wife.'

As he slipped the ring on her finger the table erupted into loud cheering and yelling. Grandpa got up and did a jig and Liam jumped up and down, clapping his hands. Even Simon stood up and punched the air in excitement. A weight lifted from Bobby's shoulders. He had finally done it. He had wanted this for a long time but had held off, not wanting to ruin a beautiful relationship. Ruby deserved it though. She had come looking for him, found him, dragged him back to reality and they had fallen in love. Now she had taken on his family as her own. She deserved the best. He looked at her, her green eyes sparkling, excitement all over her face. Wrapping his arms around her he pressed his lips on hers, a long passionate kiss that caused more cheering and clapping. Simon stood on his chair, Rusty barking loudly beside him. 'You may now kiss the bride,' Simon declared. 'For evermore.'

CHAPTER 47

By the beginning of the new year everyone had settled into some sort of a routine. Bobby and Ruby married on the seventh of January. The ceremony took place under the bunya nut trees in the front yard, the sweeping views of the valley a perfect backdrop as they took their vows. A small group of friends as well as Sarah, Simon and Liam gathered around as they were announced husband and wife. Sarah took Ruby's bunch of native flowers from her, before Bobby swept Ruby into his arms and kissed her tenderly.

The five of them stood together for a family photo, the two boys dressed up in their new jeans, shirts and boots that Ruby had bought for them. Sarah watched the boys as they talked to some of the guests. They appeared so confident and happy, unlike when they had first arrived. She'd come to think of them as brothers and the three of them often walked together or sat under the huge trees talking about school and what they wanted to do when they were older.

Simon turned and waved to her. She was proud of how grownup he sounded when he talked to Ruby and Bobby's friends. He had been angry and disappointed that his mother had declined Bobby's invitation to attend today. 'She doesn't care about us at all,' he'd told Sarah. 'It's like she's forgotten we've existed.'

Sarah tried to say the right words but it was hard not to agree with him. 'She knows you have a good life here, so I guess she doesn't worry.'

'Mothers are supposed to care for their kids, not neglect them. One day I'm going to have my own kids and be a good parent.'

'Liam doesn't seem worried about it,' Sarah replied, 'He just shrugged his shoulders and said that's good, when Bobby told him.'

'He used to argue so much with her. He'd talk back until she was so angry she'd go for him. He just couldn't keep his mouth shut. The trouble is he's a lot smarter than she is. She couldn't deal with it.'

Sarah laughed. 'Yeah, he's too smart for his own good. He corrects me on things I say sometimes. It's a good thing though. You can both stand on your own two feet. You're like me and Bobby, we've had to learn the hard way too.'

'Aunt Ruby said it will make us stronger and a better judge of people.'

'Ruby is generally right. She's the kindest person I know.'

***

Ruby came to stand beside Sarah, the two of them

looking out over the valley. The sun was dipping lower in the sky, the glowing colours of the sunset beaming over the hillside. Ruby linked her arm through Sarah's. 'Thank you for everything you've done to help out for the wedding.'

'I've loved it. It's been perfect.'

'It has been.' Ruby squeezed her arm. 'I love that I can see the cemetery from here. The jacarandas are all out in flower so it's easy to pick out the exact spot. Mum and Dad would have loved today.'

Sarah looked towards the spot. 'I wish I could have met him.'

'Your grandpa reminds me of my dad. Kind and gentle, they're good men.'

'Like Bobby.'

'Yes, like Bobby.'

CHAPTER 48

*S*arah was surprised how nervous she was on her first day at university. Ruby had helped her enrol in a science course at the nearby campus, a pathway into the eventual vet course she would study. She was completely out of her comfort zone. Her school studies had all been done through distance education. Even though Ruby and Bobby had done a practice run with her the week before, today was different. Traffic and people went in every direction and even finding a park had proven difficult, making her late for her first lecture.

As she sat in the crowded auditorium she looked around. There were hundreds of students in there, all different ages and nationalities. Some seemed to know each other while others were like her, sitting silently, waiting for the first introductory course of the year to begin.

When the hour was over she waited until most of the others had left. Her head was full of information and she looked over the notes she had taken. A girl with purple hair sitting behind her, had remained seated too and she leaned forward and introduced herself. 'Hi, my name's Bree. You look like you don't know anyone.'

Sarah swivelled in her chair, intrigued by Bree's hair colour and the variety of colourful tattoos that covered her arms and legs. She looked about the same age and had a number of facial piercings. The edge of her left ear was also covered in a row of silver studs. Sarah thought about what Grandpa would say about a young girl looking like she had a bull's ring through her nose. She held out her hand for Bree to shake. 'Hi, I'm Sarah and you're right, I don't know anyone. This is my first day.'

Bree stood. 'I'm meeting with some others I know, at the café. You would have passed it when you came in here. Why don't you come and have a coffee with us?'

'Oh, I'd love to do that. Thank you. The university is a huge place.'

The two of them talked as they walked through the crowds going to and from lessons. 'This is my second course,' Bree told her. 'I started doing education but now I've moved into Vet Science. I'll see how it goes but I've heard it's a hard course.'

'You know your way around then.'

'Yeah, it's easy once you've walked around a few times. Where are you from?'

'Western Queensland. A property near Boulia.'

'Where? I've never heard of that.'

'It's out west, south of Mount Isa.'

'I have heard of Mount Isa.' They'd reached the café and Bree waved to a group of boys and girls who were already seated around a table. One of the boys pulled a couple of chairs up for them and Bree quickly introduced her to everyone.

They were all friendly and soon started asking her questions about where she came from and what she was studying. She relaxed and enjoyed her coffee. The other two girls looked similar to Bree. They didn't have quite as many tattoos but all had lots of earrings and wore similar dark clothes and boots. Two of the boys had very dark skin and tight curly hair. When she asked them where they came from they said Ipswich. She didn't know where Ipswich was. 'I think Sarah meant where are you originally from?' Bree added into the conversation.

'Oh, you mean our heritage?'

'Yes, I guess so,' she said, hoping she hadn't sounded impolite.

'We're from Africa originally. Ben's family is from Sudan and mine are from Ethiopia. Our parents came here as refugees before we were born.'

'Wow, she said, trying to not stare at how dark their skin was. 'I've never met anyone from Africa. I've lived on the property out west my entire life. When I came to live with my father a couple of years ago I hadn't ever seen the coast or the ocean. Everything is new to me.'

Ben and the boy, Stanley, who had answered her, both laughed. 'We could tell that from the look on your face.'

The other boy's name was Marcus and he seemed a bit quieter than the others. Similar to the girls, his arms were covered in an assortment of tattoos. Unlike the other boys, who were tall and thin, Marcus was muscly and solid, his calf muscles bulging when he got up to get another cup of coffee. He returned with four cupcakes and placed them in front of the girls, ignoring Ben's and Stanley's complaints about where theirs were.

'Just for the ladies,' he said, throwing a wide smile Sarah's way.

Ben talked with his hands, his white teeth flashing brightly as he jibed Marcus. 'And which lady are you trying to impress today?'

The other girls looked at each other and Sarah realised they were all looking at her, Marcus included. She remembered her manners. 'Thanks Marcus. Where do you live?'

He turned to her and she scrutinised him, a few days of dark growth covering his lower face. His eyes were green and they seemed to be laughing at her. 'I live on the Sunny Coast. Mooloolaba. How about you?'

She chatted to him while the others talked about what they'd done on their holidays. Marcus knew the area well where she lived. 'I camp up there a fair bit. I've got a four-wheel drive and I like getting away from the noise at the coast.' He lowered his voice. 'Maybe I could take you camping one weekend. I've got all the gear.'

She was flattered at the attention and could feel her face reddening. City boys were forward and Marcus hadn't taken his eyes off her since she had sat down. 'I'd like that. I don't know anyone around my age so I gener-ally stay at home when I'm not studying.'

Marcus filled her in on his engineering course. He was in his third year and knew Bree and the others through some other friends. 'We're all at the same parties. You'll meet heaps of people once you get into the swing of uni life,' Bree told her.

'How about I walk you back to your car,' Marcus

offered. 'I'll show you somewhere better to park next time. That way you won't have to pay.'

She'd taken him up on his offer and they'd stood at her car and talked for a long while. He'd even put his hand on her arm when he said goodbye and for the first time she'd felt flutters of excitement in her stomach. Taking deep breaths she blinked hard when he leaned over and kissed her on the cheek. He had a sexy deep voice and she loved the way he looked at her. 'I have a feeling you and I are going to be seeing a fair bit of each other,' he said.

She stumbled over her words. 'Thanks, I'd like that.'

With that he had turned and walked in the other direction, leaving her to stare after him. What had just happened. First day and she'd accepted a date from a very good-looking boy. Wait until she told Ruby.

CHAPTER 49

*M*arcus was waiting for her outside her lecture the next day. She was in the same course as Bree so it wasn't hard for him to work out where she was. He grabbed her hand when she walked out of the building. 'Hey gorgeous. I have something for you.'

She squeezed his hand. 'How did you find me. There're a thousand people here.'

'Follow me,' he said.

She walked beside him as he led her out of the buildings and across the park to the other side of the campus. Here there were expansive bush zones, dotted with areas where you could sit on the grass and relax. She snuck a few sideway glances at him. She'd worn one of the new dresses Ruby had helped her pick. It came to just above her knee and fitted loosely, the hem of it kicking up and showing her legs. Marcus wore the same as yesterday. Shorts and a t-shirt. He'd shaved though and she noticed his square jawbone and rugged features. He led her to an area with no one else around. Pulling a rug from his backpack he spread it out and then pulled out a container with sandwiches in it. 'I made these and thought we'd have a picnic. Celebrate meeting each other.'

She was in awe. Who did something so thoughtful? Taking her sandals off she sat down on the rug, stretching her legs out in front of her, enjoying the warmth of the sun on her skin. The rest of the time she spent either laughing at one of his funny stories or watching him as he explained where he was going to take her camping.

'We could go this weekend if you're not busy,' he asked her.

She sat up, her mind suddenly thinking a bit straighter. 'Um, it might be a bit early for me to go away with you for a weekend. Unless we have separate tents or something.'

He laughed loudly and she wondered what she'd said that was so funny. 'How old are you Sarah?'

'Twenty-three. How old are you?'

'The same age. Surely we don't have to waste time on worrying about things like that. I like you and you like me. Let's get this relationship off to a good start.'

She chewed her sandwich, thinking carefully. 'I'm not in the habit of rushing into anything.' She stopped talking as he reached over and stroked her leg. Her leg felt like it was on fire and she tried not to squirm, his hand smooth on her skin. She didn't want to add that it was a long while since she'd slept with someone. That had only ever happened twice before when she was younger. There had been a couple of times she'd been with one of the boys from Boulia she'd known. He'd been working on Western Downs and taken her out for a few months. The experience had been pleasant but had made her realise that she didn't have those type of feelings for him. She'd felt terrible that she'd hurt him and led him on but also glad that she'd stopped it before it went any further.

This was different though. The feelings for Marcus were there from the minute she met him. She thought hard. She was twenty-three. It was time to be in a relationship. If not now, when?

***

Ruby and Bobby were surprised when she announced that she was going camping for the weekend. 'Is there a group of you going? Bobby asked. 'You mentioned you'd met a few people.

She felt bad lying but she didn't want their advice. 'Yeah, I think so. They're all friends, some girls and some boys.' She'd scowled at Simon when he gave her a funny look. He could always tell when she wasn't telling the entire story.

'Maybe Liam and I could come too,' he joked.

'I don't think so. These friends are all in their twenties.'

Simon raised his eyebrows and threw another suspicious look her way. She turned away from him. 'Anyway,' she said, 'directing her conversation to Ruby, 'We're only going for two nights and they have all the camping gear. I'm going to drive out there myself though and meet them there.'

Ruby seemed pleased. 'That's great that you've made some friends straight away. Uni life is a wonderful place for making solid friendships. I still see some of the girls I went to uni with.'

***

Marcus was well set up for camping and all she needed to bring was her clothes and herself. She'd put in some extra food and wine, and her own pillow. The thought of where she was going to sleep made her nervous but she had talked sternly to herself about letting go a little and making the most of being the age she was.

He'd obviously gone to a lot of trouble in readiness for her arrival and she couldn't have asked for anyone to be more organised. They'd taken a long walk to a waterfall before lunch and she'd loved the coolness of the rainforest and the different birds and plants he pointed out. He'd camped in this area numerous times with his friends and knew the best spots to pitch a tent. 'No one to disturb us here,' he'd told her as he pulled her close for a kiss when she first arrived.

The rest of the day had been magical and when they went to bed at night and Marcus zipped the tent as he crawled in behind her, she knew she was falling for him. He was everything, handsome, smart and caring. What a start to her year!

***

The first few months went past in a blur. Marcus seemed to have every weekend and spare moment planned and they spent all their time together. He was attentive and very clever at finding time for the two of them to be together with no one else around. Her shyness in bed was quickly forgotten and they slipped into a solid romance. She had been careful from the start with birth control. She didn't want anything like that going wrong. Her aim was still to finish her studies. Past that, she hadn't really given much thought and it wasn't something they'd talked about yet.

This weekend she insisted that he come to the farm and meet her family. She'd explained the living situation and although he wasn't that keen to come to her place she talked him around.

On Friday afternoon he'd come home with her after uni. 'I can only stay the one night,' he'd said. 'I've told the boys I'll go to the pub on Saturday night. They're complaining that I haven't been around much.'

'That's because we've been away every weekend since you first asked me,' she said.

'I just need to be with you every second. I don't like sharing you with anyone.'

She giggled, pushing his hand away from where he had placed it on her leg. 'I need to concentrate on the road.'

He hadn't said much on the drive and she got the impression that he wasn't that keen on visiting. Her concerns were pushed aside however when they arrived.

The others were waiting on the verandah, the table set for dinner and the smell of meat cooking on the barbeque a welcoming smell.

She'd introduced him to everyone and tried to relax. It was nerve wracking and she breathed a sigh of relief when they all finally sat down to eat. Liam and Simon were talkative and had everyone laughing with their stories from school. Liam was now in year ten and Simon in Year eleven. Both were excelling at school and Liam plied Marcus with questions about his engineering course.

Overall, the night went well and she avoided Bobby's gaze when she mentioned that Marcus would spend the night in the cabin with her. The two boys had already gone inside and she noted that Ruby placed her hand on Bobby's arm. 'That's fine, Sarah. You're old enough to make your own decisions.' Ruby had smiled at them both and said goodnight, leading Bobby back into the house.

Sarah wasn't that worried about what Bobby thought. She was in love and Marcus was the priority in her life now. Bobby should be pleased for her, he'd often told her that he hoped she'd meet someone one day. Now she had, and all caution was thrown to the wind. She had a steady boyfriend, a group of friends and her study. Life was good.

CHAPTER 50

*B*obby remained calm and friendly while Marcus was still at their house. He had watched him carefully the night before, noting that he was very attentive to Sarah, passing her food and making sure she was looked after. He'd even stood up and pulled her chair out when she got up from the table. Bobby had presumed that Marcus would sleep in his car or up at their house, not in her cabin. She'd only been at uni for a few months. Why would she jump into a relationship so quickly.

'I'm worried about how fast this has happened,' he confided in Ruby the next day after they'd waved the two of them off. Liam was inside studying and Simon had gone for a walk across the paddocks.

'She's her own person, Bobby. We can't make her decisions, she has to make them herself.'

'Tell me the truth, Ruby, apart from his handsome looks and doting manner, what did you make of him?'

Ruby twisted her mouth in that way that showed she

was trying to get her words right. 'He's seems nice and treats her like she's very special to him.'

'Go on.'

Ruby thought hard. 'For me, he's a bit over-attentive, but then again, they're a different generation.'

Bobby's eyebrows drew together, a frown on his face. 'I can't believe she'd sleep with him so quickly. She's usually so rational.'

'Once again, times have changed and besides it's not really that different to when we were young.'

'At least we used to wait a few months or longer, you know, make sure it was the right move.'

Ruby wrapped her arms around him. 'I think you're being over-protective. They've been together a few months, I don't think we realised at the start that he was her boyfriend. This is what happens when it's your daughter.'

'I just want the best for her and I'm not sure about him.'

***

Simon added fuel to the fire that night at dinner. 'Nup, don't like him. Don't like him one bit.'

'What?' Liam was shocked. 'He's really nice and super smart.'

'What don't you like?' Ruby asked.

'I'm not sure. I get a bad feeling about him and I wanted to push him away from her. He's all over her like a rash. How embarrassing.'

Bobby laughed. 'It was a bit much.'

'You're all being so cynical,' Ruby said. 'It doesn't

matter what we think anyway, and it will be the same when you two boys get girlfriends. You have to work it out for yourself.'

***

Ruby thought about that conversation a couple of months later when Sarah came to her in tears. They'd hardly seen her on weekends and she seemed to always have an excuse why she needed to stay at Marcus's place, even during the week. The fact he hadn't been to visit them again was also irritating Bobby and she always seemed to be trying to placate him and keep the peace between him and Sarah. 'I wanted to go away with Bree and the other two girls for the weekend. We were going to go down the coast and stay in a fancy motel. There's a big dance party on and we just want to dance and drink.'

'And the problem is?' Ruby asked, not used to seeing Sarah upset.

'Marcus said I shouldn't go. He said I was supposed to spend the time with him. He'd organised to go to a new camping place and said I was being selfish after everything he does for me.'

Alarm bells rang in Ruby's mind. 'Does Marcus get jealous, Sarah?'

Sarah wiped her nose with the tissue Ruby had passed her. 'He gets really jealous. He's even come and sat in some of my lectures because he said he wants to make sure people know we're together.'

'What? That's ridiculous. Why didn't you tell me this?'

'I don't want to say bad things about him. He's lovely otherwise. Everyone has faults, right?'

'What else does he do like that?'

Sarah sniffled and looked away. 'I don't want you to think he's a bad person because he's not.'

Ruby waited. 'What else?'

Picking another tissue out of the box, Sarah spoke quietly, as if she thought someone was listening. 'He told me I shouldn't wear short dresses to uni and that my jeans are too tight. He reckons Ben and Stanley are perving on me and that I'm sending out the wrong message to them. I'm not allowed to have coffee or talk to them anymore.'

Ruby's words came out too loud and she heard the door open behind her and Bobby come out to where they were sitting. 'What!' he said. 'He told you you're not allowed to do something. That's bullshit!'

'Whoa, calm down, Ruby. What's going on.' Bobby sat down opposite them. 'What's wrong Sarah? You look upset.'

Neither of them replied.

Ruby eventually spoke. 'Tell your father. Go on, tell him what you just told me and see what he says. He's a male, let's get his perspective on this.'

Sarah repeated what she had told Ruby and also added some more disturbing information. 'He said he doesn't think I should live here with you. It's not that he doesn't like you, he just thinks I should move in with him. He says that he doesn't want to visit here and it would do me good not to have so much to do with either of you.'

A shocked look crossed Bobby's face. 'That's called a control freak. To me it sounds like he's trying to rule you and not let you be your own person. Is that what you want? To be in a relationship where you don't get to do your own thing. Look at Ruby and me. Have you ever seen either of us try and stop the other from doing something. You're a couple, but you still have to be an individual.'

Sarah started crying and Ruby put her arm around her shoulder. Bobby's voice was harsh and it was unusual for him to show anger when he talked. His tone had upset Sarah even more. She could tell he was wound up though and his previous doubts about Marcus appeared to be right. It worried her that Marcus was trying to distance Sarah from her family. She'd seen that before and it was often a sign that he wanted full control. 'Do you want to keep going out with him?' she asked Sarah.

'I thought I did, but now I'm not sure. A couple of weeks ago I tried to tell him I wanted to have a break for a while. He went crazy. Told me he'd drive his car into a pole if he couldn't have me and that I'd break his heart and ruin his life if I left. We made up and he seemed to go back to normal. He even gave me a bit of space for a while. He's adamant about this weekend though. He just said said outright that I can't go.'

Bobby was lost for words and let Ruby talk. 'This is serious. You need to break it off now before it gets any worse. It's only been a matter of months, imagine if you leave it any longer.'

Sarah stopped crying. 'I know. It's not that easy though. I'll run into him at uni all the time.'

'I'll come and sit next to you every day if that's the problem,' Bobby said. 'Get rid of him. Look at you. You're not happy.'

A fresh flood of tears flowed and Sarah's words were hard to hear between her sobs. Bobby came to her and pulled her up, holding her tight. Her words were muffled.

'I don't know what to do. I haven't been in this situation before. He scares me and I'm worried he'll hurt me or himself if I try and end the relationship. I don't want to worry either of you with all of this though, you have enough to do with bringing up the boys. I should be old enough to look after myself.'

Ruby stood beside them. 'We're always here for you, no matter what your age is. Look, this has probably come to a head at a good time. The holidays are coming up. Why don't you break up with him? Cut it clean. Bobby can drive you to his house and you can talk to him while Bobby waits in the car. Then you can go back out west to Grandpa for the semester break. It's a long one and that will give you time to sort yourself out and for him to move on.'

'That's a good idea' Sarah looked up, for the first time her voice sounding calm. 'I need to get away for a while. I don't want to be with him anymore.'

'You do need to get away,' Bobby said, 'but you also need to make sure you come back refreshed and ready for more study. You're going so well and you shouldn't let that mongrel mess up any of your plans.'

They'd worked out a plan of action over the dinner table. 'Told you so,' Simon said, stuffing food into his mouth.

'Don't put so much in your mouth, Simon,' Ruby scolded. 'You eat too fast, like the food is going to run out.'

Liam listened quietly, taking it all in. 'You're quiet, Liam,' Sarah said. 'What do you think.'

'I think you should tell him to go and jump in the lake. Who needs a boyfriend anyway.'

They'd all laughed and Ruby was pleased to see Sarah

looking a bit happier. It made a difference for all of them to be there together and help solve each other's problems. Sarah had lost weight over the last weeks and they should have been quicker to pick up on what was going on. Hopefully she'd be strong enough to make sure Marcus knew her decision was final.

***

No doubt, Marcus would be surprised to see Bobby arrive with Sarah, and Ruby waited up until they returned home. It would be interesting to see how they went.

Car headlights alerted her that they had eventually returned and she waited patiently. They sat in the car for a long while before they both come up onto the verandah.

Sarah gave her a hug. 'I can't believe how stupid I've been. Thank you.'

Ruby replied. 'People like Marcus are good at manipulating. Don't feel bad, it's a learning curve.'

Bobby walked slowly up the stairs, his hands running through his hair. She could tell he was stressed. 'He's certainly a mongrel. You should have heard the abuse he threw at Sarah when she came back out to the car. He didn't care if I heard or not. Called her all sorts of names and told her he was seeing someone else anyway. We'd heard enough and I just drove away.'

'Thank goodness you were there with me. He was just horrible,' Sarah kissed Bobby and Ruby goodnight. 'I'm going to bed. It's been a long day.'

CHAPTER 51

*B*obby drove out west with Sarah the following weekend. They hadn't heard anything from Marcus and although she was quiet for a few days it appeared she was getting back on track.

Bobby stayed for a week, enjoying working with the cattle and talking to Thomas. Beth had fussed over him and once he was sure that Sarah was okay he hitched a ride back on a cattle truck, leaving the ute for Sarah to drive back home when she was ready.

There was plenty to do on the farm and the boys had another few weeks of school left before their holidays. Every week there were discussions and decisions around subjects and sport at school. Life was busy and Liam had made the state debating team so there were extra practice sessions at some of the schools on the coast. Simon had also scooped a major prize in an academic contest and now they had decisions to make as both he and Liam had been offered scholarships to two of the private schools on the coast.

Ruby wasn't sure about the offers and they needed to discuss it further, between themselves and with the boys. Life was coasting along nicely after Sarah's relationship breakup and it would be good to keep it that way for a while. They didn't need any further dramas, they just wanted to concentrate on what they had in front of them at the moment, particularly the boys' schooling.

CHAPTER 52

*S*arah took a week or so to settle in on Western Downs. It wasn't because Beth was living there, or anything to do with Grandpa, or being away from the property for so long. It was all because of that stupid Marcus. Ruby and Bobby must think she was an idiot. All the years on the property that she had pushed away anyone who had tried to get close to her, only to fall so hard and quickly for an absolute mongrel in her first week of uni. The romances she had experienced when she was younger had been easier to get out of. They'd both walked away and even said hello to her whenever they ran into one another in town. Marcus had been a different kettle of fish as her grandpa liked to say, and she needed to be careful in the future not to be taken in so easily. What hope was there for her if even Simon had picked up on the fact that he was not a good choice!

***

After a while she relaxed back into her old lifestyle and when it was time to leave she was sorry to say goodbye. 'I'm sad to go, Grandpa, but I'm keen to get back into the study.'

'Don't you let anyone else stand in your way,' Beth had said. 'Everyone makes mistakes, you just need to learn from them.'

***

A feeling of contentment filled her when she drove through the gates to Tall Trees and followed the track through the tunnel of trees. This was home, her cabin on the hill, the boys, and Ruby and Bobby. She slowed and peered up, tiny bats flitting in and out of the branches, her headlights making them surge upwards into the darker heights of the trees.

The headlights of the car lit up the yard gate and she wound her window down and called out to Liam and Simon who had run down from the house to open the gates for her. She laughed as she watched them in her revision mirror sprinting up after her.

CHAPTER 53

Sarah had been home a few months when she noticed Liam and Simon stopping their conversation when she neared them. There was no doubt they were up to something and she pounced on them as they wrote on a piece of paper. 'What are you two up to? Something is going on?'

Liam put on his grownup voice. 'Nothing my dear. Nothing is going on.'

Simon chuckled, his deep voice startling her.

'What happened to your voice?' she asked.

'It's called puberty, Simon said. 'I'm sixteen now. Look I'm even getting a moustache.' He ran his finger over his top lip, pushing his face towards her.'

'Good Lord, you do have one. What about you Liam?'

Liam frowned at her. 'I have bigger things to worry about than a scrap of dark hair on my upper lip. We Carlons have the curse of that black hair that appears all over our bodies.'

She grabbed the piece of paper away from him. 'What's this? A shopping list?'

Liam snatched it back. 'You might need to know that you must be in attendance on Saturday night here on the verandah for dinner. Simon and I are cooking, so don't be late.'

'What's the occasion,' she asked.

They looked at each other. 'End of the term for us,' Simon said quickly. 'Make sure you wear something nice. We're getting dressed up.'

'Since when do we do that.' She pulled a face.

'Since we said so,' Liam said. 'If you could put your manners back in and inform us that you will be in attendance.'

She giggled. 'Of course, I will be. I'll be interested to see how your cooking goes.'

***

Saturday night rolled around and Sarah was amazed at the trouble the boys had gone to. The table was set with Ruby's good china and the best cutlery set had been polished and placed on the table. A new tablecloth covered the surface and there were candles in between the dishes. Ruby and Bobby avoided her questions about why the night was so special when Sarah asked. She figured the boys just wanted to show off their cooking.

Once her study was finished she got changed, making sure to wear something nice as requested. The weather was cool and she pulled on a new pair of jeans and a floral shirt she'd bought last week. Brushing her hair, she looked in the mirror. She pushed her finger across her brows, thankful she'd had them thinned the week before. They appeared in a high arch and she knew that always made her dark eyes appear bigger. Her hair as usual was curly and loose and she pinned one side back. She must remember to tell the boys that she'd done that, gone to the extra trouble just because they were cooking for her.

Both of them had been more protective than usual after she'd broken up with Marcus and Simon had even phoned her when she was at Grandpa's to check how she was going. He'd whooped and yelled down the phone when she told him that Bree had contacted her to let her know that Marcus had left uni and gone travelling over-seas. She was relieved. At least she wouldn't run into him.

They'd talked for a while and she appreciated that Simon had thought of her. They'd became closer as he matured and she really felt like he was her brother. Liam was just so cute she wanted to cuddle him all the time which was getting harder as he grew older. They were great boys and she talked about them a lot to Grandpa and Beth. 'You'll never be lonely Sarah,' they'd said as they waved her off. 'We have a big family between us all now.'

She thought about Grandpa now as she watched the boys bringing out some nibblies and drinks for the special dinner. She must get him and Beth to come and visit. They hadn't been able to come to Bobby and Ruby's wedding, but one day she'd get them to come to the coast.

She sat down on the chair Liam pulled out for her, trying not to laugh at the white serviette he had draped over his arm. 'You've put one chair too many out,' she quipped, 'I thought you were supposed to be good at maths.'

Liam put on his posh voice, watching intently as

Simon poured wine for the adults. 'It's so funny you should say that, my dear. Tonight, we have also asked our math teacher from school. We wanted to thank him for all the work he put in this semester and show him our gratitude for the marks we got. We got As, of course,' he added.

Sarah took a sip of her drink, pointing to her hair clip to show them how she had dressed up for the occasion. 'Of course, you did. I expect nothing less. Is this teacher Mr Miles?'

Simon sat down beside her. 'Mr Miles has retired. I reckon he was nearly eighty!'

She laughed. 'I met him once in town, he was pretty old.'

Car headlights shone up the driveway, a four-wheel drive eventually pulling up beside the house.

'We've asked Mr McIntosh who is our teacher this year. Here he is now.'

Sarah was curious, she hadn't heard them talk about Mr McIntosh. He must be pretty special if they'd put all this on tonight for him.

Ruby leaned over and spoke quietly. 'Mr McIntosh is not quite thirty and he's very nice, according to the boys.' She paused as Sarah narrowed her eyes, a suspicious look on her face. 'He also happens to be single.' Ruby held her hand up to stop Sarah speaking. 'Sorry Sarah, nothing to do with Bobby or me. This is all the boys' doing. Let's relax and have a nice night.'

*A*t first Sarah was annoyed. This was a set-up and she'd been tricked. She pulled the clip out of her hair and flicked her sandals off. No wonder they wanted her to dress up. They were match-making. Wait until she got her hands on them in the morning. They'd pay big time.

It was obvious that Mr McIntosh, otherwise known as Matthew or Matt, was also unaware of the setup. Simon introduced him and they all shook hands. They'd shown him to his seat which happened to be right opposite Sarah. Simon and Liam had rushed back and forth, bringing out entrees, then a delicious main meal and eventually a dessert of cheesecake and strawberries which had gone a long way to pacify Sarah.

To begin with she hadn't talked, knowing that her silence would annoy them. Simon had glared at her at one stage and tried to will her with his eyes, but she had just smiled sweetly back at him and looked innocently over the top of her glass.

Bobby and Ruby made sure the conversation flowed and soon the questions they asked unravelled where Matt was from. 'I grew up near Broken Hill. I don't know if you've ever been there but it's in the middle of nowhere. Dust, mining, sheep, and cattle. That's about it. It was a great place to grow up as a kid. We had motorbikes and horses so we were never bored. As soon as I finished year twelve though, I knew I wanted more. I've spent over six years studying science and maths.'

She couldn't help but be drawn into the conversation. 'Do you like teaching? I think you deserve a medal for putting up with these two.' She gave them both a look that still said, wait until I get my hands on you.

He looked straight at Sarah when he spoke and she admired his honest eyes and handsome face. His hair was dark like hers was and she guessed he was about the same height as she was. Trust the boys to think just because he was handsome and fit looking that she'd fall for their tricks. Now she was wiser and smarter. It wouldn't hurt to have a conversation with him though. 'I love it,' he replied. 'I've come to a good school and this year I feel like I've found my feet. It's a lot of work when you start but it's worth it.'

'Are these two as smart as they say they are?' she asked.

Both boys sat up and Liam poked his tongue at her. She gritted her teeth. 'Sometimes they can be a bit sneaky, you have to watch them,' she added.

He laughed. 'They play tricks on me all the time. Lucky I have a good sense of humour. And to your question, yes, they are both incredibly smart and sometimes young Liam here corrects me.'

'In a polite way, I hope,' Ruby said.

'Always.' He turned to Ruby and Bobby, 'You should be really proud of what they've accomplished this year. They have a fantastic future in front of them and Simon tells me that it's all because of you two and Sarah.'

So, they had talked about her, Sarah thought. Sneaky little buggers. Boy was there going to be some payback for tonight.

Liam piped up, his face turned to Matt, 'Sarah's single, Mr McIntosh. She had a boyfriend but he was trying to control her so that didn't last.'

Sarah nearly fell off her chair and Ruby spoke loudly. 'Liam, that's enough. We don't need to share everything.'

Liam and Simon smiled at each other while Matt put his hand over his mouth, trying not to laugh. 'That's what I love about kids. They just tell it as it is. Maybe you and I could have a good chat, Sarah. My last relationship ended because she was a crazy, controlling person who wouldn't let me out of her sight and even stalked me at school. Nearly destroyed my career at my last school. Who would ever think it could happen? But it does, even to the best of us.'

It was as if everyone breathed a sigh of relief and Sarah relaxed and for a moment even forgave the boys for their devious ways. The chatter flowed around the table and loud laughter and funny quips rolled back and forth. When Matt stood to go it was nearly midnight and she was sorry he was leaving. She walked to the car with the boys to say goodbye, chasing them off to the gate so they could shut it behind Matt when he drove out.

'Thank you for such a lovely evening,' Matt said as he stood beside his car. 'I miss my family and it's nice to sit and make fun of each other, the way families do. What lovely people Ruby and Bobby are. No wonder the boys have flourished living here.'

'We all have,' Sarah said. 'Hopefully I'll see you again, maybe around town.'

He opened the car door and got in. 'It could be sooner than that. Those two have lined me up to come riding with them next weekend. They said you'd be in that also.'

She leaned down and talked to him through the open window. 'They are sneaky, conniving boys and at the start of tonight I was ready to throttle them for setting me up. Now, well, I won't. It's been such a lovely night.'

He started the car. 'I'll see you soon.'

She held her hand up and waved. 'See you soon, Matt.'

CHAPTER 55

*S*he'd waited around the side of the shed until the boys walked past in the dark. She could hear them talking about how well her and Matt had got on. Waiting until they were directly level with her she leapt out of her hiding space and grabbed them both, screaming loudly in their faces. Both had jumped and squealed like frightened kids and she was delighted she'd scared them. 'That's just the start,' she threatened, chasing them as they ran back to the house.

Over the next few weeks, Matt was invited to quite a few events at the farm. She hadn't been surprised after the success of the riding day that he had also turned up at the markets on the following Sunday. 'The boys said I should come and buy my fruit and vegie from here.'

She'd taken off the bag with the market money in it and handed it to Simon. 'Here, seeing this was your idea, you can serve the customers. I'm going for a coffee with Matt. Have fun.'

They sat on metal chairs, their coffees balanced on the

tiny tables in front of them. She found it hard to keep her eyes off him this morning. He had jeans and riding boots on and a thick coat to keep him warm. It was winter and she had the urge to cuddle into him. He must have been thinking the same. 'It's the sort of weather you want to be in front of a fireplace with a nice glass of red and good company.' His eyes looked straight into hers. 'You know, Sarah, those two boys might have been right in thinking that we'd get on well. We're from similar backgrounds and now want to make our lives here on the coast. Maybe we should go on a couple of dates and see how that goes.'

She sipped her coffee, warming her hands on the cup. 'I'd like that. I'd like that a lot. My only problem is I don't want them thinking they were right. However, I'm happy to put that to the side.'

His face split into a wide grin and she found herself beaming back, feeling like she was a teenager. 'I want to go slow though,' she said. 'I haven't dated much and my last episode was disastrous.'

He put his hand on top of hers where it lay on the table. 'Yes, nice and slow. Me too. There's no rush, let's just see how we go.'

He'd laughed when she sat up and waved at Liam who was spying on them from behind one of the stalls. 'Those boys, honestly, I'm going to get that little one, 'she said. 'he's too smart for his own good.'

'One day it might be him, falling for a girl.'

She laughed and then spoke her mind. 'I really like talking to you. It's so easy.'

He chuckled. 'That's a good start. That's why I asked you out.'

CHAPTER 56

*M*att started to visit the farm on a regular basis and soon became like part of the family. On Sunday morning he could be found with Sarah, the Sunday papers spread out in front of them as they did the puzzles together. She shielded the questions from Liam and Simon, who knew all the answers. 'I hate it when kids are smarter than adults,' Matt said.

'Me too,' Sarah replied. 'I know how to get rid of them.' She leaned over and kissed him on the lips, his hands coming up around her face as he kissed her back.

Both Simon and Liam put their hands over the eyes. 'Please stop. We can't stand it,' Liam said.

Sarah threw a tea towel at him. 'You started all of this. It's you two to blame.'

Simon looked through his fingers. 'Look here comes Bobby and Ruby. They've been into town. I wonder if they bought me a cream bun?'

'They usually do,' Matt said. 'Maybe they got me one too.'

Ruby hopped out of the car carrying white paper bags. She waved them in the air before walking up to them, Bobby following with Rusty running around him, as usual, barking loudly.

They sat at the table, dispersing the bags. 'One for each of you,' Bobby said. 'This is becoming a weekend ritual.'

Liam and Simon were already eating theirs before the others had opened their bags. They grinned at each other, cream and jam on the side of Liam's face. 'This is the best!' he declared.

They all laughed and Bobby passed Liam a paper towel. 'You two always eat like there's no tomorrow.'

'I don't know how you keep the food up to them,' Matt said. 'They remind me of my brothers back at home.'

'Actually, talking about Matt's home.' Sarah looked around the table. 'Matt and I are going to go for a road trip on the two weeks we have off. He's taking me to meet his family.'

They were all quiet, Liam and Simon, high fiving in the air.

'When are you going?' Ruby asked.

'We'll leave after Sarah's helped you at the markets on Sunday,' Matt said. 'We'll take it slow and have a look around on the way down there. I've promised Sarah that next holidays we'll go out and visit her grandpa.'

Bobby grinned broadly. 'Good on you. You both look so happy. Ruby and I love that you're making plans together.'

Simon joined in. 'Yeah, thank goodness. If we'd left it up to Sarah …'

His conversation was cut short as Sarah kicked him under the table, glaring hard.

'Hey, what did you kick me for?'

'What?' Sarah said, an innocent look on her face.

***

Bobby finished his bun and relaxed back in his chair. Ruby's hand was resting on the table and he put his hand over it and squeezed lightly. She turned and smiled at him and he was sure his heart missed a beat. Her green eyes looked into his and he leaned over and tucked a strand of wavy hair behind her ears. She looked exactly the same as when he'd first seen her when she came to look for him years ago out west. Elegant, kind, and always wanting to help everyone. He loved her more than life itself and all he wanted was to grow old together. Around them was their family and a home where he felt at peace. Her long legs stretched out in front of her, a clingy dress coming to just below her knees. She prodded him with her foot.

'Are you two playing footsie?' Sarah asked.

'Please don't kiss,' Simon said. 'I can't take any more mushy stuff this morning.'

Ruby blew Simon a kiss. He wiped his face as if it had landed. 'Bobby and I went into town this morning,' Ruby said. 'We went to the bakery and then had a look in the real estate window.'

'I wondered why you were gone so long,' Sarah asked. 'The boys were getting frantic that you'd forget their cream buns.'

Bobby reached into his pocket. 'We actually had to make another stop and that took a bit longer than we thought. It was well worth it though because we came away with this.'

He placed a white plastic object on the table. 'What's that? Liam leaned forward. It looks like a thermometer.'

They all stretched forward to see the object that Bobby had placed in the centre of the table. Sarah stood up, her eyes wide. 'Oh, my goodness. Is that what I think it is?'

Bobby stood up and stood behind Ruby, his arms around her shoulders.

'What is it,' Simon and Liam said in unison.

Ruby picked it up and turned it around so they could see the front of it. 'It's a pregnancy test and those two pink lines tell us that is it positive. I'm nearly twelve weeks pregnant.'

For a moment there was silence and then everyone was talking and yelling all at once.

Bobby bent down and kissed the top of Ruby's head, waiting for the noise to stop. 'The baby is due in March and Ruby's had scans done last week and everything is fine.'

'What? You knew and didn't tell us,' Simon said. 'Talk about sneaky.' He got up and came to Ruby, giving her a gentle hug. Bobby could see the tears in Simon's eyes and he started to become emotional himself, his words coming out all over the place. 'Ruby, she, Ruby, she was told...' He stopped and wiped his eyes, placing his arm around Simon.

'I'd tried to have a baby when I was first married,' Ruby said. 'There were a number of medical reasons going against me and I accepted the advice that I was unable to fall pregnant. When Bobby and I found each other, our lives were complete. That was made even better when the three of you joined us. We could never have asked for more. For Bobby and me, a family has come in a different way than we had ever thought possible.'

Bobby had regained his composure and looked around the table. 'You need to remember that a family doesn't necessarily have to be your regular type. We've proved that here with all of us coming together. You are the best family anyone could wish for.'

'That's so true!' Sarah jumped up and clapped her hands, before wrapping her arms around Liam and squeezing him tightly. 'But now we will be a family of six.'

Liam jumped up and down. 'I can't believe you knew and didn't tell us until now.'

'This has come completely out of the blue,' Ruby said. 'Even when I felt a bit sick and put on some weight it never even entered our minds. I went for a regular check-up and the doctor picked up on it straight away when he asked me how I was feeling. I am forty-three so it does carry a few more risks but so far everything is great and the doctor is really happy with the way it's going. We just didn't want to say anything until we were sure everything was okay.'

Bobby sat back down. 'Ruby's fit and healthy and we'll make sure she rests and doesn't do too much.'

'We can do everything,' Liam said.

Simon added, 'I love babies. We can all help. This is the best thing ever.'

Sarah and Matt asked questions and everyone offered to help. There was an excited buzz of conversation around the table. Bobby looked at Ruby, her face flushed with excitement. She leaned over, her lips brushing his cheek. Their eyes locked and they stared at each other. She whispered. 'I love you, Bobby.'

He gently squeezed her hand. 'Forever more, Ruby-Rose.'

~~~

A gentle breeze filtered across the massive trees that threw their shadows over the paddocks. The air swirled past the leaves and wove its way through the grasses before reaching the trees that stood tall on the grassy slopes. The breeze rested briefly as it flickered across Sally's gravestone in the cemetery, slowing as it brushed lightly over Francis and Mary's grave, just visible in the moonlight. The wind picked up speed, gathering a few dry leaves, moving through the delicate flowers of the towering jacaranda tree that stood guard. Further on it gathered small sticks, throwing them back to the earth before swirling around the sacred mountains. Finally it made its way back up the slopes, following the well-worn paths of the cows, causing the cattle lying together under a tree to lift their heads, watching as the hurtling breeze raced back up the hillside.

The family of five, with another soon to join them, nestled in for the night as a chorus of crickets and cicadas sounded, the noise filling the night air with life as the moon eased higher into the sky. The clouds and the valley far below were luminated as orbs of golden light transcended across the paddocks and over the buildings of, Tall Trees, perched high on the hill.

'When I'm up here, it's like I'm floating. Like everything else has been left below. My mind settles as I climb the mountain and I feel at peace. The ancient trees with their rough bark

wrap around me like silk cocoons. Their solid trunks and tendril roots grip the ground as if to say, I will hold you, I will not let go. My life with Ruby Rose and our family is balanced and steady. The air is clear, and there's a breeze that wings its way through the branches, the leaves and across my face. The world below sometimes ceases to exist. If I close my eyes I float above the surface of the earth and ... I am calm.'

Bobby Carlon

ABOUT THE AUTHOR

Rhonda Forrest is an Australian author who juggles writing and publishing, alongside teaching high school students. She writes captivating contemporary and historical/romance fiction about relationships, family life and social issues, set amidst beautiful and uniquely Australian landscapes.

After bringing up three daughters and traversing several careers, Rhonda went on to teach creative writing, English and history. Her passion for literacy, history and travelling around Australia fuels her novels. Along with her husband, she divides her time between Tamborine Mountain and a century-old cottage with a rambling garden overlooking the waters of the Whitsundays.

Recent novels bring to life the remarkable characters and settings that make up the unique Australian heritage and take the reader on a journey from bush to beach, with steamy romances, riveting history and eclectic characters.

Some books are available in audio and large print and you can also find some titles available in Portuguese, Publisher- Leabhar Books Brazil.

If you enjoyed this book or any of Rhonda's other books, you can make a big difference by writing a review, or leaving a star rating on Amazon, Goodreads or Bookbub. A personal recommendation to family, friends, libraries and book clubs is another great way to share the books with others. You can also follow Rhonda on Facebook, Instagram, Goodreads and Bookbub.

Website - https://www.rhondaforrest.com/

BOOK 1 - *We'll Meet Again* Series

ELIZABETH'S STAR
by Rhonda Forrest
Sample chapters are included at the back of this book.

'A dingo howls, a star falls.
Don't worry for me, I'll be home soon.'

In 1941, Queensland drover, Michael McTavish leaves behind his young daughter Gracie and joins the 2/22 AIF, his destination, Rabaul, New Guinea, a small town surrounded by impenetrable jungles and steep jagged mountains, its shores lined by tranquil bays and active volcanos.

Joanie has also arrived in New Guinea, with a chance

to manage a trading store with her father, Reg, too exciting an opportunity to pass up.

As the tendrils of war creep closer to the islands north of Australia, some who call Rabaul home are given an opportunity to return to Australian shores. Others have no option but to stay. Will separation and distance affect the destiny of those who live in the path of the approaching enemy or will the power of love prevail?

Based on actual events, Elizabeth's Star begins the story of Michael and Joanie, unfolding the lives of their families and friends while following the life of Gracie, a little girl left behind when her father went to war.

A moving tale of love, loss, and separation.

Maree Page-Gear — *An absorbing, sweeping saga that harks back to a period in Australia's pre-World War II history that has been largely ignored. Compelling historical authenticity based on research and familial connections to this era.*

Susan Mackie (Author) — From the first few pages the story of Michael and his family, then Joanie and hers, drew me in. Rhonda Forrest must have lived and breathed the locations; her descriptions take you right there - to breathe in the humidity, sometimes the dust, hear the rain, feel the heat, see the stars. The characters are well-rounded, the dialogue flows and the adventure is real.

BOOK 2 - *We'll Meet Again* Series

UNTIL WE MEET
by Rhonda Forrest

'When you go home, tell them of us and say, for your
tomorrow, we gave our today.'
John Maxwell Edmonds 1918

In early 1940 Bud joins the United States Navy, his aim,
to become a US Submariner. Less than two years later,
Japanese forces bomb Pearl Harbour. Those living on the
islands of New Guinea lie directly in the path of the
oncoming enemy.

Along with other Australians, Joanie prepares to

depart Rabaul, leaving behind her fiancée, Michael, her father, and many others she loves.

As the volcano, Tavurvur, gathers its forces and bursts forth from its crater, the ill-equipped, small Australian defence known as Lark Force is left to secure the small town. Overwhelmed by the large enemy forces, the order is given, 'every man for themselves.' Although some will survive, over a thousand men lose their lives when a US Submarine sinks the POW Japanese ship, Montevideo Maru. The seeds of destiny are sown and the lives of Bud and those in Rabaul, intrinsically linked.

Will Michael return to fulfil his promise of marrying Joanie and what will be the fate of his young daughter, Gracie, who still turns to the evening star for guidance, for her questions to be answered, and above all to be reunited with her father.

Until We Meet is an epic war saga based on actual events that continues the story of Elizabeth's Star. A tale of survival, love and family, set amidst the backdrop of World War II.

Review - Author Leanne Lovegrove

Following on from the first book in the series, this is another moving account of a time in history I knew nothing about. This story traverses continents and with sensitivity and warmth, details events during this period of time told from the point of view of various characters, some new, others we are familiar with and they continue their journey. The author depicts the locations beautifully and transports the reader with obvious meticulous research. Not long to go until the final instalment!

BOOK 3 - *We'll Meet Again* Series

WE'LL MEET AGAIN - 2022
by Rhonda Forrest

*'My troubles are all over, and I am at home; and often before I
am quite awake, I fancy I am still in the orchard at Birtwick,
standing with my friends under the apple trees.'*
~ Black Beauty

The 1950s are a carefree time for a young woman like
Grace. The war is over and when her family moves to
Brisbane, plans are made for her to complete her studies
at the University of Queensland.

Ewan is also studying the same course and when he
meets the beautiful, head-strong Grace, the differences in

their backgrounds are pushed aside as they plan their future together.

However, not everyone is happy with the romance and when the young couple are forced to separate, decisions are made that will determine their path in life. Will the path taken, lead Grace to the story behind a star she knows as Elizabeth's Star and will a fortune teller's prophecy 40 years prior, be proven.

We'll Meet Again is a story of love and family, a connection between those who suffered loss and separation and a sweeping tale of hope, chance and love.

Review - Author Susan Mackie

A triumphant finale to the trilogy. Lush descriptions of Brisbane and Mt Tamborine and the development of characters we love from previous books and the introduction of new ones. I began reading a little at a time, pacing myself, but the last twenty percent I read in one big gulp, as I had to know what happened. Twists and turns and delightful characters. I think I need another one ... that's a challenge Rhonda Forrest.

SILKWORM SECRETS - Dark Secrets from a Distant Past

'The ancient trees with their rough bark wrap around me like silk cocoons. Their solid trunks and tendril roots grip the ground as if to say, I will hold you, I will not let go.'

SILKWORM SECRETS - Silkworm Secrets Series Book 1

In the 1960s the rural suburbs of Brisbane should have been an idyllic place for Ruby and Bobby to grow up. Their treehouse retreat, set high in a mulberry tree is a place to share friendship and watch the events of the yards nearby. However as the two become teenagers, the naive Ruby is exposed to the sinister events that Bobby has to deal with in his family life. As the years pass and the best friends go their separate ways, childhood events become a distant memory. Will the dark secrets remain uncovered or will Ruby and Bobby be forced to face up to what they witnessed so many years before.

This is a story about the secrets that children keep, the strength that comes from a childhood friendship and a special family love that overcomes the hardships of the past.

***

Mary – reviewer Goodreads - *Yes it's true this novel explores deeper and darker issues, - but life can be like that, complex, difficult, unfair. A rollercoaster ride of emotion but well worth it. This quintessential Australian novel is a must-read.*

Brenda – Reviewer Goodreads - *'Silkworm Secrets' absolutely blew me away! It was beautifully written - filled with deep emotion and heartache, love and abiding friendship.*

TWO HEARTBEATS

When Jess heads west for a fresh start in a small mining town, the dusty, outback plains are a far cry from her former life in the city. Despite having no knowledge of country life, she finds herself loving the isolation and local people who she lives with. All she has to do is keep her head down and work hard to create a better life for herself and Johnno, the only person she has ever truly cared about.

Happy Valley BooksRead — *Amazing authentic relatable characters, the harsh but beautiful Australian country settings and a storyline of realness that you can connect to. This wonderful Australian writer knows how to pull her reader into the plot and bring all the feelings bubbling to the top!*

Chapter Ichi - *I could not put 'Two Heartbeats' down. Rhonda Forrest has such a beautiful style and describes the Australian land in a way that makes me feel a closer connection and appreciation of the country I live in. The scenery described is breathtakingly realistic.*

Brenda - Goodreads' Reviewer - *Two Heartbeats' by Aussie author Rhonda Forrest is a story of second chances; of hope; sadness; love and trust. Set in the vast and drought-ridden Australian outback with nothing but dust, flies and heat for company, Two Heartbeats is another emotional novel from an author I thoroughly enjoy.*

Also available as an audio book - Two Heartbeats Audible

TIME WILL TELL - Sequel to *TWO HEARTBEATS*

A rural love story, where friendship, romance and hearts
entwine.

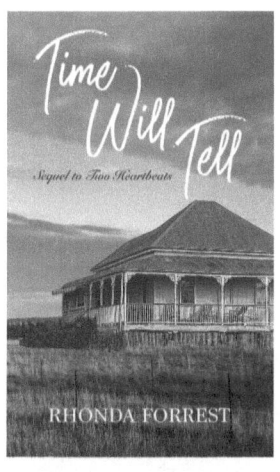

When Jess discovered love with
Daniel in the tiny outback town of
Gowrie, her previous troubled life
was cast aside. However,
differences in their backgrounds,
her doubts about real love and the
urge to return and support her
twin brother Johnno, forced her to
make a decision to leave.

A new home in the small
community of Tamborine
Mountain provides an
opportunity to contemplate how
she really feels and what is important. Johnno lives nearby and
new friends and a romantic encounter give her a fresh start, but
is this what she really wants? And if it isn't, will Daniel welcome
her back with open arms?

The tranquil setting of Tamborine Mountain joins forces with
the outback of Queensland to continue the story of *Two
Heartbeats.* Will the decision be taken out of Jess's hands, pushing
her further away, or will her heart lead her to where she will
find true happiness?

*When I read Rhonda's work, I think "authentic". There is no pretense.
Just raw, honest and beautifully crafted characters and dialogue.* The
Mad Hatter – Book Reviews

DISCOVER ROMANCE IN THE
WHITSUNDAYS

WHITSUNDAY ROMANCE SERIES

Love by the Jewel Sea - Book 1

Summer by the Jewel Sea - Book 2

Will the serenity of a tiny beachside community full of local characters, change Frankie's perspective on what is important in life?

THE SHACK BY THE BAY - by Rhonda Forrest

An isolated fishing shack on a beautiful bay in the Whitsundays provides Luke with a retreat where he can find peace and solitude. However, the discovery of family war relics, and a developing relationship with the beautiful Lily, connects family histories and reveals a story that threatens to destroy his chance at real happiness.

Will the wartime secrets prove to be the breaking point for a beautiful romance? Or can two families put the deeds of the past behind them?

Romantic and purely Australian, The Shack by the Bay captures the pristine beauty of the Whitsundays and the wartime memories of older Australians while introducing an eclectic blend of friends and family.

***

Review comments - *An intriguing mix of historical romance, a coming of age, love and its complications against the backdrop of World War II.*

Praise for The Shack by the Bay - *A novel that offers a linkage between the present and past while showcasing the natural beauty of a spectacular slice of Australia.*

KICK THE DUST

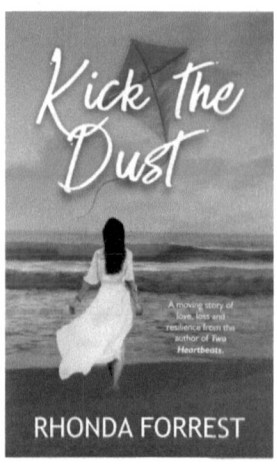

'If I close my eyes, it's easier to hold onto a memory. When I open them, I think it might really be there in front of me.'

After three tours of duty in Afghanistan, Liam Andrews is home safe in Queensland. His weekly life drawing class, full of colourful local artists, helps him manage his post-traumatic stress disorder. But he's struggling to open up about a past that still haunts him.

Belourine 'Billy' is an Afghan refugee who lost everything before arriving in Australia as a child. She finds joy in her daily swims in the lake. After years of upheaval, she's still searching for a place to call home. But her past makes it hard to trust people.When Liam and Billy meet, they form an instant connection. But will they ever overcome the past? And will it be together?

***

Telma Rocha - *Canadian Author* - *Rhonda Forrest's books always captivate and touch my heart, and this one did too, just as much as all her other books. Her story telling style is unique, full of emotion, and her characters come to life instantly. This book deals with themes of: war, refugees, immigration, PTSD, friendship, and art.*

The MadHatter Book Reviewer - *When I read Rhonda's work, I think "authentic". There is no pretense. Just raw, honest and beautifully crafted characters and dialogue.*

ALSO BY RHONDA FORREST

Writing with 4 other Australian authors to bring you -

Love in a Sunburnt Land - Anthology 1 and 2

…or purchase Love by the Jewel Sea novella separately.

 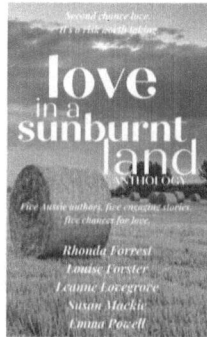 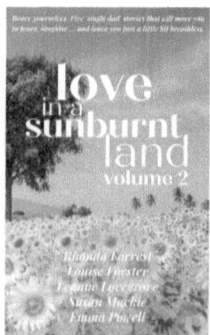

5 AUSSIE AUTHORS BRING YOU 5 RURAL ROMANCE STORIES IN EACH VOLUME

Love in a Sunburnt Land Volume 1 and 2, will take you on a journey from the tropical coast to the fertile plains and magnificent high country, where quick thinking and endurance is a way of life and where love might happen, right when it's least expected.

hapter 1

Bundeen Station – Channel Country, Queensland
1929

Michael sat at the kitchen table, running his fingers across the five names carved into the well-worn timber top. His name was in the middle: Michael McTavish, 1916. Two names were written above his; his twin brother, Dan, and elder brother, Rory. Below Michael's name was a star and the year 1918.

'That was the year the Great War ended,' Michael's father, Hamish, said. 'It was the war to end all wars, and Australian men from all over the nation signed up, with sixty thousand never coming back.'

'How many died altogether in the whole world?' Michael asked.

'Millions. Millions and millions. Fifteen, sixteen

million they say, but probably more than that.' Hamish grimaced. 'They wouldn't take me because of this bung leg. Let's hope there'll never be anything like it again.'

'Surely, with so many people dying, they've learnt not to start wars.' Anxiety tugged at Michael —the thought of going off to war and dying, never seeing his mother again, stopped him from eating his dinner, just for a moment.

'Let's hope so.' Hamish turned to his wife, Edith. 'Your mother and I are blessed you five boys were born after the war, so we didn't have to suffer the loss of sons like so many others.'

Michael returned to the carvings in the table. Below the star and year 1918 were the names of his two younger brothers, Frank and Lachie. He ran his fingers over the star, the shape familiar, the edges smoothed by the hands that had touched it over the years.

His mother never talked about it, but there had been a baby girl born before he and Dan turned two. Michael often sensed there was something that bothered his mum. Sometimes her eyes dulled, or she stared vacantly across the paddock at nothing in particular. Often, when she sang a lullaby or sat resting in the evening, tears moistened her cheeks. When he asked what she was looking at, she would wipe her face and turn away. 'It's nothing, Mickey. Just something in my eye. Nothing for you to worry about.'

Michael had quizzed his father, but it wasn't until he was older that he found out why his mother was sometimes a bit distant, or sad without reason. Michael would always remember the night their father told the story. It was the night after his and Dan's thirteenth birthday, and they were camped out on the long paddock, the stars filling the night sky above.

Earlier in the afternoon, Michael had ridden ahead to pick the best campsite for the night; by the time the others arrived, the spare horses were hobbled and the damper on the fire. By dusk the cattle were settled, the sun dropping quickly below the low scrub lining the horizon. There were no fences to hold the mob, and Michael chose the camp and fire area carefully, so the smell of preparing dinner wouldn't drift near them. The cattle hated the smell of cooking meat. Even the water used for cooking and drinking was carefully poured out so they wouldn't get wind of it and become unsettled. Camps needed to be tidy and well ordered, with nothing left lying around to be kicked during the night, spooking the cattle and causing a stampede.

The three brothers sat around the fire with their father, the silence of the night settling in. Michael wrapped his heavy coat tighter, warding off the winter chill as he repositioned the billy in the dancing sparks. He watched the fire flicker brightly as slivers of flames licked the dry logs, the branches and twigs crackling in the still of the evening.

Dan placed more logs on the blaze and looked up at the night sky. 'That star to the west is always the brightest and the first one to come out in the evening.'

'That's Elizabeth's star,' Hamish said, casting his eyes upwards.

The three boys waited, looking at each other silently. Michael knew better than to ask questions. His father always thought and paused before he spoke. When he did talk, his Scottish brogue was like music, lilting on the night air.

'You know, your mother and I came here from the home country with only a suitcase each and that old bugle my brother brought back from the Boer War. All the way from Glasgow to Sydney, the two of us, your mother a young lass. We found our way here to Bundeen and it was a lucky day for us, and all of ye, that Bill and Charlotte gave me work and offered for us to buy the hut and block.'

Dan stoked the fire. 'You were going to tell us about Elizabeth.'

'Ah, I was, wasn't I? She was born after you boys.' Hamish nodded towards Michael and Dan. He picked up a stick and stirred the embers of the fire, pausing for a long while before continuing with the story. 'The healthiest chubbiest bairn, with eyes as blue as the sky above Loch Lomond on a clear summer's day.'

The silence hummed with tension as they waited for him to continue. The silhouettes of the cattle in the distance remained motionless, not a swing of a head or bellow of a calf. The dogs lying next to the boys were also silent, two of them lifting their heads and watching Hamish, as if they too were listening to the story. Rory got up and took the billy from the fire, his father holding out his tin mug for a refill.

'Thanks, son.' He took a long sip, his stare fixed on the fire's embers. The glow lit up the boys' faces, the flames throwing flickering shadows across their coats. 'Aye, she was the bonniest baby you ever saw. At six weeks old she was already smiling and reaching up to my face.' Hamish's voice shook, and he pulled his hat lower over his face. 'She'd grab my beard and make those sweet sounds babies make. A wee noise that pulls at ye heart-strings.'

Their father sat upright, wiping his eyes with the back of his leathery hands. 'There's something about a wee girl that affects a man; it's a softness, a love different from that of a son. She held my heart from the moment she was born.'

Michael waited while his father took a deep breath.

'Your mother would never talk about it, not to you boys. Sometimes she and I talked, when it first happened, but after a while she couldn't bear it. I think she always blamed herself.'

'What happened, Dad?' Dan asked.

'It was the middle of winter. You three boys slept in the wee bed together, out near the fireplace to keep you warm. Elizabeth slept right up next to your mother's side of the bed in a crib.' He looked up at the evening star for a long time before continuing, struggling with his words.

'She went to get her from the cot in the morning. I remember lying in bed waiting, because your mother always passed Elizabeth to me after she fed her. It was a morning ritual and it kept us all warm. You know, a special time for the three of us.' A tear rolled down his face and the boys looked at each other, unused to such a show of emotion and unsure what to say.

He placed his cup of tea on the ground, his voice barely audible. 'The wee baby had died. She was dead in your mother's arms.' His hands ran through his hair. 'Your mother screamed my name, yelling at me to wake Elizabeth up. But there was nothing to be done. She was gone.'

Dan's voice was a whisper. 'What made her die, Dad?'

'We never knew. The doctor said sometimes it

happens. Babies go to bed healthy and don't ever wake up. Your mother blamed herself. But the bairn had plenty of warmth and it was nobody's fault. Just the will of God, maybe.'

'If that's the will of God, then I don't want anything to do with him!' Michael declared. The thought of his parents' suffering was too much for him to bear.

'I remember her.' Rory spoke up. 'I have a memory of holding a baby in front of the fire. I remember the smell, a soft baby smell.'

'That would be her. You were about four and you used to nurse her. You were only a wee fella yourself.' Hamish's voice broke again. 'She smiled when you talked to her.'

Michael sat by the fire for a long time after his father and Rory turned in for the night. Not far away, Dan played a wistful tune on his harmonica, his silhouette and that of the horse he sat on visible as he rode around the mob. Dan was the night watchman and in charge of the cattle, the tune letting the mob know where he was so they didn't startle. The music, as usual, settled the cattle and, before long, lullabied Hamish and Rory to sleep, their snoring accompanying Dan's tune. Michael's gaze turned towards the evening star, a vivid, winking diamond pointing directly down at him. He stared hard, imagining what his baby sister would have looked like, how her voice might have sounded. A shooting star blazed across the sky. A streak of light, in slow motion, its sparkle fading before it reached the ground.

Chapter 2.

Bundeen Station – 1929

Bundeen Station was situated in the Channel Country of far Western Queensland, the nearest town, Windorah, over one hundred miles to the north. The Diamantina River and several of its tributaries ran through the forty thousand square miles of mostly flat, arid land. In times of high water, the tentacles of braided channels cut through and over the floodplains, leaving in their wake nutritious grasses that were excellent for grazing cattle. The shallow waters, sometimes stretching fifty miles wide, brought moisture and nutrients to the soil, heralding the beginning of plentiful seasons to come.

Michael barely remembered what the plains looked like in flood. The baked, cracked earth and dying trees were a familiar landscape, no matter which direction he travelled, the wet years a distant memory. Bundeen Station was owned by Bill and Charlotte Roberts, who had many years ago sold a one-hundred-acre block to the McTavish family, the small hut on it providing a starting point for the family, who increased its size as their own numbers grew.

It was a harsh environment, but the five boys thrived, all of them loving the lifestyle of working and living among cattle and horses. By the time Michael and Dan were thirteen, and Rory fifteen, they were already skilled stockman. Along with Hamish, who was known as the best ringer in the area, they made a reliable team for moving mobs of cattle.

Bill Roberts was full of praise for them. 'You boys are as good as any of my men. You two,' he nodded towards Dan and Michael, 'you've got different skills from one another and you make a solid team.'

'Dad says we're like chalk and cheese, both the way we look and the way we are,' Michael said, stretching up tall to look Dan in the eye.

Dan continually reminded Michael, or 'Mickey', as he called him, that he was the eldest. 'Don't forget, I'm older than you by ten minutes—and *way* taller.'

Dan had always been taller, making him an ideal kitchen helper who could reach the tins on top of the hutch. Michael was easy to spot, with a mop of unruly blond hair, unlike Dan's straight, brown hair, always combed back or hidden under a hat. Their facial features were similar: the broad cheeks of their father, the long eyelashes and deep-set eyes of their mother, and a mixture of the two in their full lips and straight white teeth. The fact that the boys all had good teeth was put down to the fact that their pet goats supplied them with plenty of milk, particularly when the boys were little.

Their mother often caught them drinking from the goat or hiding some other stray animal they'd found. 'Lachie, get yourself out from under that goat. You're covered in dust, and not much of that milk is going in your mouth. And Dan, you're squeezing the poor goat dry.' Her eyes missed nothing. 'Mickey, I wasn't born yesterday. What have you got in that box? If it's another lizard or baby bird, you'll have to find food for it—and make sure you use those old rags to keep it warm.'

Lachie and Frank always wanted to help look after the animals, and they followed Michael everywhere, their cries of '*Mickey!*' echoing across the paddocks as they tried to keep up with him. Even the pet parrot had picked up on his name, screeching '*Mickey!*' every afternoon when it wanted feeding.

Michael always made sure to take care with his chores, because although Edith was short in stature, she was in charge of the household. Their father told them that when she first came to Australia at the age of twenty, her waist was tiny, her arms and legs thin and short like a child's. Now, although she had gained a little weight and her face was tanned, she still looked like a youngster, her dark brown eyes and deep dimples an attractive sight.

Edith's wavy hair intrigued Michael, the long blonde tresses hanging down the middle of her back, the colour the same as his and his younger brothers'. At night she sat patiently as Michael plaited it, her eyes closed, talking to him while he braided.

'It's the best feeling in the world, having you boys all together with me.'

Dan often interrupted the tranquillity. 'Ha, Mum, look at Mickey's hair. I plaited it while he was doing yours. He looks like a girl.'

'That's the worst plait I've ever seen.' Rory joined in. 'There's more sticking out than in.'

'Look, everyone, I've tied a pretty ribbon in it. Now he'd pass for a young lass.' Dan tugged hard on the plait, pulling a silly face as he jigged around Michael.

Michael's mother turned around and patted him on the arm. 'Leave him alone, Dan. If only you were all as easy-going. Not through all the years has Michael ever given me a second of grief, unlike the rest of you.'

'What about when he puts the fear of God into you with the tumbles and jumps he does on the horses? You always say the twins give you grey hairs and wrinkles,' Rory said.

'Aw, Mum, you love us.' Dan wrapped his strong arms around her, lifting her off the ground. The boys huddled, hugging her tight, not letting her move, even when she started yelling out to their dad. 'Cheeky bairns, the lot of you. Get out of my way and let me do my work! You're nothing but a bunch of troublemakers and a terrible example to those younger two.'

'Ah, the spoilt ones', Rory said, 'they're the real trouble. Only yesterday Mickey rescued them from the big house. Stealing fruit from right under the nose of Ah Lee. Poor old gardener, with his one ancient tree in the dusty dry paddock and barely a piece of fruit on it. Those two were up it and ready to take what they could.'

Michael's favourite times were when they moved large mobs of cattle across the plains. The days were long and hot, but at night they sat around a campfire, listening to Hamish as he reminisced about life in the old country. It was hard to imagine a country where the landscape was covered in snow for more than half the year and cattle had shaggy coats and long wide horns.

It was a stark contrast to the vast plains of outback Queensland and the robust, short-haired cattle that spent their lives flicking away swarms of flies.

'Was your house like the one we live in?' Michael asked his father.

His father shook his head and wiped the sweat from his forehead. 'Nothing the same at all. It was a thatch-roofed blackhouse, with stone walls on the outside, lined with earth on the inside. The roof was made from rye grass, keeping out the rain and warming your mother and me through the long winter months when the sun hardly shone.'

'Our walls are thick slabs of bark,' Rory said. 'The roof

is tin, and Mum says it's hot enough to fry an egg on in summer.'

'Aye, it's a different life. It's hard for ye to believe, but back in the old country our animals slept inside. Us down one end, them down the other. Now we're working with hardened cattle and horses, as well as with men who can tell stories about tracks that are drier and wilder than ours here on Bundeen Station.'

Michael hung on Hamish's every word, his father conjuring exotic images of a different world. 'Are you glad you came here, Dad?'

'Aye, at first it was foreign territory and I had to work hard to earn my place among the cattlemen. Men back home were tough and could withstand the harsh winters and the bleak mountain countryside. But the men here,' he shook his head and stoked the fire, 'when I first arrived, I was in awe of how they'd kill a black snake as thick as your arm, or wrestle with cattle as wild as the devil himself.' He paused for a long while, casting his eyes out into the blackness surrounding them. 'Here the distances are huge, the people are rugged and,' he looked back to the boys, 'this country has everything a man could ever want or need.' He sniffed the air. 'There's nothing better than smelling the cattle nearby, the burning wood there in front of ye, and feeling the isolation that comes from being surrounded by thousands of miles of scrub and desert. Aye, it's a rare country, and it was the best day of our lives when we arrived here.'

*

Although the hut Hamish bought from Bill was small to start with, over the years—as the family grew—several rooms and a long sleepout had been added down one side, and the iron roof extended accordingly.

A new floor with timber boards was a welcome comfort after years of dampening down a dirt floor. The houseproud Edith had turned the hut into a cosy retreat that not only kept them out of the weather, but also had some tender touches of the old country. Straggly sweet peas grew over an arch, welcoming visitors to the house, and there was always a vase full of whatever wildflowers or foliage Edith could lay her hands on.

It was a difficult time in Australia. The Great Depression had begun, and throughout the country—in city and rural areas alike—legions of men were unemployed, having to survive on handouts.

Occasionally a swagman stopped by their hut, his face gaunt, a small bag of belongings hanging from a stick resting on his shoulder. These men were down and out, moving from property to property in search of work. Edith would always find something for them to eat and let them spend a night in one of the sheds, sleeping on the feed bags, or send them on their way with a full belly and perhaps the possibility of work over at the main homestead.

The men were grateful for anything they received, and their gratitude was a reminder that not everyone had food in their belly, or somewhere safe to sleep at night. Michael never wanted to be lonely like they were. Their faces came to him at night when he closed his eyes, and he promised himself to never be in a position where he needed to beg for food or with no family around him.

· · ·

Chapter 3.

Bundeen Station – Winter, 1932

Michael sat warming his hands at the wood-fired stove. He watched the younger two as they helped set the table in readiness for the special dinner tonight for his and Dan's sixteenth birthday. A large pot bubbled and boiled on the stovetop, a delicious aroma filling the room. The availability of sheep on a nearby property catered for the family's traditional meal of haggis, and Michael's mouth watered in anticipation.

'Sit down, the lot of you.' Edith's quiet voice was commanding, and immediately the five boys sat around the table, waiting for their father to join them.

Hamish was a quietly spoken man. He rarely raised his voice but had a canny way of making sure the boys all toed the line. He only needed to tap his finger on the table and someone would be up and getting the milk out of the cold box, or filling the water jug for their mother. Out in the paddocks, a nod of his head or a wave of his hand was enough to command not only his own sons, but any man who was working for him, to ride in the direction he indicated.

Edith was adamant Hamish was the boss and every idea had to be run past him, but Michael and his brothers all knew that the backbone of the family, and the one they needed to heed, was their mother.

For many years, Hamish's work had been out on the stock routes, the droving taking him away from the family for months at a time. He covered countless miles with thousands of head of cattle, mixed with tough men and endured isolation and hardships while battling the heat and cold of the outback. Back at the station, Edith persevered without complaint, continuing to carve out a life for her family. It was a sweet day for the family when Bill offered Hamish the position of homestead stockman, in charge of the activities of the nearby cattle and horses.

'When cattle go astray or I need someone to find water, I can rely on your sons,' Bill said. 'Your boy Michael has an extraordinary gift for finding water. He can track down a steer and find those hidden waterholes that only the Aborigines know about. It's uncanny, like he's one with the land.'

'Maybe he learnt from the Aboriginal kids he played with. They were always out yonder together,' Hamish replied. The two men leaned on the fence, looking over the latest mob of cattle they had brought into the yard.

'I can tell you, that boy would survive in the middle of the desert. His sense of direction is unerring, and his mind is as quick as any.' Bill shook his head. 'Your other boys work as good as any of my older men, but Michael, he's going to be a big asset for you in the future.'

'Aye, he's a grand lad with a heart of gold,' Hamish replied.

Bill chuckled. 'I saw your two boys in the home paddock the other week. It was the day after they brought that big mob in. They were letting off a bit of steam and having a wonderful time doing tricks on their horses.'

Hamish grunted. 'It'll be the death of my poor Edith, watching those two on the horses. I've never seen anyone do what they can.'

'I counted the tumbles in the air and then every time, they landed back squarely on the horse's back. The amazing thing was, the horse never faltered either.'

'They've had their share of falls, but nothing too serious. They've been doing those tricks since they were wee lads.'

'You should be proud of them—and all your boys.'

'Aye, we've been blessed alright. I hope they never have to go through war like our generation did.'

Bill shook his head. 'They say never again will there be a war like that one. It's good times ahead for all of us, once these Depression years roll by. And they will.'

Hamish smiled as he gazed out across the vast expanse stretching in front of them. '*Aye khoi*, never again. They are indeed a lucky generation.'

Chapter 4.

Bundeen Station – Spring, 1933

Working with stock in the paddocks was what Michael loved most. The land swarmed with life, and he never tired of watching the many creatures that shared the area where he rode. His keen eyes followed trails of spiky dragon lizards that scuttled through the red dust, their short legs moving at a million miles an hour, seeking safety away from the hooves of horses and cattle. The ambling echidnas were not as fast. Michael would stop and loosen the reins, giving his horse a sniff of the spiked animal that had decided its safest bet was to roll up in a ball and wait until the stock moved on.

The sky was also alive. Enormous flocks of corellas soared overhead, their white bodies stark against the vivid blue sky, their screeches echoing across an emptiness as they flew eastward in search of water. Black kites glided high above, wings spread wide, eyes cast downwards in pursuit of prey. And every so often, thousands of striking blue and yellow budgerigars flicked across the heavens, also seeking to quench their thirst.

At sunset, huge mobs of kangaroos bounded effortlessly in front of the cattle, their bodies partially hidden by clouds of dust stirred up by movement, hazy particles dancing in the glare of the sun. As the sun sank lower, brilliant golds, pinks and reds filled the sky, a few low distant hills the only break in an otherwise flat land. The burning colours of the sky cast their reflected glow back onto land and, for a short while, rich hues of gold and red covered the earth, the cattle and the men who moved across it.

As the sun dipped below the horizon, its last, lingering rays cast long shadows. This signalled the end of the working day, and time to head home and clean up for dinner.

*

The lounge room was a cosy after-dinner retreat, a place and time to reflect on the day now past and what tomorrow might bring. Michael stretched his body out on the long lounge chair, stretching his neck from side to side to relieve the aching and stiffness that had built up during the day. The muscles in his arms were tight, and he rubbed them hard, noticing the hairs on them getting thicker and his once-gangly forearms starting to thicken and look more like a man's. He enjoyed the sight of his body developing, maturing, his limbs now thicker, stronger—no longer those of a boy.

He glanced at Rory and Dan, who lay on cowhide rugs, a serious game of draughts in play. The two younger brothers lay next to them, propped on their elbows, while Hamish watched from his armchair in the corner, a pipe tucked into his mouth, the sweet smell of tobacco wafting through the room.

Edith usually had mending to do, and the golden light from the lamp next to her cast a warm glow over the family as they enjoyed the quiet of the evening. Michael lay on his back, looking at the pictures hanging on the walls. His mother had hung gilded frames, filled with paintings of green pastures and babbling brooks—rural idylls from the old country. There was a carved wooden frame with a photo of Hamish's brother before he went to fight in the Boer War. On the shelf next to the pictures, taking pride of place, was the 'good luck' bugle, brought back from that same war.

Sometimes his father took it down and passed it to Dan, who was the only one of the boys with any musical ability. Dan had inherited his mother's gift for music—he could also play a lively harmonica.

An old drover had given the harmonica to Dan when he was a kid. Edith had invited the drover, who brought a mob of cattle down from way up north, to have a meal with the family. The wiry stockman entertained them for hours on the small verandah, his Scottish tunes a melancholic sound across the plains. For the first time Michael could remember, his mother cried, the music bringing back memories of the people and places that had once been her life.

Hamish passed her a handkerchief and, once she'd composed herself, she sang along, her voice a melodious accompaniment to the drover's music. As the drover was leaving the next day, he gave the small harmonica to Dan, who sat mesmerised at his feet the entire time he played. 'This old tin sandwich belonged to Sid Kidman himself,' he told Dan. 'I'm running out of puff to play, so you learn it now. Your mother knows the tunes. It'll calm the cattle and horses when you're out on the track.'

Dan drove them crazy, the tinny notes shrill to their ears, until he learned to play in tune. His determination paid off and within a few months he mastered every tune his mother could remember. At night Edith's strong voice filled the hut, with the boys joining in, their deep voices blending harmoniously as they sang the haunting lyrics of her favourite songs.

*

Not long after Michael turned sixteen, a mystery load arrived at the hut. Not only was there equipment and supplies for the main house, but hidden behind a cover was a surprise delivery for Edith. It was an upright wooden piano that had made its way on the back of the supply cart all the way from Brisbane.

Hamish grinned like a mischievous boy, laughing loudly when Edith threw herself into his arms. He swung her around like a doll, and his arm stayed around her shoulders as the precious piano was lifted down. The boys manoeuvred it through the front door and positioned it in pride of place in the lounge room, directly below the bugle on the shelf.

After the piano arrived, every night was spent in the lounge, with Edith often playing for hours on end. Her singing was accompanied by the boys, filling the house with music and love. Hamish told them that no man was as lucky as he. Sometimes, he'd lean back in his chair and close his eyes, the only sign that he was awake the smoke that continued to puff from his pipe. Michael knew he was thinking of the tiny baby, Elizabeth. He moved closer to his father and sat on the rug next to him.

'She'll always be with us, Mickey. With us in spirit.' Hamish ruffled Michael's hair. 'Life can be harsh and full of ups and downs. The best day of my life was when I met your mother. Treat a woman well and you'll have a friend for life.'

Chapter 5.

The Channel Country – 1933

It was the first night of the New Year, 1933. Edith gazed around the table as the five boys and Hamish devoured every last scrap of the hearty stew she had cooked. She closed her eyes and tried to hold the moment in her heart. The boys were all getting older—sooner or later they'd be wanting to spread their wings.

Only last week she overheard Hamish talking to one of the station managers from further south. The McTavish family had known John O'Donnell for years, and he was well aware of the stockman capabilities of their three older boys.

'You should send those older boys down to work for me at Durham Station,' he told Hamish. 'I'd give them different work and it would do them good. They could see a bit of town life and mix with other folk in the area. Bill won't mind; it was him who suggested it.'

'I'm not sure my Edith will be wanting to part with any of them.' Hamish pushed tobacco down into the funnel of his pipe, puffing heavily to ensure it caught. He dragged on the pipe, holding it like a treasured friend as he drew it away from his mouth. 'You're right, though.

Sometimes they don't talk to anyone outside the family for months.'

'With us being a Kidman property, they'll get to move from one station to the other,' John said. 'There are runs into town for supplies and a special job coming up. I'd be interested in Michael. I'd pay him well.'

'I thought you'd be after my older son, Rory. He's more settled. Michael's only young; he's just turned seventeen.'

'I'll take him and his twin brother, or him and Rory. You're a lucky man, Hamish, having five sons.'

***

Hamish had discussed John's proposal with Edith and now she nodded, indicating that tonight was a good time for a discussion on the matter. No-one would leave while there was still food on the table or left-overs to be scraped from the big pot, warming on the wood fire stove. Besides, no boy or man, would be game to leave the table until she excused them.

Hamish's voice caused them all to stop chattering. The only sounds were his Scottish brogue and the clinking of cutlery on plates.

'John O'Donnell from Durham Downs came to see me.'

'Aye,' answered Dan. 'That's one in a line of Kidman properties on the Cooper Creek. In full season it can carry more cattle than anywhere else in the area.'

Rory chipped in. 'I've talked to men from there. When it floods, they say the water is like an ocean and deeper than a man is tall.'

'When they had the last big dry, they lost ten thousand

head of cattle.' Dan added. 'They also have trouble with wild horses—they eat the good pickings.'

Michael listened with interest. He'd travelled long distances with the cattle, but there were thousands of miles to the south and north he'd never seen. With a trusty horse and a swag, a man could ride the length of the country stretching endlessly in every direction, with ranges to the north, green pastures to the south and, in the east, oceans that rose and fell with the pull of the moon.

He'd only ever seen pictures of the ocean in the geography and history books his mother used for their lessons. She'd tried to be strict with their education, but it was only ever him and the two younger ones left after the first hour passed.

Michael was drawn in by the black-and-white pictures showing cities and villages in other parts of the world, as well as oceans with waves that were high and curled at the top. He plied his mother with questions, his finger running over a page showing mountains covered in snow.

'Life can't stay the same forever. One day you boys will move on, maybe marry and build a life somewhere for yourselves.' Edith patted Michael's hair down, flattening the unruly curls and pushing a few stray strands from his face. He looked up from the book, the dark brown of her eyes similar to his own.

'The younger two will be around for a while,' Michael said. 'Frank told me he wants to get married and have ten children, and Lachie said he's going build a house for himself right next to you and Dad.'

Edith laughed. 'Wouldn't that be grand. All those little ones running around and you boys close by. Mind you,

you'll all have to become a bit more social for any of that to happen.'

'I want to see other places, Mum, but I'll always come back here to you and Dad. This is my home and where I belong.'

'There's a big world out there, Mickey, but we'll always be here for ye to come back to.'

*

Now Michael waited for his father to continue. He looked to his mother for clues, but she shook her head, not giving anything away.

Hamish sat back in his chair, his arms crossed as he looked at the boys. 'John O'Donnell has asked if ye would like to go and work for him. He's willing to pay good money, and you'd be on the properties as well as droving cattle to stockyards further south.'

Frank and Lachie sat upright, their faces taut, their eyes wide, as if they were soldiers at attention in the army.

'He is, of course, only after ye older boys.'

The younger boys' faces fell. They scowled at each other across the table.

Rory was the first to break the silence. He lay his knife and fork down and pushed his plate to the side. 'I'm not wanting to leave this place. I'm happy here.'

'I'm not forcing any of you to go, but your mother and I have talked about it and it would be good to see what's on the other side of these paddocks.'

Michael looked out the window. Out there were places and people he could only imagine.

He looked towards his mother. 'What do you think?'

She hesitated then spoke softly. 'You'd learn new things, and John O'Donnell is a good man.'

Michael held his mother's gaze. 'I wouldn't want to leave this place or any of you,' he cast his eyes around the table, his hands clasped and resting on his lap, 'but if it's for a short while, it would be fine.' He paused and looked at Dan. 'But I understand if Dan is the one to go.'

Dan sat upright. 'I've wanted to do something different for a while and,' he grinned at Michael, 'there aren't too many girls around here.'

Edith smiled. 'It's okay, Dan, to admit missing the company of women your own age. You're young men now.'

Michael's shoulders slouched. He may have to wait his turn. Dan was bigger and stronger, and full of confidence.

*

Edith listened with interest as she poured Hamish a cup of tea, the steam wisping up in spirals before disappearing into the rafters of the hut. Silence drew down upon them again as Hamish methodically placed three teaspoons of sugar into his cup and began to stir. It was a habit of his, and no one would dare hurry him when he was stirring his tea. He stirred it for what seemed an eternity before tapping the spoon on the side of the cup. Initially this was to rid the spoon of any drops of tea threatening to blot Edith's clean tablecloth. But they all knew that the number of times he tapped the spoon signified the seriousness of whatever conversation was taking place.

The tapping went on and on as Hamish concentrated, his eyes fixed on the spoon. After a while it was too much for Edith, who leaned over and gently stilled his hand. He lay the spoon down on the table.

'John said he'd take two of you. Are ye sure, Rory, you don't want to go?'

'I'm sure, Father. I'm nineteen, but I want another couple of years here. I want to teach these youngest boys a thing or two.'

It would be a different stage for the family without the twins, but it had to happen sooner or later. Dan needed to spread his wings, he was restless, itching for adventure. Edith's gaze lingered on Michael; her kindred spirit, the most soft-hearted, caring and kind son a mother could ever wish for. She would miss them, but they weren't boys any longer, rather two young men on the cusp of a new adventure.

Far to the west a dingo howled; another, nearer the small hut, took up the mournful cry. Edith looked around the table in the golden glow of the kerosene lantern. The dingoes howled again, and a shiver ran down her spine.

A spider running over my grave, she thought. Was this a premonition of what lay ahead, or was it normal anxiety for a mother experiencing the impending separation of her family for the first time? It would take her a long time to find out and, when she did, she would think back to this night so many years earlier, when they had all sat together as a family, looking forward to a bright future.

~~~

ELIZABETH'S STAR is Book 1 in a series of 3 books - We'll Meet Again Trilogy